RAINLIGHT

ALSO BY ALISON M<small>C</small>GHEE

Was It Beautiful?

Shadow Baby

RAINLIGHT

ALISON McGHEE

PICADOR
NEW YORK

To Bill O'Brien,
who fits the forces of evil
and makes the world safe
for democracy, and to Min–Min,
who came from China

www.picadorusa.com

Picador® is a U.S. registered trademark and is used by St. Martin's Press
under license from Pan Books Limited.

For information on Picador Reading Group Guides, as well as ordering,
please contact the Trade Marketing department at
St. Martin's Press.
Phone: 1-800-221-7945 extension 763
Fax: 212-677-7456
E-mail: trademarketing@stmartins.com

ISBN 0-312-27703-2

First published in the United States by Papier-Mache Press

10   9   8   7   6   5   4   3   2

ACKNOWLEDGMENTS

For their generosity in reading this book in draft form, and for their greatness in general, I thank Julie Schumacher, Bill O'Brien, and Karla Kuban.

To Holly Smith and Cheryl Harris, thanks for advice on medical terminology and occupational therapy.

To John Bai Laoshi Berninghausen, thanks for long ago imparting a love of China.

To Patricia Anderson, Laura Caton, Jeff Clarke, Lenny Dee, John Hake, Christine H. McGhee, Frances O'Brien, Susan Schickel, Amy Sheldon, Ellen Harris Swiggett, Meredith Wade, Garvin Wong, and John Zdrazil, thanks for years of unshakable friendship.

My gratitude to Nita Bernard and Elizabeth Horton, who, each in her own way, provided peace of mind.

Thanks to Mikhail Iossel, a wonderful writer and teacher.

Thanks to Shirley Coe and the rest of the perceptive and talented staff at Papier-Mache and to Reagan Arthur and Liz Hronkova at Picador.

Thanks to Laurel and Holly and Doug, who know Sterns.

Thanks to my students, who know so well the transformative power of words.

My deepest thanks go to Don, who knows how to tell a story, and Gabrielle, who knows how to listen.

I had two pigeons bright and gay,

They flew from me the other day.

What was the reason they did go?

I cannot tell for I do not know

—nursery rhyme

TIM WILLIAMS

Johnny Zielinski who loves shinies, you would have thought he'd love a sunshower, light broken and glittering through rain. But no. He moaned and cried in his speechless way. I saw him come out of Jewell's Groceries holding a red Popsicle in his good hand, the sweet that my son, Starr, bought him because Johnny carries no change. Too shiny, it mesmerizes him. Johnny Zielinski will throw change into the sky, a whirling sparkle of coins, and laugh when it falls to the ground.

He looked up and down the street like his aunt Crystal took five years to teach him to do, and stepped off the curb with his bad foot first, the same way he does on stairs.

Tim, you want french fries with your hamburger? Or coleslaw? said Crystal.

Coleslaw, I said. Like always.

Then it started down, the rain, a passing shower falling from blue sky. I watched Johnny freeze.

Dammit, said Crystal from behind the grill. She was frying hamburgers for Starr and me, and I saw the way she hesitated with the tin spatula, then laid it on the countertop. Across the street from the diner Johnny stood frozen on the curb with the Popsicle in his hand. Crystal ducked under the latched grill gate, heading for the door, calling his name—Johnny, Johnny.

Starr and I, we come to Crystal's Diner for hamburgers mostly, and milkshakes, which are Crystal's specialty. When we walked in Johnny was sitting in his booth, his face turned to the window, muttering.

What is it Johnny? asked Crystal from behind the counter. What do you need, more ketchup?

She heard him over the sputtering grill and the clinking mugs. Crystal always hears Johnny. He turned at the sound of her voice. In front of him was a pile of french fries on a red china saucer; Johnny likes small red things. Crystal brought him the ketchup squeeze bottle and stood waiting as he squirted with his good hand. His Mickey Mouse lunch box stood on the shelf next to the window.

He spoke again, in his words that almost no one besides Crystal can understand. But Crystal's raised him from birth. She knows everything he says.

What is it Johnny? asked Crystal, patience of years in her voice. Take your time.

He wants a Popsicle from Jewell's, said my son, Starr, from his counter stool. And I know just the man to get him one. Come on, Zielinski.

Johnny lined up a few of his shinies on the sill so the sun made them glitter. Then out he slid, pushing along the red vinyl, holding his good hand out to Starr. They went through the door together, tall Starr and small Johnny, his head bent as if listening to a voice from outer space. I watched Crystal watch them walk to Jewell's. Crossing the street, Starr waiting until Johnny's bent head turned each way, looking for nonexistent cars. Through the dark hole of Jewell's screened door, white butcher paper signs plastered over the windows: Eggs $.75 doz., 5 lb. Sugar $2.15, Bear Paws 3/$1.00. Today Only.

Some children, they have nothing but their need. They come

into this world with skin and soft bones and sinew and pumping hearts. They fight their ghosts from the day they are born.

My sister's having a hard time, Mr. Williams, Crystal said to me twelve years ago, when she brought Johnny back to Sterns with her. I'm going to raise her baby for a while.

Crystal Zielinski, nineteen years old. She set up his baby seat in the booth and draped a string of bouncing toys across the front of it. But he strained away from the toys. There was a window behind him, flooded with sun. Johnny reached his fingers up to it, as if he could pull it inside himself.

Taken, said Crystal when strangers came in looking to sit down at that booth. He slept a lot at first, like babies do. The diner murmured around him, lulling him to sleep, his aunt Crystal's voice at the grill, *How do you want that done? You want onions with that, mustard?* and her eyes cutting sideways to where he slept. Watching over him, her baby nephew.

In the diner now Johnny sometimes gets up from his booth and makes his way among the tables, holding on to the backs of chairs for support. Chrome-backed, with red vinyl seats, the light strikes them sometimes and he stops, waving his head back and forth to catch the sparkles. Spoons, glasses filled with water and ice, all are Johnny's treasures. Wedding rings or, better, engagements because of the diamonds. He reaches with his good hand and picks up the hand of its wearer, bringing the ring closer to his eyes. He'll twist a hand so that the diamond pierces his clouded sight and sends rays of hard light into the center of his eyes.

What's with the retard? said a woman once, snatching away her hand, covering her chip of diamond.

Aunt Crystal burned behind the counter.

Babies don't get born in North Sterns. They just appear, then grow, like corn that's dropped on a hard dirt road. Like rust. Like love. Cerebral palsy gave Johnny his twisted hand and crooked foot, his slowed mind. At the elementary school he walks close to the wall for the balance its support gives him. He hums in passing, the same high-pitched chant. Johnny's tune of appreciation, his aunt Crystal calls it. If he doesn't show up in class the other teachers and I check the washroom, where he likes to stand next to a window by the sink, watching the sunlight play off water that he lets run and run.

But he hates it falling on him.

Crystal and I turned at the sound of the rain, first of the April rains, looked out the window to see the drops starting down out of a sunlit sky.

Damn, said Crystal, waving her arms at Johnny. I saw her mouth moving: Johnny, stay there, don't move. And he wavered on the edge of the curb, crippled foot touching down and then coming up.

Crystal'd do anything to save that boy. She dropped the spatula, ducked under the gate to the grill, headed to the door when the rain started falling from the sky. Johnny held his red Popsicle in his hand and moaned. Rain on the window blurred the sight of him.

The hamburgers sputtered on the grill, flesh singeing above the heat.

Hang on, Johnny, Crystal said as she squeezed through the tables on her way to the door. I'm coming.

It was one of those freak sunshowers, unexpected on a soft spring day. Johnny stood with his red Popsicle, his mouth stained red. Turned his face up to the rain that my granddaughter Mallie once said was heaven crying.

Nights, Crystal closes the diner late. After my wife, Georgia, died I started staying sometimes to talk with Crystal, to sit with Johnny in his booth. When the grill is cleaned Crystal turns the lights off and puts his jacket on.

Come on, Johnny, push your arm in. Now pull the zipper up.

He bends his head and squints, trying to find the zipper pull in the dim light from the street lamp. We walk into the snow of a Sterns winter. I watch Crystal load him into her pickup that's painted an unearthly red, fasten his seat belt, and head home to North Sterns, her taillights winking all the way up the slippery slope that leads into the Adirondacks. Next morning she's back, mixing up the pancake batter, setting out little white pitchers of syrup. Starr and I, we stop in once or twice a week.

So, said Crystal to Starr when we walked in. Your father here tells me you got the airplane tickets already.

Right here, and he patted his breast pocket.

So it's really going to happen then? asked Crystal, dunking the basket of fries into hot oil. You're really going to China?

I'm really going to China, said Starr. To Xian, the City of Western Peace. To the tomb of the terra cotta warriors. Each warrior modeled after a living soldier. Like looking into the faces of ghosts, one of the books says. Xian first, and then I'll walk the Great Wall.

You always did love China, said Crystal. Even in fourth grade, I remember you doing a book report on the Great Wall.

Crystal is right. Starr always has loved China. My wife thought it was funny, this little boy from the Adirondack Mountains of upstate New York, fixated on China the way he was. She used to take him to the library in Sterns once a week in the summers, and every week he wore out the lady at the desk, making her thumb through the card catalogue looking for books and more books on China. You've got a peculiar child here, the librarian finally said to Georgia; he is literally obsessed with China and let me tell you— Sterns, New York, is not a hotbed of Chinese culture.

Will you bring me back a souvenir, Starr? asked Crystal as she shaped hamburger into patties for our lunch. A clay ear or something? Or an eye. A finger. Something from one of those soldiers, I'm not fussy.

Sure, said Starr. A body part, that's what you're in the market for?

In his corner booth Johnny stirred his spoon softly in ice water. Clink, clink. Crystal whipped her towel out from behind the counter and slapped Starr on the butt.

5

Don't forget now, she said. And don't forget something for Johnny. Something shiny and Chinese.

I would have wanted to go to Xian too, if I were younger, to see the terra cotta warriors in their dark tomb. Their sightless sculpted eyes, their voiceless mouths. I heard my wife, Georgia, once on the phone: Tim used to paint, she said. Tim used to sculpt. But he started teaching art and all the art in him got used up.

I did used to paint, I thought. And I did used to sculpt. But the years took it out of me, the years and years of molding the hands of children like Johnny Zielinski over paints and brushes, shreds of paper, and pots of glue. I'm sixty now, closer every year to being an old man. I could retire any time.

The special ed kids file into elementary art, some holding hands.

Hi, Mr. Williams, the ones who can talk clearly enough say.

The others tilt their heads, smile their smiles that are usually crooked, reach out to swing at my shoulder, my hair that's grey now: Mr. Williams their art teacher.

Johnny Zielinski limps into the classroom sideways, like a crab. He goes to his chair and his desk next to the window, where the light's brightest, and I bring him his red box from its shelf. Tinfoil, old keys, scissors. A tube of golden glitter that he uncorks and sprinkles onto the lines of glue he draws with a glue stick. And Johnny's favorite: a kaleidoscope that Starr gave him for his ninth birthday, full of silver stars that he holds up to the buzzing fluorescent light. He twirls it and he shakes it, he screws his eye up to the opening; that boy longs for light.

Johnny Zielinski's blurred eyes focus best from the side, and so he turns his head away from the crystals and prisms that I hang for him in the window by his desk. Johnny bends his head while the sun pierces and splits the crystals into pieces of colored light. He hums his tune of appreciation. At her easel Brenda dips her fingers into jars of bright colors and trails them against big sheets of rough paper. Marcy fingers textures in her box of fur and flannel and sandpaper.

Sometimes my granddaughter, Mallie, appears in the window of the classroom door. All I can see in the fraction of a second as she jumps up to reach the opening on her way to lunch is a little piece of her smile. Up she jumps, and then she's gone. Johnny Zielinski and his friends love what their eyes see and what their fingers tell them but my granddaughter, Mallie, loves smell. When she was a baby she used to bury her head in her mother, Lucia's, neck, scrubbing her face back and forth against the pastel wool of the sweaters Lucia always wears. Starr feeds his daughter's craving. He brings her treasure from the woods where he spends his days. Juniper twigs in the fall; in the spring baby ferns, with their heads unrolling on green stems that Mallie once said were swan necks. Red maple leaves and chunks of rough bark sticky with pine sap.

Starr has promised Mallie some ten thousand-year-old dirt from the tomb of the Yellow Emperor.

What do you think, Mal? he asks. Anything ten thousand years old'd have to have an unusual smell to it, wouldn't you say?

When the lunch bell rings at school I can look out into the hallway to see Mallie walking just to the left of Johnny Zielinski as he bobs up and down. Skinny Mallie with her dark brown hair, holding her book bag like a shield over Johnny's weaving shadow. Mallie, who'd do anything to make him happy.

Some children, they have nothing but their need.

Crystal's rusty-bottom trailer leaked baby toys when Johnny was a toddler, crawling around after other kids his age were walking, holding onto the sides of things for support. Then he started to walk. He held his bad hand high, and his foot with its high arch hesitated where other people were solid and sure of themselves.

Ice floating on spilled water from a glass keeps Johnny busy for half an hour. He'll drag his fingers through and swipe the wetness down the pane of glass next to his booth. He has a thing for water. But only at a distance. Crystal keeps her eye out for that, for the thunderstorms that are his terror, for the swimming pool at school that they tried to put him into when he was a little kid, for the tin tub the Sterns Town Hall fills with water each Halloween so the kids can bob for apples.

A warm washcloth, that's how Crystal keeps him clean. I've seen her, swabbing it over his face and hands, stained red with ketchup or dark with chocolate milkshake around his mouth.

The rain fell through the sun and sprinkled the pavement outside Jewell's.

Oh, God, said Crystal and I watched her, her thin body duck under the gate that led to the grill. She laid the spatula on the counter and let the hamburgers sizzle. Johnny's face turned in dread to the warmth of the sunny rain, eyes closed against the bright shards of water you would have thought he'd love, foot melting the ice of a red forgotten sweet.

The rain hit his turned-up face. His twisted foot hesitated midair then came down in the street. Crystal was nearing the door, her mouth opening—Johnny, Johnny—but I heard the brakes at the same time she did.

The rain came down in a soft blur. It fell on the concrete and dripped off the budding trees. Johnny Zielinski closed his eyes and clutched his twisted hand to his neck, cradling his own thin bones.

Crystal threw herself past the tables. A chair went sprawling.

Johnny stepped eyes closed into the street.

Oh, God, screamed Crystal.

The air horn moaned. There was a smell of burning meat from the grill.

I watched my son, Starr, come flying out the door of Jewell's.

A waterfall of sparkling water and ice whirled up into the sky as it left Starr's hand. His arms spread wide in the empty air and then pushed Johnny out of the way. Starr's white T-shirt hung bright in the sunny rain. Then it disappeared.

I couldn't see him anymore.

All I could hear was a cry.

Crystal's clean glass window pinned me like a fist yards away from where my son flung himself onto the howling metal. I can picture him still in my mind, like the pictures I used to paint. A flame, leaping into rain.

2

MALLIE WILLIAMS

We believe in reincarnation, Charlie and me. We talk about it at breakfast while our parents Lucia and Starr sleep.

Remember Road? I say. I start with Road, which is our cat that died, because Road is the only thing that's died that Charlie can remember. Charlie is three.

Road died.

And where is she now?

Under the rock, Charlie says. More toast.

I get him more toast.

Remember Grandma Georgia?

Yes, says Charlie. I know he doesn't remember Grandma but I say, Good, anyway. Then I tell him about reincarnation, that Grandma is a baby somewhere else now.

Charlie thinks it's funny. Where *is* that baby? he asks.

She could be anywhere, I say. She could be in Utica, a baby Grandma just learning to walk. She could be in Paris, France. She could be in . . .

China! says Charlie. *Wo ai pijiu!*

That means "I love beer" in Chinese, which our dad taught him from his Chinese practice books. My dad is going to walk on the Great Wall, which is three thousand miles long. My dad is going to see the terra cotta warriors. He says he's going to bring me back some ten thousand-year-old dirt. Charlie does love beer. Whenever dad and mom drink some he gets a sip. Me, I hate it.

Charlie sings nursery rhymes that our dad, Starr, teaches him. *Hey diddle diddle, the cat and the fiddle, the cow jumped over the moon.*

Imagine that, I say. A little Chinese grandma, just walking around over there on the Great Wall.

The little dog laughed to see such sport, and the dish ran away with the spoon. He laughs. He loves nursery rhymes. They sing them together, Charlie and my dad. I get tired of them, the rhymes, over and over.

Wo ai pijiu! says Charlie. More juice please.

That's the kind of thing we talk about at breakfast, Charlie and me, when we talk about reincarnation and some of the other things we believe in.

Keep your eye on the curve ahead and don't blink your eyes. If you blink them even for a second that means that a car will come whipping around out of control and smash into the school bus. You look at Tiny Eddy, the bus driver, and you imagine him with his head just tipped back for another mouthful from his quarter pounder of M&M's he keeps on the dashboard, trying to grab the wheel but he can't. It's too late.

So I keep my eyes on the curve ahead and do not blink them even though they burn and itch.

If Tiny took the short way I could be the first one off the bus. But he goes the long way, through North Sterns, with the North Sterns boys sitting behind him, their mean dark heads and old army jackets. There's a story that Tiny keeps dirty pictures underneath his M&M's bag.

Do you know that you can peel the inner foil off a gum wrapper and stroke it onto a desk, or the back of the bus seat in front of you? It is the thinnest foil imaginable, and you have to stroke it on with the back of a fingernail otherwise it will split. It curls in your hand, this thin piece of foil, but if you stroke it on right it will stick and never come off.

Every piece of gum I chew, I add another layer of foil to the back of the seat that's Johnny Zielinski's and mine. Now the seat is almost covered with foil so on a sunny day it shines in Johnny's eyes, which he loves. Sometimes Johnny hugs me; he presses his head into my neck so that his hair floats up at me, smelling like sun and the shampoo his aunt Crystal used to rub on with a washcloth. Because Johnny Zielinski is scared of water, water that falls.

Far away on Star Hill I looked down over the hills to where the village of Sterns sits in its little valley and saw the sun come through a cloud. It looked like a sunshower from where we were, ten miles away in North Sterns. Sprinkles of rain through the slanting sun, so pretty through the window that I almost forgot to duck when we went by the tree where my grandmother Georgia died. Then I remembered, and I scrunched down in time to miss the tree and miss the sunshower, but I kept my eyes trained on the plastered tinfoil that makes Johnny Zielinski happy.

There's a ghost on Star Hill, the hill that is the same name as my dad only my dad has a double *r*. The high schoolers say the ghost is there when they drive up after midnight, an eye of light coming toward them out of the woods. It shakes and floats toward them but no one's ever stayed to see how far it comes. You can't look at it straight on; you have to look at it out of the corner of your eye. That's the only way you can see it, is what they say.

You have to do the routines. I missed once, I'm not sure how, and that was the day my grandmother Georgia died. Driving at night is how she died. The next morning there was her car, crumpled against the tree, and they cut her out with the Jaws of Life, but she was already dead. My grandfather Tim was out looking for her that night, driving around with the lights on, swerving back and forth across the roads so that the headlights would shine into the ditches and the fields and around the trees. So that he could see the shine from her car if she had gone off the road. He drove all night looking for her and when the sun came up, there was the reflection of her car.

Every day the bus goes by and every day I have to scrunch down below the level of the window so I don't see it. Three years later there it still is, a tree taller than a barn. I have to bend down below the window so that I can't see the white scar turning grey from rain and sun and wind. I stare at the gum wrapper tinfoil plastered on the seat back in front of me. Johnny Zielinski scrunches with me when he goes to his trailer instead of the diner. His stop is the second one after Star Hill. Johnny thinks it's a game. He tilts his head so he can see me better and laughs the way he laughs, which is not making a sound. I pretend to laugh with him so he doesn't feel bad. I open my mouth and rock back and forth in his rhythm, but all the while inside I'm counting: one, two, three, four, five, six, up to eighteen, which is how long it takes to get past the tree that my grandmother Georgia died against.

Charlie comes into my room in the morning before Mom and Dad are up.

Mallie, he whispers. Maaaaaaaallie.

My name used to be Madeleine until Johnny Zielinski learned to call me Mallie. That's as far as he could get with a name like Madeleine.

Mallie, he whispers.

I pretend to be asleep, that's the routine. He slips the covers back and crawls in next to me.

Mallie, he whispers. Should we go down and get some breakfast?

This is what we started doing a year ago. I was eight and he was two. I can get toast and cereal and milk and juice for him and me.

Charlie and I eat toast the secret way. First you eat all the crust off, then you nibble off the bottom crisp part, on the side that wasn't buttered. Then you mush the butter part into a ball and put it into your mouth.

We talk about the things we believe in, like reincarnation. And every day I practice Emergency with Charlie. He talks with his mouth full of toast but still, I can understand him. Charlie smells like butter and grass and in the morning, sleep.

What's your name, Charlie?

Charles Timothy Williams.

Where do you live, Charlie?

Sterns, New York, in the foothills of the Adirondack Mountains.

Charlie, what is your telephone number?

315. 865. 7836.

He's getting good, Charlie is.

I imagine my dad tripping in the woods while the chain saw is running. It grinds through his leg, and I imagine him ripping his shirt and wrapping it tight around the stump, tight enough so that no blood can get out. He crawls to his truck and gets in, shifting and gassing and braking with the one leg that's left, steering through the woods, between the trees, onto the road that leads through North Sterns, past Carmichael Hill, past Star Hill, down the long hill that goes to our house, past our house, into Sterns, blowing the horn, leaning on it so there's a solid blur of horn, and stopping at the diner. I imagine Crystal and my grandfather Tim running out the door when they hear the sound of the horn and dragging my dad out of the truck. Mom will meet them at the emergency room in Utica. I imagine them stopping the blood, sewing up the leg. I imagine it, the blowing horn, the truck blurring onto the curb by the diner, and them all heading out to get him out of the cab. They would stop the blood. They would sew him up. He would be alive.

The day she died I must have missed something. I keep thinking back. There was something I missed, that later that night caught up with my grandmother Georgia as she drove her car around the bend. Something I missed that stole into her car, a ghost that stole the controls and steered her car into the tree.

Johnny Zielinski, who is Crystal Zielinski from the diner's nephew Johnny, carries a different shiny every day from his collection. He loves them all, his pieces of tinfoil, his marbles that shine with eyes of light trapped inside. The rocks that when you're little you think are gold, but when you get older you find out are fool's gold.

I wonder what Johnny ate for lunch. Not his milk, because C. J. Wilson and the other boys took it out of his Mickey Mouse lunch box and spilled it into the rubber gutter. Not his chips, because they ripped open the bag and ate them themselves. It was a little bag of barbecue chips that I know came from the diner where his aunt Crystal took them off the metal claw board where all the bags of chips hang. Not his sandwich wrapped in wax paper, because the boys shook it out of the wax paper and wadded it into a peanut butter-and-white bread ball and threw it like a snowball. Splat, it went against the back window. Dawn Moskin screamed and started wiping goo out of her hair.

The boys have got off the bus now, the ones that tried to tell Johnny this morning that he wet his pants. I knew it was the milk stain from what they spilled on him, but he turned his head to the side and bent down, trying to see his leg.

Don't worry, Johnny, I said. They're just joking.

Still he bent his head down there, squinting, and tried to feel his pants with his hands.

Later Johnny walked sideways down the hall, hopping from his bad foot to his good the way he does. I walked next to him holding my books over the stain. I knew it was milk, but everyone else thought it was pee. I took him into the girls' bathroom when no one else was in there and rubbed at the stain with toilet paper, but what happened was that the paper shredded with the scrubbing, rubbing off onto his pants leg in a whitening way that only made it worse.

My grandmother Georgia died in her car, alone at night, crumpled against a tree. No one told me if she died fast or slow. I imagine the car going off the road, my grandmother alone in her seat and screaming because the tree was coming at her and she knew what would happen. I imagine her dying alone, feeling the blood leaving her body, knowing what was happening to her. I imagine her not wanting to go but feeling it happen.

This morning my dad played a trick on Charlie.

Charlie, said my dad. Hey, Charlie.

Charlie turned around and screamed.

There was my dad, Starr, with a pillowcase over his head and his hands in white gloves, waving like spiders.

Chaaaaaaarlie.

He started coming toward Charlie, and Charlie was too scared to move.

I'm a ghooooooooost.

I reached out and grabbed Charlie with my arms and shoved him in back of me.

Cut it out, Dad! I said.

The white spider hands reached for what they thought was Charlie but it was me instead.

He's only three! I said.

Charlie started to cry in a way that didn't make any noise.

Stop! I said.

I hit my dad. I hit him and pulled the pillowcase off his head to see him laughing.

I'm a ghost! he said. I'm Starr, the ghost of Star Hill!

Then he saw the look on Charlie's face.

Hey. Charlie, Charlie. I'm sorry.

See what you did, I said.

I turned my back and I wouldn't hug him or kiss him even though that was part of the routine.

Well, OK then. I'm going now.

Then I heard the truck start up and I heard it shift into reverse. I imagined him alone in the woods, the chain saw grinding through his jeans. I went flying out the door with my arms out to hug him.

Wait! Wait! I forgot to say good-bye!

But he was gone, the taillight red eyes winking up the hill.

She died. My grandfather walks different now. I see his mouth moving sometimes. He tries to hide it but I know what he's doing. He's talking to her, as if she's a ghost that stands next to him and makes him happy. On my way to lunch I jump up beside the door to his art room, during the hour when he's teaching Johnny and the other special eds. I jump up so that I can see inside through the glass pane high in the door, the window into his room. At first all I see are colors, construction paper and easels with their pots of paint, and pictures tacked all around the walls. I have to keep jumping until I see my grandfather Tim. That's the routine that I have to do, to keep him safe.

This is a secret, I said to Charlie at breakfast. Do not tell anyone.

OK, he said. Could I have some more toast?

I killed Grandma.

Grandma died, he said.

It was me that killed her. I missed something and that was the night she died.

Road died, he said. Road is under the rock.

It was my fault.

Grandma is a baby cat in China, he said. With a fiddle, like in hey diddle diddle.

In my closet I have a box for my grandmother Georgia. Inside is her obituary that I cut out of the *Utica Daily*.

Williams, Georgia, sixty. Lifelong resident of Sterns. Beloved wife of Timothy, mother of Starr (Lucia), grandmother of Madeleine and Charlie. Will be sorely missed by her many friends and relatives.

When I unravel time, the furthest back I can go is this: my father was ahead of me, climbing up brown stairs that had little bits of grey on them. I know this because I was crawling on the stairs, looking down at them very close to my eyes. He was carrying a bucket. I was wearing diapers. I still can feel the plastic and the heaviness rubbing on my legs and back. I looked out through the railing on the stairs and I saw the world going by and time passing, and he was climbing, climbing up beyond me and even though I didn't think in words yet I told myself, *Remember this.*

At the end of the bus ride it's just me, Mallie Williams. Tiny's quiet by then. He doesn't laugh after the boys get off, he just keeps sliding M&M's into his mouth. I sit quiet in my seat, fifth from the left front. I smooth the tinfoil wrappers onto the back of the seat so Johnny Zielinski can tilt his head and smile at them next day when he gets on the bus.

Charlie is too young to ride this bus, but when he starts kindergarten I will still be riding it, a sixth-grader, two more years to go before I have to ride the high school bus. Charlie will sit between me and Johnny Zielinski, in our seat fifth from the left front. The boys from North Sterns will not bother my brother, Charlie, because I will be there, sitting next to him. If he wants to sing nursery rhymes on the bus he can, because already I am getting ready for the day when Charlie rides the school bus, when I will take care of him.

The bus pulled into my driveway to make the turn that is called a three-point turn, and there was my mother walking toward me with a look on her face and her arms held out, waiting. There was my grandfather standing on the porch holding Charlie's hand, and there was my dad's friend Brian crying by his car.

Tiny stopped eating his M&M's.

I quick closed my eyes before it all got burned into my brain, and I went over everything: I had practiced Emergency with Charlie at breakfast; I had jumped up till I saw Grandpa at lunch; I had scrunched down past the tree where Grandma died; I had hugged Dad.

I had not hugged Dad.

I started to hum. I willed Brian to fade away. I willed Grandpa to laugh and throw Charlie up in the air. I willed Mom to just be walking out to check the mail. I willed Tiny to laugh his coughing laugh and pick out a handful of just reds.

My mother kept walking toward me as I counted them up: Mom, Grandpa, Charlie, Brian. Mom, Grandpa, Charlie, Brian. I did not let myself think, Dad. I twisted around in my seat, looking back down the road, remembering how the sun glinted through rain down in the village. If I could just see that sunshower, if I could just see that sunshower, if . . . I . . . could . . . just . . . see . . . that . . . sunshower.

But all that was left was a rainbow.

Always remember Mr. Roy G. Biv, my dad says. That's the secret code for the colors of the rainbow.

I remembered how I crawled up the stairs after him. How he was ahead of me. I was a baby. I loved him.

LUCIA WILLIAMS

You're dreaming again, Starr says when I moan in my sleep and he shakes me awake. Poor Lucia.

My mother steals me at night while I lie dreaming and defenseless. Her gravelly voice surrounds me, singing to me, lulling me with soft words. Starr's hand becomes part of the dream, pulling me away from the woman whose face I can't see but whose voice fills my ears.

You're calling for her again, he says.

She comes often, my faceless mother whose voice haunts my sleep, but there's Starr to drag me back, to pull me into the land of the living.

In my shadowed soul, eighteen-year-old Lucia, the girl that I was, wears her hair long. In the salty ocean air it's full and dark, separating in thick strands. Laughing, she brushes it out of her eyes. At night she plaits it, drawing the length of it around to her chest so she can see it, her fingers moving swiftly, drawing the locks over and under until the braid hangs heavy over her breast. She bands it with rubber and lies on the bed by the window, listening to the crickets, listening to the waves, smelling the beach roses that seem more fragrant at night. Watching the moon rise over the water, a flickering trail of light leading to its fullness.

This is where I will live, I said all that summer that I lived with my grandparents and walked along the water. The water is where I belong. Along that line of sand, where I can stare out and out and never have my vision obstructed, where the glittering water can draw my eyes out and there is nothing to make that line of sight stop for thousands of miles, until the lines of another country appear, another continent. Where the people speak another language, where they would look at me with the eyes of a foreigner. That girl lives in me still, frozen in time, not knowing that I chose another life, here in a tiny Adirondacks town, wife of Starr, mother of Madeleine and Charlie.

That girl lives in me still. She will hear her mother's voice singing to her for the rest of her days, a tune without words, a lullaby just out of reach.

The day I stole him, Starr wore a blue work shirt and his boots were scuffed a worn-in brown. He stood there pulling on a soda. I watched Crystal looking up at him. I watched her with the ice cream scoop behind her back, digging unseen in the sunken round carton of vanilla.

You don't know that a minute can change your life. Twelve years later you look back and you see how your days have been constructed around a single act, my entire life a penance for my act of evil: taking Starr away from Crystal.

We were eighteen years old. I didn't know anything of Starr then, not how years later he would get up early and make coffee, bring me a cup when I was still sleeping and set it on the table so its smell would draw me out of dreams; not how he loved nursery rhymes and would teach all the ones he knew and their endless variations to Charlie; not how he would feed his daughter Mallie's love of scent by bringing her gifts from the forests where he spent his days, ferns and jack-in-the-pulpits, juniper twigs, and even skunk cabbage; not how every morning he would make our bed and fold the quilt in a different artful way, one day in a precise square, one day in a triangle, one day draped so that the interlocking rings of its wedding ring pattern made a lacy circle on the white cotton sheet.

Crystal in the diner looked up at Starr behind the grill.

Crystal, he said, and the white towel licked out and slapped her softly on the bottom. *Crystal.*

I wanted that voice turned to me. I wanted it to be dark, a summer night. I wanted the sound of crickets and the sight of stars, and I wanted that voice in my ear: *Lucia.*

We were eighteen years old.

I hear there's a ghost around here somewhere, I said.

They turned to look at me, Starr and Crystal.

Is that true? I asked, looking at Starr. In the corner of my eye I saw Crystal start to shrink.

Star Hill's got the only ghost I know of, he said.

Her white apron started to disappear.

I'd like to see a ghost, I said.

Out of the corner of my eye I knew she was melting away, she was fading into the periphery. I kept my eyes on Starr, with the white towel still in his hand. I could feel how his hands would circle my waist, play on the insides of my thighs. He gave my look right back at me. Crystal melted away while I kept my eyes burning into Starr's, burning like the hot sun that burned away the fog and uncovered the fishing boats that whole summer that I lived with my grandparents and walked the beach.

Whispers rose from downstairs this morning, as they do every day. I heard cereal rattling softly into a china bowl and the kiss of the refrigerator opening up. Their voices, a murmur nearly indistinguishable from sleep.

Starr slept on. I strained my ears to hear what Mallie said to Charlie. He laughed.

I thought of joining them, of rising from our bed and slipping into the kitchen where they sat talking softly, eating their cereal and drinking the juice that Mallie pours for them into plastic cartooned glasses.

I remembered the sun-soaked day she was born.

You have a daughter, they said.

They pulled Mallie from my body and laid her on my stomach. Baby girl, I said, and I reached down for her. But she was slippery. I almost dropped her.

Whoa, said Starr, and he plucked her up. Cord still dangling, he cradled her against his chest.

And there I lay, arms reaching for her baby's body, still covered with white wax and blood, gasping with the shuddering cries of a newborn.

Give me my baby.

Surprised, he did. But she looked at me and cried. Even then she preferred Starr.

The years go by and Mallie grows. Mallie grows, and the years go silently by. She is six, and seven, and eight. There are secrets held by parents, secrets held by children; when I was younger I didn't suspect all the mysteries of my children that I would want to unravel.

My daughter, Mallie, and my son, Charlie, will carry with them all their lives the memories of their parents. All their lives they will know how we loved them. This is what I pray every night as I watch Starr bathe his daughter and his son, every night as he sings them the bathtub song that I taught him when we were first together. A song with a rambling tune and nonsense words, sounds that make no sense, that I don't even remember learning. We call it the Young Shoe bathtub song, for the only words we know: *young shoe yeah la la la.* La is the only sound we put to the tune, a melody with a cadence to it that's foreign somehow, that's strange. But it calms them. It's lulled our children to sleep since they were born.

It was my mother who taught it to me when I was a baby, too young to remember the words she sang after she was dead and there was no one left to sing it to me. It's her who comes to me in dreams, her low voice whispering in the shadows of my mind, where nothing else of her remains.

Mallie laughs as Starr sings to her, helps her wash her long dark hair that's the same color as his own. As he slides his fingers over her scalp she holds the bottle of baby shampoo to her nose, Mallie who loves smells. Charlie sings along, all the nursery rhymes Starr's taught him meandering out in his tuneless three-year-old voice: *I had a little pony, his name was Dapple Grey, I lent him to a lady to ride a mile away.*

At work James Howard lay on his back in the oversize crib and I sat alongside, bringing his arm up and laying it back, trying to get him used to the feel of the button under his fingers. James Howard has lived here at the Foothills Home for Children all his eleven years of life.

If you press it your music will come on, James, I said.

Then I covered his hand with mine, and together we pressed the orange plastic circle. Zydeco filled the air. He smiled.

He thinks he's in New Orleans, I said to his mother who was on her lunch break from Hemstrought's Bakery.

The strawberry doughnuts are selling like wild again this year, she said. They're actually not bad if you can get around the bright pink. I told them not to bother with the food coloring, but they didn't listen. Do they ever?

On Mother's Day she brought in three dozen doughnuts, boxed and tied with white baker's string. When we opened them up thirty-six miniature women stared up at us, hair and eyes dizzying shades of red and brown and blue.

You like them? she asked. I came up with this idea myself. They were going to do just as usual—put up the advertising sign on the door, *Buy Your Mom a Dozen to Munch On*—but I said why not make some actual mom doughnuts?

She took a bite of a tiny woman, scalping her.

Not bad.

She leaned back against the vinyl armchair. I watched her nibble on a pair of bright blue eyes while James Howard felt for the orange button, seeking to bring music into his world.

I see them every day at the Foothills Home, parents thickened or worn thin by the years. They drive up in their green Novas, or their new Toyotas. One at a time they emerge from the doors, mothers more often than fathers, their pocketbooks held firmly against their sides. They are older parents, or maybe they just look older.

Hi sweetheart, says Grace's mother. Grace hums her greeting, rocking her head back and forth so her hair swings. She inclines her head to her mother.

A special treat today, says her mother. She brings forth a new brush from her pocketbook, still encased in its plastic bubble. Picks at the hard edge of the plastic to free the brush.

Let me help you with that, I say, and I snip the edge off with my orange-handled shears.

Grace's mother draws the brush over her daughter's head, the dark hair like my daughter Mallie's. Strands fall limply into place, electrified ends rising to meet the nylon bristles. Smoothed, Grace's head looks smaller than usual.

Don't you look pretty, says her mother.

Grace sways and hums.

She liked the balls this morning, I say to her mother.

Did she?

She was in there for quite a while. Probably half an hour, paddling around.

She didn't get scared this time?

I think she's getting used to them, I say.

The big circular pool filled with bright plastic balls sits in a corner of the room. I lower the children into it and watch their dark heads, brown eggs in a wild nest of colors.

A white waxed bakery bag sat next to me in the passenger's seat as I drove home from work, every Friday's gift from James Howard's mother.

For your kids. I know they like the glazed ones.

Huge and puffed, the glaze dripped solid and white down the sides, the cinnamon sugar crumbling in the whorls of the doughnuts. I smelled them all the way home to Sterns.

Their scent rose heavy in the enclosed air of the car. Up and down the hills I drove, Route 12 north out of Utica and then Glass Factory Road, through the foothills of these old Adirondack Mountains that wind their way, silent and unpeopled, through upstate New York. By the time I got to Sterns I could no longer smell the cinnamon and sugar.

Your heart pounds when you see an ambulance and a solemn crowd in a town of five hundred. A white semi leaned against the curb by Jewell's. I slowed down.

Behind the wheel I watched, sun beating through the window onto the back of my neck. Dark prickling light filled the cells of my bones as I watched them carry his broken body away.

When I was eighteen I walked the beach and knew the hugeness of the world, wondered what would be. Within myself I held secrets, secrets of the body: eggs of my unborn children, skin I would touch with my long fingers, footprints lost on sand.

I could not have imagined then the Lucia who walks empty-handed from her grey frame house, who has been waiting for the winking lights of the school bus, who stares at the dark small head of her daughter, Mallie, outlined against a grimy window.

I walked out to the bus. I could see her little head, dark and motionless against the window a few seats back. The enormous bus driver that they call Tiny sat unmoving in his seat, staring out at me as I walked up. I saw the craving in his look, his instant awareness that something had gone wrong. The awfulness of his curiosity that by next morning would have spread the news all over North Sterns: Starr Williams is dead.

My little girl sat on the bus and turned her head away from me as I walked.

If you want, I'll tell her, Tim had said.

I'm her mother, I said. I will tell her.

We watched and waited. Tiny opened the door with a hiss of escaping air.

She sat in her seat with her books piled neatly next to her, her head turned away, her eyes straining down the road.

I'm trying to find that sunshower, she said. Did you see it?

No.

It was there just a little while ago. A rainbow too.

I looked at the back of the seat in front of her, covered in a patchwork of dulled tinfoil wrappers. I tried to speak.

Sshhh! said Mallie. They were just there a little while ago, the sunshower and the rainbow.

When I was eighteen I walked into a diner, still wearing my pink cotton skirt and T-shirt, scratchy and rough from the salt ocean wind. I saw a boy leaning up against a grill, flirting with a girl named Crystal, who was digging ice cream out of a tub smoking with cold.

Lucia, I think now. Turn around, girl. Go back the way you came. Mornings by the ocean are waiting for you, with light from the sun trailing fire to the horizon.

That girl was too young to know how important a second is, a moment of time. She thought her life still stretched ahead of her, limitless as the sea. She didn't know that if she turned her head the sun and the sea would disappear. She had no parents, no husband. She had no children. She didn't know the price of that kind of love, its immeasurable cost.

But I do.

CRYSTAL ZIELINSKI

Tim's hand jerked and his arm swept over the counter where I had piled the rest of Johnny's shinies, a bunch that I had collected and Starr had brought in for him over the last month. I watched them fall, squares of tinfoil and some tinselly wrapping paper. A hammered silver key chain, somebody's tiny silver dancer earring that I loved, her arms held out and both legs scissoring the air.

Tim crashed against the window.

Somebody kept saying god, god, god.

Shut up, I said.

But it was me, it was me who was saying it.

Far off I heard the ambulance coming. Up and down the hills that led the eighteen miles from Utica to Sterns. Soft and then louder it came, blowing its way into the town. The Sterns Volunteer Fire Department clustered around the semi.

No one went to Johnny, moaning and sobbing by the curb.

In third grade I was Pocahontas and Starr was John Smith. We walked down an aisle made by pushing aside all the desks and got married as part of the third-grade play. I remember his hand was cool and dry in mine. I remember the boys laughing and the girls standing, watchful as Crystal Zielinski from North Sterns promised herself to Starr Williams for better and for worse.

I ran to Johnny.

Hi, baby, I said.

I checked him over. There was a bruise coming out on his thigh, the size of an orange already, and bluish-red. I felt around it with my fingertips while he moaned. He covered his eyes with his hands.

It's OK, Johnny. The rain's gone.

The sun shone down in the stark blue air.

The ambulance came closer.

Johnny sobbed in my arms. His hands clutched at my shirt. Outside in the air I could smell the grill on our hair and clothes, the close smell of hot grease. A fainter one of vanilla and pancake syrup, mingled.

When Starr and I were eighteen, we left the others behind at the Baron von Steuben Memorial field trip.

Crystal Zielinski, are you paying attention?

That's what Starr said when the groundskeeper started the Baron lecture. He surprised me. Starr Williams had not said anything to me since *I do* in the third grade.

No, Starr Williams, I am not, I said. Seeing as this is the thirteenth time I've heard this lecture.

Every year they carted us up in a school bus to North Sterns, a couple of miles from where I live, and we all got off at the Baron's Memorial. The cabin, the walk through the woods, the grounds, the stone memorial, the lecture: North Stern's one historical attraction.

Let's go then, he said. I've got my truck.

And I went with him where he took me, to the old Welsh cemetery outside Remsen where they had buried the founders of Sterns.

Look at all these dead Welshmen, he said. Someday we'll end up here.

Not me, I said. I'm a Polack.

The grass in the cemetery tickled my ears. I ran my hand through my hair, which was long then and light brown. The sun softened and warmed my skin. I could feel the ground move when Starr got up and where he was heading by the vibrations underneath my body.

Robert Roberts. Evan Evans. Hugh Hughes, he said. I'm counting them up, Crystal. Three so far.

Three what?

Three double-named Welshmen.

Any double-named Welshwomen?

Women don't count.

I opened my eyes to see him laughing at me.

I knew I could get you to open your eyes.

You could get me to do a lot of things, I said. The only time in my life I said anything like that.

Silence thick as a funeral. His hand, his tan strong hand, played on one of the tombstones.

I picked up Johnny, big as he was, and carried him into the diner. He struggled against me and I saw I was pressing into the bruise on his legs. I slid with him into the booth, where his soda pop-top and old silver key were still lined up on the sill.

Your mouth is red, my boy, I said. Something to say, something to keep me busy, to keep me from looking out the window, through the glass that separated us from the crowd so still around the white truck.

He rocked on the seat. I took down a pointed crystal that Starr's daughter, Mallie, gave him and twirled it in the light. It flashed small rainbows across the booth. He quieted, tilting his head to catch the colors.

I went behind the grill where the hamburgers had shrunk to three black lumps, the burnt smell heavy in the air. Johnny's red washcloth hung in its place on the tap. I ran the water until it was hot and rinsed the cloth in it. Rinse and squeeze, rinse and squeeze.

In his booth Johnny sat with the crystal, waving it in the sunshine. The water hid the crying that was tearing up my throat.

Across the street the truck still leaned against the curb. The ambulance was there, quiet now. Its light that was still on flashed rhythmic red through the diner. Johnny looked up entranced. He smiled and waved for me to look.

I know, baby, I said, rinsing and squeezing. Pretty.

After a while I brought the cloth over to Johnny. The sun was starting to drop.

Here we go, I said, passing it over his mouth and over his thin white face. We'll get that stain off now.

He brought his good hand up to my face.

What are you doing now, Johnny Z? I asked.

He stroked my cheek.

You're washing my face? Is that what you're doing?

We wandered around the graves.

Look at these, I said. Girls and their babies, girls and their babies.

It was true. Sixteen-year-olds and then right next to them, a tiny head-stone with an infant's name on it. Reading those tombstones made me cold. I saw girls with huge bellies screaming on their backs in bed, trying to force life out of their bodies as their deaths rose silently before them.

Why would you even bother? I asked. Why do any of us bother?

He reached out his hand. I stood perfectly still. Heat came from his fingers, the same way you feel it when the eye doctor sits you in that chair in a darkened room and moves instruments in front of your eyes, telling you to focus on the light. And all the while you're feeling the hot blood sending out heat from his fingers.

He brushed grass from my hair with his hand.

Because we can't help it, he said.

You're washing my face? Is that what you're doing?

He stroked my cheek. Up and down, soothing. On the sill the

shinies lay still, dulled by the passing of the sun. Around his mouth I saw a faint outline of red, where I'd missed with the cloth. His T-shirt revealed the bones of his neck. When I undressed him for bed later I would ease the shirt off his arms, stretch the neck to get it over his face quickly, before he got scared. He would sit on his bed while I ran the washcloth over his skin, warming it under the tap when it grew cold. He would rock and hum. Shadowed valleys would lie above his collar bones, and his shoulder blades would jut like angel wings.

I twirled away from Starr Williams and threw my arms out to the graves. All I could see were dying girls.

Boring! I said. Boring Welsh names. Nothing interesting like Zielinski. They're as boring as John Smith.

Is that right? he asked, coming up close. *Pocahontas.*

Let's leave these old Welshmen, he said when I didn't say anything. I want to show you something.

A half hour out of North Sterns we were up into the Adirondacks, where the hills start to turn into mountains. We walked through woods that I could tell Starr Williams knew well.

I found this place, he said.

It rose up out of the ground. It came up on me before I knew it was there, a shimmer of water hidden between rocks that also opened up. A chasm in the earth, unexpected.

They've found ghosts in China, he said while I stared at the quarry. Did you read about it?

No, I said. You still love China? I remember you loving China when we were just little kids. In kindergarten even, you were talking about China.

Clay warriors. Buried for thousands of years. They dug them up, they were guarding the tomb of the Yellow Emperor.

That's a long way from Sterns, I said.

I'm going to go see them, he said. Mark my words. I'm going to the City of Western Peace to see the clay soldiers.

I had not touched him since the third grade. With warm hands he slipped off my T-shirt and we lay down next to water that shimmered up from that vast split in the earth.

I'm making you miss the lecture on the Baron, he said.

The Baron's dead, I said.

He pulled me to him, and his hands and tongue on my breasts were so good that I groaned and rubbed and drove against him. All I could feel was his body on mine, and with my eyes closed it was dark; I couldn't see a thing ahead of me.

Later we found our clothes on the rocks. They were still warm. We dressed in the darkness, worn fabric clinging to our wet skin, and walked back through the woods to Starr's blue truck.

The double pane of glass separated us from the scene outside. Inside it was warm and Johnny played with the shinies. With the sunshine gone he never looked outside. Movement caught my eye and I looked up: flashes of white coats, tall shapes of people in the crowd moving away, the circling red light of the quiet ambulance.

The summer Starr and I were eighteen we hid, hiking in maples and oaks that turned to pine the further up we got. He had an Adirondack Mountain Club trail book for the south-central Adirondacks that we followed, and he knew of other hikes too, that he had found on his own. He wore jeans and old shirts that smelled of sun and salt and sweat. I rubbed my cheek on the back of his neck, where the dark hair grew straight and fine. My legs cried for lack of air. On the way down the mountains my thighs trembled and my knees hurt from braking, step after step, on the steepness of rock and loam.

That summer he talked about Chinese warriors while I waited for the hikes to end, to get back to my trailer, to lie with him on my bed with the cool sheets.

How come I've never met your father? he asked one night in the truck. Driving through the woods, the windows wide open with cool night air rushing in.

Well he's a trucker, I said. He's gone.

I stuck my head out the window and sang along with the radio. Always? he asked.

Pretty much, I yelled with my head still out the window. I could barely hear him with the wind filling my body, pushing against my skin, and blowing my hair straight back.

He pulled the truck over to the side of the road. Turned it off. Turned off the lights. We sat in the darkness, the roar of the lost wind still filling my ears and skin with tingling.

Crystal are you all alone? he asked.

Everyone's all alone, I said. It's a law of nature.

He looked at me in the darkness, his eyes shining like the wild animals that crouched in the ditch, waiting for the truck to fling itself past.

I'm eighteen, I said. Of age.

He put his hands on the steering wheel and rocked.

I still have Johnny's baby toys, stored on the shelves above his bed in the trailer. His favorites even then were the shinies: mirrored rattles, a plastic cube that snowed stars over a sleeping village when he shook it. The bigger wheeled things, the tricycle and scooter, he never used. I put them away one day when he was still little. Just for the time being I thought, but I never took them down again.

When it was fully dark and everyone had disappeared from the street, I hung the Closed sign on the diner door. Then it was just Johnny and me. I put my arm around him, disturbing the rhythm of his hand patting my cheek. I remembered how he smelled as a baby, how I used to bring him into bed with me when he cried at night, curve my body around his and rock until he fell asleep again.

My eyes burned from crying. I rubbed my cheek into the hollows of his neck, smelling his particular smell, sweat and syrup and tears.

Dead, I thought, the dark word crawling through me. *Starr's dead.*

But Johnny, Johnny was alive.

MALLIE WILLIAMS

At night my bones hurt. They are growing in the dark. When I lie down, they start to stretch. I curl on my side and press my knees together. I hold my ankles with my fingers, but nothing I do stops them.

You're growing, Mallie, voices from the black dresses and suits said. What a tall girl you're getting to be.

They all stood around. The table had the extra boards in it, and it was covered with plates and bowls of food. I saw Charlie's foot disappear, and I knew what he was doing. I used to do that too, hide underneath the table and watch the legs go by. Stick my finger out and wisp it across someone's foot or ankle and watch them jump or slap it with their hand, as if I were a bug that they couldn't see.

The white lace hung down. I kept looking over and there it was, Charlie's foot, the edge of his blue sneaker poking out under the salad end.

They all wore black. A forest of black.

Charlie wonders where it went, but I didn't tell him.

Mom, he said. Where'd the swimming pool go?

She didn't hear him, I don't think. She didn't say anything. But later she hooked up the old green sprinkler to the hose, the one we used to play in before my dad brought home the new swimming pool. I'm too old for the sprinkler. But Charlie loves it. He dashes through the falling water. It's a warm spring this year, warm and dry. Charlie sings his rhymes that my dad taught him. *Ride a cockhorse to Banbury Cross, to see a fine lady upon a white horse. Rings on her fingers and bells on her toes, and she shall have music wherever she goes.* Sometimes he changes the words to Charlie. *To see a fine Charlie upon a white horse*, which is what my dad used to do when they were playing.

It has been six weeks since my father, Starr, died.

I've got you a dress to wear, my mother said.

Navy blue. Puff sleeves. That decoration stuff they call smocking.

I can't wear it, I said.

I'll help you with the buttons, she said, if that's the problem.

I'm not going to wear it, I said.

I can't wear something that he never saw.

Are you my baby girl? my father used to ask. Are you my baby girl?

I remember that. At night when he got home from the woods he used to pick me up, one arm under my back, one arm under my knees, and rock me back and forth. That was before we had Charlie. He always had something for me, a flower or a pinecone that he called a fir cone because that's what Winnie the Pooh in the book I liked when I was little called it. He twirled me around the living room. I remember hanging my head down so my hair flew out, watching the couch and the chairs, the pictures, and the fireplace flash by. Everything a blur. I remember shutting my eyes to block it out, so all I could feel was my father's arms under me and his voice saying, Are you my baby girl? Are you?

In the book it says that people are born again, over and over. They can live hundreds of lives.

I started looking around at the new babies in town. There was only one. Dena Jacobs's new baby girl. Jacobs Number Six because her husband keeps wanting a boy. I saw Dena at the post office after school when we were getting gas. I jumped out of the car and ran in. She had the baby laid on the counter.

Could a man be born as a girl?

I looked at the baby. Dena had her all wrapped around with one of those flannel blankets that was pilled from being wrapped around so many Jacobs babies. It was sleeping. Dena was licking stamps in the corner so I quick put out my finger and pushed up one of its lids. They said that the eyes reveal the soul. I looked into its eye, but it just rolled up in the baby's head, and I couldn't stand to look at that so I let the lid back down again.

It was me, me who dragged the swimming pool up the stairs while Mom was sleeping. It squeaked against the sides of the railing and the wall. Then I pushed it into my closet, as far back as it would go, all squeezed up into a lumped ball, like the twisted balloon animals that they make at the fair. My dad blew it up for us the same day he brought it home.

Mal! Charlie! Got something for you!

It bulges in the back of my closet, filled with his air.

When I do seances I put the incense that I got at the state fair in its ring. I light the incense with a match. The smoke curls out in a wisp that lazes up in a spiral, reaching up to my nose and making my nose shiver with the smell. It's pitch dark in the closet, with that smell that makes my nose close in. There's the incense smell and the vinyl smell from the swimming pool. It closes in around me, the pool, and I squirm into its center. The air in it gets warm after a while, and it keeps me warm in the dark closet.

What if there was nothing? is what I say. *What if there was nothing?*

That's the way to go into another world. To think of what if there was nothing, nothing at all—no sun, no moon, no spinning earth, no colors, no people or animals or anything. Think hard enough and it closes in on you. It suffocates you: *What if there was nothing?*

I keep the door to my closet closed. A sign: Keep Out, Violators Will Be Prosecuted. Inside I have all my clothes on their hangers, all in a row, my shoes lined up below, so if a violator walks in anyway they will think, What a clean neat closet, and they'll shut the door. The swimming pool no one can see; it's stuffed on the way left side behind my sleeping bag. I check the plug every day. There it sits, bulging, with fish and seal and mermaid pictures stamped all over it, hidden behind my sleeping bag and that navy blue dress.

At night my bones ache with the growing.

You're going to be tall, my grandfather Tim says. Like him.

My father was my grandfather's only child.

I will not grow, I say to myself. I will not grow. If I grow, how will he know me? My father who's a baby now somewhere in the world.

I'm waiting for a sign. He will give me a sign. *What if there was nothing?* I think.

The swimming pool sits in the back of the closet, smelling like vinyl. That's not the kind of smell we like, me and my dad. We like forest kinds of smells, grassy kinds of smells, smells like the kind my dad brings me from the Adirondacks.

Now Charlie plays outside in the sprinkler, the old green sprinkler that I'm too big for. He runs through sparkles of light, around and around, singing his rhymes. The grass gets wet and he slips and falls and jumps up again to run around and around. I started singing with him. *Little Bo-Peep has lost her sheep, and doesn't know where to find them.*

Stop that, he said. That's me and Dad's and you can't sing that.

He won't let me sing them anymore. Only he can sing them, is what he says. In the back of the closet I hung the stickums. I took them down from where my dad hung them: *zhuozi* on the table, *chuanghu* on the window. *Diandeng* on the lamp. In the back of my closet I stuck them to the wall, all in a row. On the back of each one I wrote down where it came off of, so that I would not forget. It was my father's handwriting. He printed the names on each stickum and then put what he told me was a tone mark on top of each one, to tell him how to say it.

He was studying Chinese for his trip to China. That belongs to the other world now, his trip to China that isn't going to happen, the other world when he was alive.

What if there was nothing?

I got his tape recorder from the shelf in the kitchen. I put it in the back of the closet too. At night after I was tucked in I got out of bed and rewound the tapes. There was one of a Chinese man's voice talking and another one of my dad, trying to say the words the way the man said them.

Zhuozi.

Chuanghu.

Diandeng.

There were sheets of paper covered with Chinese marks that meant numbers.

I'm only going to learn how to write the numbers, my dad said. That's all I can handle.

I remember the night when I heard them talking about the trip.

It's something I want to do, he said to my mother. All my life, I've wanted to go to China.

By yourself, she said.

By myself.

Just get in an airplane and go to the other side of the world? You can just do that? she asked. What if it goes down?

It's not going to go down.

But what if? she asked. What if?

At the service my grandfather sat in the corner. I saw his lips moving, talking to himself. Other people saw. They started to walk around him, carefully, like people do around Johnny Zielinski. Johnny saw Charlie's sneaker poking out underneath the lace. He tilted his head and started to laugh like he does. I saw people watching him.

Come on, Johnny, I said. You come with me.

I got a plate for Johnny, and I took him down the line of the table.

You want some Jell-O? I asked. You want a roll? Butter with it? You want some baked beans or some ham? Mustard? How about a pickle?

I got him a pickle and some chocolate cake.

You come with me, I said.

I took him upstairs. I showed him my room.

Now this is secret, I said. There's nobody who knows about this, just you and me. He was eating the pickle. Pickle juice dripped off his fingers and chin.

See that swimming pool? I asked.

He licked his fingers. There was a drop of green pickle juice on his chin. That's my secret, I said. That's my dad's last air. And he's going to come give me a sign.

Then I took Johnny outside so he could eat his cake where it didn't matter if he made a mess. Johnny likes to go outside.

On the bus the morning I went back it was just me and Tiny at first. First one on, last one off, even though I'm closer to the village than anyone. If they went through North Sterns first I could be last on, first off. But they don't.

Tiny opened the door and I went to my seat. The tinfoil was still there.

The boys from North Sterns got on, one by one. They sat in their seats behind Tiny. Tiny said something and they laughed. I saw them, one at a time. They turned around and looked at me quick, then they turned back.

Johnny got on. He was happy to see me. He said my name the way he does. I took his hand and put it on the tinfoil.

I'll bring you some more, I said.

I was wearing my blue shirt and my pants with the flowers that come to the top of my ankles. Three months ago they were the right length. At night I lie and hold my ankles, rocking back and forth. The shoulders of the blue shirt pinch in and hold my arms back. My hair is getting longer.

Starr Williams.

I heard the boys saying his name. Whispering it like it was a dirty word.

Starr Williams.

I stood up.

Starr Williams, I said. STARR WILLIAMS.

Next to me Johnny moaned.

My father smelled like trees. Like sap from the pines, blobs of it oozed onto pinecones that he used to bring me in the spring. Like the moss that we put in the terrarium that we made together. He brought me dirt from the forest that he called loam, and we put in twigs for trees, and the moss, and some rocks and a toad.

I thought, maybe he wasn't born again as a person. Is that possible? Could he be born again as an animal, like a toad? Maybe a cow. In India they don't eat cows because they think that people are reincarnated as cows, is what the teacher said.

After a while they started lifting their glasses in the air, making toasts. I remember when Starr. There was this one time when Starr and me. Starr and I used to. Johnny Zielinski's aunt Crystal stood in a corner with a glass in her hand. My grandfather sat in his corner. My mother stood by the stairs. None of them said a word. I moved down the line with crumb cake for Charlie. Nobody was swatting their legs or kicking their feet. Charlie was staying still as a stone underneath the lace.

The bowls and dishes looked worn down. Dribbles and spills of baked beans and juice littered between the hot mats and the spoons. I took a piece of crumb cake, and I held it in my hand. Down the line I went. When I got to Charlie's sneaker toe I poked the crumb cake under the tablecloth and held it there. I shook it like you shake a bone for a dog. It was taken away from me.

Starr Williams. I kept turning to see who it was, but I could never catch it. Then when my attention was back to Johnny I would hear it again, *Starr Williams*, and it was gone and I had missed it.

Anywhere in the world, he could be. He could be a baby born already in China, wearing those split pants that our teacher told us babies wear there instead of diapers. When they have to go they just go anywhere, right on the street. He could have slanting eyes.

I don't know of any babies due soon in Sterns. The book said we were born and then born again. I'm waiting for the sign.

One, two, three, four, all the way up to eighteen, to get past the tree where my grandma Georgia died against. But how to get past the place where my father died? How to get past Crystal's Diner, past Jewell's?

Do you remember, Johnny? I asked him on the bus. Do you remember when my dad bought you a red Popsicle and it started to rain?

He tilted his head.

Every night I listen to my father's voice: *yi, er, san. Yi, er, san.* One two three, over and over. Then he goes on, all the way to ten. Every night I listen to my dad's voice, until his air in the swimming pool is warm and incense burns my nose. Then I rewind it and listen some more. I don't know what the sign will be. But I'm looking. I'm on the lookout.

6

CRYSTAL ZIELINSKI

Mallie? I said. There she was, hovering around the counter, so skinny with her dark hair falling onto her face.

I got some shinies for Johnny, she said. Can you give them to him? She dragged up a pocketful of glitter sticker stars, with a sheriff's badge thrown in.

I'll take the stickers, I said, but you keep the badge. He'll stick himself on the pin.

She pushed the stars across the counter. She looked skinnier to me, and squeezed, as if she couldn't get enough air into her lungs.

Come on, sit up here, I said. She got up on one of the stools. I started making her a shake.

You want chocolate or vanilla?

Thank you, was all she said.

So I made her a chocolate. She started pulling it up through the straw I gave her, but she couldn't get it. I saw her cheeks sucked in, her jaw muscles working.

You look like me when I try to blow up a balloon, only in reverse, I said. I've never been able to blow up balloons. Here.

And I gave her a special thick milkshake straw.

Thank you, she said.

She managed to suck up a little bit with it.

I've been hearing some things about you, I said. From Dena Jacobs.

She darted a look at me then went back to pulling on the milk-shake.

Do you believe in reincarnation? she asked.

What were you hoping to find in that baby's eyes? I asked.

She didn't say anything.

Do you want me to make you a hamburger or anything? You could use it, it looks like.

She sat there pulling on her milkshake, so seriously I couldn't stand looking at her.

I don't eat meat, she said.

Since when?

Do you know they don't eat cows in India, she said. Because they think it could be their grandmother reincarnated into the body of a cow. All cows are actually dead people, in India.

Oh, I see, I said. So if you eat a hamburger you might be eating your daddy. Is that it?

Someone in a window booth wanted more water so I brought the pitcher over. After a while I looked over again and saw Mallie sucking in with all her might, pulling up gobs of sweet cold while the tears ran down her cheeks.

At the memorial service Mallie dragged Johnny down the line while I stood in a corner. There was no casket. They were having him cremated.

I'll be buried here, he had said that day by the tombstones, when I couldn't stop thinking about young girls and their big bellies. Here with all these other Welshmen, he had said.

I wanted to tell someone, someone who would listen.

Hey, Starr wanted to be buried up in the Welsh cemetery, I wanted to say. He didn't want to go up in smoke.

But who would hear? Years go by and people forget; they look at you and what do they see: Crystal Zielinski who runs the diner, who takes care of her sister's retarded boy.

The truth is that I never had a sister. Nights, I lay in the trailer in my bed and dreamed one up. She was older than me, she took care of me. When our father was gone she made my breakfast and waited with me for the school bus. She was the sister I made up for myself.

I was fifteen when he got out the big green Army duffel. Started putting in his clothes.

You going somewhere, Dad? I asked after a while of trying to ignore him.

A job, he said. A new job.

When will you be back?

He pulled the ropes that shut the duffel up and slid the cinch down tight.

You're a big girl now, Crystal.

Not that big, I said after a while.

Fifteen is big enough to watch out for yourself until I get back, he said.

But when? I thought. When?

Make sure you shut the door tight when you go to bed, he said. And keep the truck filled up.

I thought, I'm not even legal to drive it yet. But I didn't say anything.

Once I asked him about my mother.

What about her?

He didn't look up from the .22 he was cleaning.

Well. Where is she? Is she still alive?

He held it up to the light.

Those coyotes are getting too bold for their own good, he said. I give them a couple more nights howling like that then I'm going to teach them a lesson.

He cleaned it some more.

Forget about your mother, he said. God knows I have.

He put the duffel in the back seat of the Nova, and then he got in the front seat.

I'll be back, he said. Now you take care of things around here.

I looked at him. He had on his red flannel shirt with the stitching across the pocket. His hair was combed flat across his head so you could still see the comb marks.

What about my mother? I asked again, the only other time I brought it up.

Your mother. Your mother didn't want a kid . . .

Still half a sentence left, but he stopped talking. Then he started the engine.

Any more than I did, is what I knew he was going to say.

It wasn't too hard to keep them in the dark at school. My father hadn't ever gone to the conferences anyway, so that wasn't anything new. Money was harder. When the envelope he left on the table ran out, I drove to the diner after school.

I'm looking for a part-time job. I can waitress.

How old are you now, Crystal?

That was Jack, the manager at the time.

Fifteen.

Looking for a bigger allowance, I guess.

Mmhm.

Well I guess we could start you on a couple of afternoons after school. How about weekends?

Weekends would be fine, I said.

This was before I had my license and was legal to drive by myself. But nobody noticed that it was just me in the truck. The trailer was owned. I had to pay the taxes and the electricity and food. I could eat at the diner so groceries weren't much. Nights I worked I ate a lot.

Crystal Zielinski you eat like a horse, said Jack. For such a skinny girl.

I had dreams that I spun while I lay in the trailer listening to

47

the coyotes. My father with a regular job. A mother. My only re-curring image of her was of her brushing my hair. In my dreams I had long hair, halfway down my back, and my mother brushed it every night and every morning before school. She made sure my teeth were clean before I went to bed and she brushed my hair. That was it for my dream of a mother, feeling her hands guiding the brush down the long hair that I wished I had.

Pregnant, I lay thinking about the baby. It was a girl, I was sure of it. I would brush her hair every day. I would grow it long, unlike my real hair which had always been short. My father used to clip it with the scissors. If it was summer he cut it really short, and then sometimes he'd shave up the neck with his razor.

Even North Sterns kids, they had families. Mean those kids were, but they got off the bus and I watched the way they walked change. They turned into kids when they were off that bus. They carted their drawings and their lunch boxes into their trailers or their houses. They stopped to pet dogs. They fought with their brothers and sisters. Me, I got off that bus and it was me, myself, and I. Except for the summer I was eighteen, when there was Starr Williams, and my dreams about my baby girl, whose hair I would brush.

Alone in the trailer, I lay in my bed and looked out the window at the stars. The coyotes howled across the field. There was noth-ing from my father, not a postcard like the kind he used to send me when I was little. Not a ten dollar bill like he sometimes used to send.

I shut the door tight and I kept the truck filled with gas, gas that I paid for myself.

And what are your plans? Jack at the diner asked after I gradu-ated from high school, walking down the aisle slowly. I made sure it was slow, so it wouldn't look as if I was embarrassed to be by myself, as if I were worried about not having anyone to clap for me when I got the diploma.

What are your plans now, Miss Crystal?

Well I'm going to spend the summer and fall at the diner and the winter in Albany with my sister, I said, the lie spilling from my mouth. So naturally, because I'd practiced it. Then I thought I might come back here and work for a while.

A winter in Albany, he said. Doesn't that sound like an adventure.

He was a kind man.

Yes, I said. And I'm looking forward to seeing my sister.

Do I recall her? he asked.

Angela, I said. She's much older than I am. Ten years.

Oh yes, Angela Zielinski, he said. Of course I remember her. Tall, pretty? Long hair?

That's her, I said. I smiled.

He nodded his head, remembering my make-believe sister with the long pretty hair.

Hello, Mr. Williams, I used to say when Tim Williams walked into the diner.

Hello, Crystal.

He smiled. He was a kind man also.

What can I get for you?

You're practically running this place, he said. How long have you worked here now?

Three years, I said the summer I was eighteen.

I pressed my belly into the counter, feeling its weight against the tiny hard lump that was growing way down low. My biggest secret.

I used to look at Tim Williams that summer, thinking of the secrets I knew about his son Starr. How he started out hiking in his blue work shirt and then took it off when he got hot, the fine blond hairs on his forearms glinting in the sun. How his favorite hike was up Bald Mountain, climbing bare rock that curved up the mountain like a rib, like a spine, because he remembered hiking it with his dad when he was three. How he touched the inside of my wrist, stroking, with one finger, and moved up to the inside of my elbow while I lay, eyes closed, against him.

Do you have any plans for the future, Crystal, now that you're graduated? asked Tim.

I'm going to spend next winter with my sister in Albany, I said. She's expecting a baby. You might remember her from elementary art class. Angela Zielinski?

Angela, Angela, he murmured.

She was tall, I said. A lot taller than me, with long dark hair?

Did she go by Angie? he asked.

Sometimes, I said. Yes, sometimes she did.

No, I don't remember her. I'm sorry.

He was the only one, the only one that admitted he never heard of Angela, my pretend sister.

But I'll be back in the spring, I said to Tim. I plan to work here at the diner for a while more, then we'll see what happens.

Starr's going to take some time too, said Tim. Figure out where he wants to go to school.

Another secret that I knew about Starr: he wasn't going to school. He didn't want to. In the woods was where he wanted to be, in the Adirondacks up beyond Sterns, where he loved it best.

That sounds like a good plan, I said to Tim.

He looked at me and I thought he would ask about Starr and me, that he knew about me and Starr. But he said nothing, he looked away.

For a few months I thought I maybe could turn them into my family. Starr Williams, who lived in a grey frame house with his mother, Georgia, and his father, Tim, Mr. Tim Williams the art teacher at Sterns Elementary. Who was *my* art teacher when I was a little girl. Starr had no dog, but everything else fit: when we were growing up he got off the bus with his lunch box and turned into a kid. He went into a house with a mother and a father. He spent his summers running through a sprinkler that his father hooked up for him, planting and weeding a garden, playing baseball. My summers were spent in North Sterns, waiting for school to start again so I could talk, so I could have someone to talk to, someone to look at my papers and drawings.

For a few months I thought that it might be mine. That I could have his father and his mother, that I could join into the life of the house that Starr lived in, be absorbed by the Williamses.

I was going to tell Starr about the baby the day Lucia walked into the diner, cotton skirt swaying around her ankles, her hair floating back over her shoulders. Starr's back was to her, his hand reaching across the counter to grab mine. Teasing.

I'm looking for a ghost, she said, looking at his back. Has anyone heard of one around here?

He turned. I watched it happen, my hand freezing onto the ice cream scoop that I had dug into the tub of vanilla. I saw him begin to flow toward her.

There's only one ghost around here that I know of, he said.

She smiled, her teeth white against the tan, and I felt him going. I watched him slide away as if he were water falling through my fingers and I knew, that was the end of Starr and me. *No, no,* a silent screaming grief, flying around the diner, bouncing off the walls, the ceiling, the floor, inside my soul.

Can you show it to me? she asked, and at that moment I felt life move within my gut, like a tiny protest, like a bubble bursting way down deep.

I kept it hid until the seventh month, then I disappeared. I had bags and bags of food in the trailer, boxes of spaghetti and cans of soup. Dry milk, which I mixed with well water. It's easy to hide in North Sterns. Even Starr never guessed until the end, that it was just me living there. I used to meet him at the end of the driveway and jump in when he drove up, tell him my father was off on a long-distance haul.

He had been with Lucia already four months when I disappeared, so there was no one to know that I wasn't in Albany, that I was living in North Sterns the whole winter, sitting in the trailer with my stomach stretching tighter and tighter against the T-shirts and old sweatshirts.

There would be plenty of time I always thought, to get in the car and drive down to Utica. The books said first baby, just wait until the contractions are five minutes apart then call. I thought I'd leave when they were ten minutes apart to be on the safe side, an easy half-hour drive to Utica Memorial, forty-five minutes if it was snowing.

What I thought might be a contraction came when I was eating a can of tomato soup with dry milk mixed in for the calcium. Let's time it, I told myself. I was used to talking to myself by then. I was putting on a sweater when the water broke, trickling down my leg. Wasn't it supposed to gush out like a fountain? But it was a hot trickle, gradually wetting through the layers of my father's old boxers and jeans that I wore unzipped with an elastic threaded through the belt loops to hold them up.

Then I had to push.

I was alone.

I had to push more than I had ever had to do anything.

I got the jeans off and I was down on the rug, my arms grabbing onto the leg of the couch, bracing my feet against the wall. I felt myself rip. A huge hot ball slid from me. I couldn't see.

A minute later I pushed again and it slithered out of me onto the rug. I kept waiting for a cry. There should be a cry! I thought. Then I reached down, grabbing for it. So slippery.

When Mallie came in next time she sat on the counter stool she always sits on. It was broken, it wouldn't twirl. I didn't want her to fall so I said, Mal, it's broken, honey. Come sit on this one. Obediently she followed me down to the other end of the counter. I wondered why it is that the seat people sit on the first time they come to a place is the one they want to sit on forevermore. Comfort, maybe?

She squirmed onto the red vinyl circle and pulled out a notebook. Her hair hung down over her eyes. You could use a haircut, I thought, not to mention a good brushing. But I said nothing. In his corner Johnny sat in the sun with his eyes closed, swaying. The heat made him drowsy.

What're you working on, Mal? I asked.

Code.

Code?

Secret messages, she said. I'm trying to decipher them.

I looked in the notebook. icnkrmf. guecnmms. 3uy8vna.

Ouija, if I'm not mistaken.

She nodded. She was using different symbols for each letter, letters equalling numbers, trying to make sense of gibberish.

Any luck?

None, she said.

She was skinnier than ever, so I made her another milkshake and put a burger on the grill. She gave me a look.

Oops. Still not eating dead grandmas, I see.

I decided to eat it myself and put a bun on the grill to brown. Mallie dragged up a piece of tinfoil from her pocket and started working at it, molding it. I put the can under the mixer and added a scoop of malt, which I had read somewhere was nutritious.

For Johnny, she said when I turned around.

There it was, a little swan made out of aluminum foil.

Now where'd you learn to do that? It's beautiful.

Dad, she said. My dad.

Give it to Johnny, I said, you know where to find him.

She walked over and pushed it across the wooden tabletop to him where he was playing with the metal flap of the sugar shaker. I watched him turn his head to the side and squint. He held the bird up to the sunshine and dangled it back and forth to catch the light.

Thanks, Mallie, I said when she dragged herself back to get the malt.

What happened to Johnny? she asked. How did he get that way?

Hemiparesis, I said. Cerebral palsy. No oxygen when he was born. It can paralyze you and cause blindness.

Johnny's not blind, though.

He can see partly, I said. When he turns his head the right way. He can't see things straight on.

His baby face was blue. The cord was white and it pulsed, a twirl like a phone cord wrapped around his neck. It was all slippery and covered with gunk, but I slid it up over his tiny blue face and pinched his cheeks.

I ran my finger into his mouth and tried to clear away the gunk from his nose.

I bent over him and blew into his mouth and nose.

I slapped him.

I snapped my fingers against his head.

I pushed air into him.

He gasped.

Across the field the coyotes howled and howled.

At the hospital in Utica where as soon as I could stand I drove him down to, they bent over him for hours. I said my husband was off on business; we hadn't expected the baby for a few more weeks. For the birth certificate they asked father's full name and I said Dale Zielinski. That was one thing I had practiced. I always liked the name Dale.

Mallie gave up trying to decipher her secret messages and closed her notebook. She sat there in the sunshine with one arm propped up by the other, dangling the swan for Johnny. I looked at her, her hair that she won't cut hanging stringy and dark in her face. Dangling that tinfoil swan, staring at it as if it had her hypnotized. My son laughed the way he laughs, that looks like he's crying unless you know better.

I remembered the night I had him, how his mouth opened in an airless gasp. I remembered my dreams of a baby girl, with long dark hair to brush. The shadows under Mallie's eyes looked like bruises, and there was a snarl twining through her hair. Johnny's skin stretched pale over his bird bones as he swayed in the sun, following the swan. Jesus, I thought. The price of love.

TIM WILLIAMS

My wife was the one who wanted to name him Starr, not me. I thought the kids would laugh at him, that a funny name like that would make his life harder than it had to be. Georgia said she wanted to name him Starr because Star Hill was where we made him.

Besides, I don't want him to have an ordinary name, she said.

Why not? I said. There's nothing wrong with ordinary names. Take Tim, for instance.

She finally got her way, but right in the beginning it was like I predicted. The nurse with the birth certificate form looked at us funny in the hospital room when Georgia told her that his name was Starr Timothy Williams.

Star? Like twinkle twinkle little?

That's right, said Georgia. But with a double *r*.

When the nurse left the room I gave Georgia a look.

See what I mean? I said. This is how it's going to be.

I don't care, she said. His name is Starr.

It'll make his life harder than it needs to be, I kept saying.

She just looked at me. She could look right through me.

You're just thinking about yourself, she said. And you know it.

She was right. It was my own life I was thinking about, I guess. How kids used to laugh at me and sometimes even adults. When we were growing up, teaching was a woman's job. And art teachers especially were always women. But from the start it was what I wanted, the art and the teaching. I wanted the kids, all around me like I was all around my favorite teachers in elementary school. I kept it to myself, though.

In high school I met Georgia in a painting class. She was one of those girls who traveled in a flock of other girls. She was always ready with an answer. She teased her friends. She wore a red skirt with a pink sweater. Maybe twice a week, she would wear that outfit.

Pink and red.

Later she had a blanket that she kept in my car. I remember she brought it out of her house in a paper bag one night when we were seniors, under her shoes to change into once we got to the party. It was winter, boots weather. All the girls used to carry their shoes to change into later.

I made this for you, she said.

I remember the sound of her voice when she said that. That's how I remember things, flashes of color, little corners of sound and shape that wouldn't make sense to anyone except me. That blanket had the feel of grass and wool mixed together. It was ivory flecked with brown. I can see a corner of it now, with a strand of Georgia's hair curling across it. All I need is to picture a corner of that blanket, to bring back the summer night on Star Hill that Georgia wanted to name Starr after. That's how my memory works.

Georgia's red skirt and her pink sweater I put into the painting I made in that class where I met her. She sat in her corner with her girlfriends, all of them working on watercolors: the Sterns village green, the view from Glass Factory Road looking down at the Mohawk Valley and Utica in the distance, a dark Adirondacks lake with a red canoe in the distance. Busy and laughing. I remember her looking over once to where I was, at my table where I sat by myself with the paper and paints spread around me, taking up room so I wouldn't look lonely to her and all her friends. We were sixteen.

Later the teacher pinned all the paintings on the line to display.

The girls' were full of trees and flowers and water and sky. Mine was a swash of grey, with a smear of pink and red in one corner and white splashes of laughter floating up near the border of the paper. That's what Georgia was like to me.

Very nice, Tim, said the teacher.

I knew she didn't like it.

But Georgia's eyes stayed on my painting. Later, after she started showing up next to me in line, behind me at my locker, at the bonfires, after finally there started to be an understanding between us, she told me that she had liked my painting.

I liked its colors, she said. That red and that pink, it's an interesting combination.

She was laughing. She knew. That was the thing about Georgia.

I remember that blanket she made, the smell of the grass, the feel of the dew on Star Hill under my bare feet. We had tried for nine years to make a baby. That was after we got married, after I got the art teaching job, Georgia explaining to my parents and everyone else that I was a painter and I liked kids, and teaching was a good steady job with summers off, so why shouldn't I be an art teacher?

I got used to Starr's name and so did everyone else. It took them a little while, but then the name was just who he was. Starr was a kid that nobody messed with, anyway. He was one of those kids. There's one in every classroom; I see them day to day. The one kid who's nice to everyone, who everyone's nice to in return. There's something about those kids, hard to put your finger on. But every class has one of them.

You think there's time. I always thought there was. I thought that someday I would talk, tell Georgia the things I wanted to tell her, the bits of shape and color and sound that were what came to me when I thought of her. At night when she was asleep I smelled her hair. There was a smell of leaves and nutmeg that came from her when she was asleep.

I could have told her that. I thought I would someday, but then she was gone.

Then I thought I would tell Starr, talk to him someday about his mother, about himself, how I felt about him.

He comes to me too, in fragments. When he was three I took him hiking up Bald Mountain in the Adirondacks. He was holding a stick to fend off ghosts and bears.

Don't worry, Dad, he said. I'll save you.

When we got to the top he was tired. I gave him a drink from the wineskin. He pretended the water was wine. Then he looked around the flatness of the rock at the summit. The sun went behind a cloud.

Daddy, is this where we are? he asked.

I can still hear the sound of Starr's voice on that day, his first day of hiking. I had thought that someday I would tell him about that.

I thought, if he had just stayed inside that store.

I thought, if he had not turned his head at that moment, not seen the truck coming down, not seen Johnny step out into the street.

Just once I let myself think it: If only it had been Johnny instead.

Piles of construction paper and jars of paint. Easels, pots of glue, scissors, and colored pencils. I watch the children come and I watch them go. And every year they move on, into their lives, growing into the people they are. Starr among them. While I pin up their paintings and put their clay sculptures up on the display table next to my desk.

The night Starr died I sat in the dark with the window open. Crickets sang. I thought of warriors, the clay soldiers that he had longed to see. The color of terra cotta wove its way through my mind.

At the wake I sat by myself in a corner. Charlie hid under the table that the women had heaped with plates and bowls and cups. Mallie tried to feed Johnny Zielinski.

Daddy, is this where we are?

The sound of his voice kept coming to me.

There was food: baked beans, lime Jell-O salad with cottage cheese and pineapple, a ham. Pies. The young ones started drinking beer. Then someone made a toast. I sat in a chair at the back of the room, watching them all in their confusion. I felt Georgia near me.

They're trying, I said to her. They don't know how to go about it yet, thirty years old is all they are.

They started talking, the young people, all Starr's friends whose baby faces I had watched when they were just born, some of whom I had taught. I saw them grow up, thin out or plump up, all of them lengthening and curving into the adults they were now.

I saw that they would go on changing. Laugh lines would appear around their eyes, the first grey hairs, the girls' flat bellies would start to sag.

They toasted Starr as if it were a wedding. They raised their beer glasses in the air. I saw that that's the way it would be now, that all these young people had left of my son was what was already in their minds.

They don't know what else to do, I thought to Georgia, they don't have much practice with funerals.

Grey-eyed Crystal watched from across the room.

Sometimes at his corner desk Johnny Zielinski loses his breath on a fall or spring day. He forgets how to breathe when the thunderstorms roll in, when a flash of lightning blinds him. I sit him on my lap and give him a brown paper bag to breathe into, to calm his overworking lungs. Now I know how Johnny must feel when a storm comes rolling in. Help me, I thought, help me, help me.

Crystal's sister never came back to claim her baby. When he was sick Crystal kept him with her in the diner, wiping his nose and spooning red medicine into him.

He hangs his head out the car window on the way home, Crystal said to me once. Like a puppy except his tongue stays in.

What's he looking for?

Stars, she said. He loves the stars but they're almost never bright enough for him to see.

You should take him to see the ghost of Star Hill.

That old ghost, she said. You believe in it?

Sure, I said. A spark of light, coming at you out of the woods. But you can't look at it straight on. You have to catch it out of the corner of your eye, so they say.

She smiled.

Get Starr to take him, I said. Starr knows those woods better than anyone. Starr cuts firewood for a living. The state marks the trees with orange slashes on state land, and Starr goes in and cuts them down, turns them into chunks of wood and drives into Utica with his blue pickup loaded down, looking for chimneys. All spring and summer and fall he cuts firewood. In winter he does construction.

Starr's seen the ghost? asked Crystal.

You'd have to ask him, I said. But it wouldn't surprise me.

The first time I saw my son, Starr, he came forced and screaming from my wife, Georgia's, body. Half in and half out of this world, his twisted-up infant face covered with blood and fluid. They gave him to me and I took him.

Mr. Williams, the nurse said. You have a baby boy.

I wished I was naked, to hold him against my skin, to take off the blue scrubs, the mask and cap they made me wear when I made them let me into the delivery room. But instead I bent down and put my cheek against the pulse of his heart, on the soft spot where later on his bones were supposed to knit together. I listened to him crying while they sewed Georgia up.

I remember Starr at three years old, whirling and leaping just outside my peripheral vision as I soaped behind the glass of the shower door. The shower fan was on and the door ajar. I rubbed off the steam on the shower door so that I could watch him as he whirled past the open door.

Was he dancing? Or screaming?

I couldn't tell. The water rushed on. I strained, listening. *Here am I, Little Jumping Joan. When nobody's with me, I'm all alone.* On he spun, baby Starr who loved nursery rhymes. The shower drummed on my skin and face, warm and hard. I closed my eyes and let the hiss grow until the water was all I heard. The smell of water and melting soap filled my nose, and I almost lost my balance, standing with my head tipped to the hard rush. Then I opened my eyes and cleared the water from them to see Starr again, a shadow shape through the steamed-over glass, running or dancing or twirling. I couldn't hear anything but the echo of his voice, his chanted nursery rhyme turned to words, a question he was asking me. All I saw was his small body, bent and dashing, flinging itself. I could have shut off the water and opened the door and said Starr, what did you say? Starr, I couldn't hear you.

But the water ran on and he whirled on and I let him go.

I didn't want a headstone in the Sterns cemetery, Starr stuck in there with all those old Welshmen. Georgia was buried in the Utica cemetery, under a weeping willow, next to her parents. Nobody thought we'd have a child. We tried for nine years. Babies were all around us, turning into children, and there we were, by ourselves.

Nobody doesn't know where we are, Dad, Starr used to say when we hid in the cornfield. The smell of young corn is the smell of green. He could sit among the green stalks for hours. Okay, I thought one day at twilight, we'll see how long he'll last. He kept me out until the moon rose. He liked to sit for hours in the dirt. He laughed when the pollen made me sneeze.

Their roots look like spiders, Dad, he used to say about the cornstalks.

Don't worry about the bears, Dad, he said on Bald Mountain. I'll save you.

Pieces of that day are hiding in me. If I could still paint, I would paint that day: the sun through pine trees, light like lace. His feet in their red sneakers. He hiked the way a child hikes, in twirls and runs and sudden stops.

There might be ghosts here, he said. Don't worry, Dad, I'll bop them on the head.

I am older now, a sixty-year-old man with a headstone that stands uncarved next to my wife's. My obituary will read: Timothy Williams, preceded in death by wife and son. Enough time goes by and no one thinks to write beloved, even if you were.

I watched Mallie's dark head bend over the buffet. Her hand dragged cake along the draped linen until I saw Charlie's hand reach out for it from under the table. Mallie, trying to take care of everyone. Her hair hung limp over her shoulder. A white dress too small for her, socks too big for her skinny legs. She hunched along.

There are things you were going to say but you didn't. There's the rest of your life to say them, you think. But there isn't.

MALLIE WILLIAMS

At night when I burn the incense I ask the Magic 8 Ball the questions.

Have you seen my dad?

It is certain.

I write down the answer in my notebook. Next I get out the Ouija board. I put my fingers on the pointer as lightly as I can. I never move it by myself. I wait for the spirit to enter into the pointer and skate it around the board. After it has answered my questions I write down the code. I lean into the swimming pool in the back of the closet and wait for it to get warm.

Sometimes it comes back over me while I wait: his red taillights going up the hill, a voice inside my head like the Chinese man's voice on the tape, saying, You didn't hug him. I close my eyes and I say, What if there was nothing? What if there was nothing? even though I don't want to. But that's the only way to stop the red taillights of his truck going away from me, to go into the other world where there isn't anything. Where there's nothing at all.

Chinese numbers I have down. I have moved into greetings.

Ni hao, says the Chinese man.

Ni hao, says my dad on the tape he made just of himself repeating after the man. Hello.

Sometimes I fall asleep in the closet, with the vinyl smell that is a smell my dad wouldn't have liked. I wake up late. The house is dark and quiet. There is no light. I reach out to the wall and feel the stickums. I turn on the tape recorder with the volume wheeled down as far as it can go. I close my eyes and listen.

Every day I quiz Charlie.

What did Dad *not* like to eat?

Black!

Charlie is obsessed with colors now. Come on, Charlie, I say. What did Dad *not* like to eat?

Blue!

OK, what did Dad *like* to eat?

Green!

I am making lists for Charlie and me, so that we will always remember.

Foods He Liked, I wrote at the top of one page.

Oranges cut into quarters.

Cinnamon raisin toast with butter only, never honey.

Hamburgers.

German chocolate cake.

Fried rice. He learned to make it himself so he could practice with chopsticks. I have started practicing with his chopsticks, which I get out of the back of the silverware drawer where he kept them.

Me too, says Charlie, so I let him try. He grabs one in each hand and tries to spear his sandwich. That's not the way, I say.

But I don't know the way either.

Karma, the book calls it. You live as many lives as you have to to pay for your sins. I wonder what it was I did in my before lives that was so bad, that made me have to kill my father and my grandmother in this one.

Now I'm working on what if a stranger takes Charlie, what he should do.

Hi, little boy, I say, I have a present for you. Open the door so I can give it to you. What do you do?

What kind of a present?

No. That is not what you do. Now think. What do you do?

Jump out.

Jump out is what you do if he puts you in a car and stops for a red light.

Green light, go, he says. Red light, stop.

Try again. If you're walking by yourself on the road and a stranger grabs you. What do you do?

We don't walk on the road, he says.

But what if?

We don't walk on the road.

Just pretend, I say.

We don't walk on the road and Daddy walked on the road. And that's no good.

He started to yell. That's no good! he said.

Hey. That was different.

He shook his head and kept crying.

Dad was saving Johnny, I said. I tried to tell him that, but he put his hands over his ears and kept crying. I started to sing one of his rhymes for him, *The Queen of Hearts she made some tarts, all on a summer's day*, but he screamed louder. I forgot; it's only him and his dad who can sing them.

Has he already come back to earth?

Signs point to yes.

Ghosts are everywhere. That's what the book says and it's true; I see them out of the corner of my eye. They hang around. Everyone trails ghosts. Charlie has baby ghosts jumping when he jumps, sitting next to him when he eats. My mother's ghost is pale and rose-colored; it holds her hands when she works with the kids. Lift your hand, she says, and the ghost helps the hand up, up. Try to raise your head, she says, and there is the ghost, supporting the weak muscles that some very retarded kids have.

Mine, I don't know what it looks like.

My dad's, I'm looking for it.

All around the house I look and outside too. Down at the wood-pile where he went every nice night, I figure his ghost might be there if anywhere. Nights, I lie awake sometimes, listening for the *chunk, chunk* of the sledge coming down on the wedge he drove into the stump where he split wood. It's there, the wedge, still standing where he left off. Sometimes I think I can hear it. I go to the window and peek, thinking I'll catch the ghost, wanting to finish out the last cord, which is only half split.

Every morning I pour Charlie's cereal and get the juice, which he hardly ever spills anymore. Then I start.

Dad's full name?

Starr Williams.

Age?

Three.

You're three. He was *thirty*.

I'm three. He was *thirty*.

What color hair did Dad have?

Purple.

Brown! Sing Dad's Young Shoe song.

Charlie starts to sing. I sing with him. *Young shoe yeah la la la, La la la la la la.* That's the only song he lets me sing with him now. Because it was all of ours song, is what he says.

I asked Crystal about the day it happened. She was mixing up tuna fish in a big bowl. First she chopped an onion into tiny bits. Then she chopped up two of the big pickles from the jar by the cash register. Then she opened a giant can of tuna and dumped it in; then she got out the big diner jar of mayonnaise.

Starr and Tim came in for lunch, she said. Then Starr took Johnny to get a Popsicle. Then it started to rain.

Johnny hates rain, I said.

Yes. Johnny hates rain. He was standing on the curb eating the

Popsicle, waiting for your dad, when the rain started. He got confused. He started to step into the street just when a truck was coming.

I watched her mix yellow-white lumps of mayonnaise into the tuna fish with a big wooden spoon.

What then? I asked.

The truck was going to hit Johnny. Your dad came running out the door of Jewell's. He was holding a soda. Starr pushed Johnny out of the way and the truck hit him instead.

She finished mixing up the tuna.

He yelled something, she said.

What? What did he yell?

I don't know. It was a yell.

But maybe it could have been a word.

Maybe, she said.

Ni hao ma, says the Chinese man.

Ni hao ma, says my dad. How are you?

My hair is getting longer and longer. He was the one who brushed it every night while I sat in the bath.

Come on, Mal, let's get the horsetails untangled, is what he said.

One of my secrets is the snarl in the hair. It's a big one. It runs all the way down my back underneath the top layer of hair, which is smooth. Every morning I brush my hair by myself, skimming the brush lightly over the surface in back so that the snarl will not show.

If my mother finds the snarl she will make me cut my hair. The snarl is too huge to untangle. It's been there too long. I can't get it cut. I wouldn't look like Mallie. He wouldn't know me, down here in Sterns where he isn't anymore.

What did my dad yell just before the truck hit him? I ask the Magic 8 Ball.

No.

No is what he said, or no I should try again?

Yes.

Crystal snooped in my notebook and saw my list of world's worst dead people, my list that begins with the Yellow Emperor.

Mallie, what's this?

The people in the world who have the most karma to work off, I said. If you know what karma is.

I know what karma is, she said. The Yellow Emperor's the guy who built the Great Wall. Wouldn't that make him a hero instead?

He was evil, I said. Slaves. Prisoners. All along that wall, inside, there are bodies.

He was a hero according to your dad.

There it was; she said the word. *Dad*. I sat perfectly still on my stool. *Dad*, I wrote in my notebook with my red pen.

The Yellow Emperor's guarded by ghosts, Crystal said. By thousands of warriors, your dad said.

There again: *Dad*.

That's true, I said. Warriors that are terra cotta, which means clay.

I know what terra cotta means, she said.

There are only three more weeks left of school. If my dad was alive he would already have gone to China and walked the Great Wall. He would already have come back from China. In my closet the yellow stickums are still stuck on the wall. The pool is still full of his air. Every day I check the plug.

I heard my mother on the phone.

But he's *dead*, she said. She twisted the phone cord around her hand.

Yes I know it's a nonrefundable ticket, she said. But he's *dead*.

Anytime in the next year, she said. Thanks so goddamned much for all your help.

That's a word I never heard her say before.

Foods He Didn't Like, I wrote in my notebook.

Mayonnaise.

Tomatoes on anything except in spaghetti sauce, which he did like.
Mint.

Anchovies, which I have never tasted.

I'm worrying about who's next. Who's it going to be? It'll not
be me because my karma is to watch who I love die. I asked the
Magic 8 Ball if it was my karma to watch the people I love die, and
the answer came: *It is certain.* I turned the page. I made a list of
the people I love who are left.

Mom.

Grandpa.

Charlie.

Johnny.

Crystal.

I only put the top five down. I left off my friends at school, like
Serena.

What are you doing to your hair? Serena asked me.

What do you mean?

Why are you always touching it like that, in the back? she asked.

No reason.

You're getting weird you know, she said. It's not just me who
says so either.

I pulled up the skin at the corners of my eyes. *Yi er san*, I said.
Ni hao, ni hao ma.

The Yellow Emperor, I could have been in a previous life. He
worked them to death building that wall, and then when they died
he mixed them in with the stones. A thousand lives that would
take, to pay. I tore the list of people left that I loved out of the
notebook and folded it into a tiny square. I put the square under
my pillow.

The back of our seat on the bus is almost covered with tinfoil.
Johnny ducks down with me when we pass Jewell's. It's up to me
to tell him when to get out, so he will get out at the diner and go
inside to sit in his booth. You can't see us ducked down, and Tiny
might forget to let him off.

I quiz Charlie on lots of things, things that he and my dad used to do together. Like when they used to go out in the cornfield. This was last year when Charlie was two. They went out there and sat, so my dad could show Charlie how corn grows, how it's trying to jump out of the ground on its stilty roots. He did that with me when I was three.

How corn smells, which is like the color green.

How the dust called pollen sifts down on you and starts to cover you if you sit there long enough.

Who showed you how corn smells? I asked Charlie.

You.

No, not me. Dad.

It was you, said Charlie, looking at me in a way that I knew he wasn't just pretending.

No, Charlie, I said. There was a sick feeling in my stomach. You're talking about yesterday. *Yesterday* I took you out to the corn-field so you would remember how it was when Dad used to take you out there *last summer*.

Charlie was quiet. Then he said, *Mallie* told me how corn smells.

It was *Dad*, I said. *Dad*.

Charlie started to cry. Stop it, he said. Just stop it.

Mom came into the kitchen.

What's going on here?

Charlie was crying, really crying, not just whining like he does. Stop it, he said.

What's going on, Mallie? Mom asked.

I swiveled in my chair so she wouldn't have any glimpse of the lumpy snarl in my hair.

Nothing, I said.

All over the house my father is disappearing. First his suits went. Tiny let me off the bus and there they were in the back of my mother's car, hanging from hangers in the back. His black one that he wore when they got married, that Charlie and I used to go look at in the closet.

What are those? Charlie asked when I showed it to him.

Tails.

No, said Charlie. He laughed.

Yeah they are, I said. Tuxedoes have those things on the back called tails.

And the other one, the navy blue one that he wore whenever he had to put on a suit. His ties were there too, hanging by the blue suit. I went into the house while Tiny did his three-point turn.

That's the tie I gave him, I said to my mother.

She was cutting the stems of flowers by the sink.

That one out in the car? I gave him that tie.

The knife crunched through the stems. She didn't even hear me.

The one with the woodcutter on it, I said. That one.

She put the peonies in a vase and filled it with water. Pink and white petals drifted from the big balls and spiraled to the floor.

Do you hear me? I said.

She turned around. She was crying.

I know you gave it to him, she said. He loved it.

Later the house was quiet when I woke up in the closet. Around me the swimming pool pressed into me. It was warm. I checked the plug, then I went out into my dark bedroom. I opened the door and went through the dark house and outside. The peonies were dark shapes next to the driveway. I sat next to them and pulled the stems down to my nose and buried my nose in the petals. I didn't even think about the ants that always crawl all over peonies.

Smell these, Mal, my dad said to me when I was little. This is the way to smell peonies. After the sun goes down.

I didn't tell my mother that she wasn't doing it right, that you should never cut peonies.

When I opened the screen door to come back inside, there it was, a voice.

Mallie.

This is it, I thought.

Dad, I whispered. *Dad, I can't see you. Where are you?*

Mallie.

It was my mother, whispering like a ghost.

Mom. What are you doing?

Thinking about the ocean, she said. I'm thinking about the ocean.

I've never seen the ocean, I said. I'm going to bed now.

Upstairs I waited by my window to see if the ghost would come and start chopping wood, to finish out the cord. But it didn't.

Will I know him when he comes to me?

Answer hazy. Try again.

My father's fingerprints are still on the sledgehammer. They are still on the ax. They are still on the pieces of wood that he started to stack down at the pile. But they are disappearing. They are slowly fading away. Soon there will be no more left in this world.

9

LUCIA WILLIAMS

I took his suits out of the closet, the black tux he wore the day we got married and the blue wool. I put my arms inside the blue sleeves and folded the jacket tight around me. I sat on the edge of the bed and felt the scratchy wool. I leaned into its stiffness.

Starr.

Outside on the lawn I could hear Mal and Charlie, their voices drifting in through the screen. She was drilling him in one of the games she plays with him each day, the games that stop whenever I come near.

The air inside his suit jacket grew warm.

I bent my head to the jacket and breathed in, imagining I could smell his smell, his Starr smell of soap and sweat.

My daughter, Mallie, is fine-boned, with narrow angles to her wrists and elbows and knees. Her eyes and her dark hair she got from her father. When she was just born you could already see the resemblance. As she grew I would turn sometimes, catch her bent over a toy or a book, her fingers playing over her painted blocks and paper dolls. In the movement of bone and muscle was Starr's imprint, passed to her in the blood.

I brought to my child my longings, and she answered them with longings of her own. At the woodpile I could find her, or in the fields. She was two or three when her shrieks drew me to the corn-field. I stood at its edge, listening to the sound of feet, of corn leaves ripping over arms and legs. I followed with my eyes the rippling rows of corn that told me of running bodies hidden.

She burst out, arms spread wide.

We're playing hide and seek, she said.

Starr came flying out after her.

Gotcha, he said.

Can I play too? I asked.

Sure.

But I hated it, the closing-in of all that green, the edges of the cornstalks that cut my arms and fingers.

She's wearing out her clothes, she's growing out of them.

How about a haircut? I say.

She shakes her head.

Violators Will Be Prosecuted, says the sign on Mallie's door, in her child's handwriting, with her unchildlike perfect spelling. Only in sleep does she allow her mother the violator to stroke her cheek, smooth her hair, pull the sheet up so that she will stay warm. In sleep she softens. The lost curves of her face return.

Darkness is what I remember from my childhood. Dark hallways that opened onto dark rooms. Prints hung on the walls, painted people that none of us knew. One I used to look at when I was a little girl: a soft young woman bathing a naked baby in a tin tub. I pretended she was my mother. When I passed her in the hall I lifted my hand and let it trail across the glass.

Hi, Mom.

Every day I did this, my ritual.

What are you doing? asked my grandmother, silent sentry, watching me from the doorway.

Other kids, they could say the words. *Mom* and *Dad*, they said, rolling out of their mouths. I searched the house for clues, for signs of the family that should have been mine. I stole into my grandmother's closet, opened the door and stood next to the shelves. My mother's sweaters were piled in that closet my whole childhood, folded neatly, arms over chests, as if inhabited by serene ghosts. Soft colors, pinks and blues and creams.

Grandma, I said when I was a little girl. Whose are all those sweaters in your closet?

They were your mother's, she said, they're not to touch.

That was before I started school, before I found out that other kids didn't live with their grandparents. Other kids went home to parents that they called Mom, they called Dad; they went into houses where other kids lived too, and dogs and cats.

Can we get another kid for me to play with? I asked my grandmother.

No.

How about a dog then?

No.

How did they die? I asked my grandfather when I was a child, when we still lived in Utica. My mother and father?

Heart attacks.

Both of them? At the exact same time?

I had seen the headstones. They had taken me there, to the cemetery in Utica a few days before we moved. Two grey stones, died on the same day.

I went to my grandmother.

How did they die?

She was scrubbing potatoes the way she scrubbed them, with a bristled plastic brush.

Pneumonia. They died of pneumonia. A very bad kind that they couldn't cure with the antibiotics.

I watched her fingers on the little new potatoes, scrubbing and scrubbing, scrubbing the red skin right off.

Jeez, Grandma, I said, watching the knobby balls whitening, shrinking. You're going to make them disappear.

The sweaters lay silent in her closet.

You can give some to me if you want, I said when I was older.

She ran her hand over the neat stacks.

You don't have enough room for your clothes with all of them in there, I said, craving them, those sweaters that had belonged to my mother. I lay my cheek against the soft piles of sweaters, breathing in the scent of wool and the pungency of mothballs. Purposely I injured my own sweaters, the plaid cardigans she bought for me.

I don't know why this always happens to your clothes, my grandmother said, examining the rips, the unravelings, the stains.

I held still as she turned me around, feeling the pressure of her hands marking each flaw. The only time she touched me.

Please could I have a dog? I said.

A dog was the least of what I wanted. What I wanted was what a dog meant, that there was someone in a house with enough love to care for a pet, to feed it every day and brush it, to take it out and walk with it, play with it, hug it. A dog meant an excess of love, enough to give to something not even human, love left over and spilling out around the edges.

When I got older I sang the bathtub song to myself, the one my mother taught me that I couldn't remember the words to. I had to hum because they wouldn't let me sing it. They hated the bathtub song.

In my grandmother's drawers, the cubbyholes of her oak secretary, between the books on her shelf, there was nothing. As if my mother had never existed, no trace of her left to define who she had been for me, the daughter she left behind.

That was so young to have a heart attack, wasn't it, I said to my grandfather three years later, when I was twelve.

What are you talking about? he asked.

I mean, they were only thirty.

Oh yes, he said. Your parents. Awfully young.

Finally I found it, the one thing remaining of my parents, either of them. In the record cabinet, hidden behind a stack of the Tijuana Brass: a yearbook. On a dusty afternoon when neither of them were home, there it was, the *Utica Knights*. I dragged it out.

Her photo took up a quarter of the page, black and white. *Olivia Wilder.* A smiling girl, hair brushed over one shoulder, held back with a barrette. She wore a soft wool sweater. I sat back and started at the beginning, at page one, and went through every page. I combed each for glimpses of my mother and found them, images here and there that I recognized by her hair, by the barrette, by the way she tilted her head back when she smiled.

There she was at a football game, on the fourth bleacher from the top. There she was at a dance, in a long tight dress and white shoes. There she was sitting in a classroom, her head bent over her desk, unaware of the camera. My father, John DeMaria, he was in there too, just a single graduation photo. None of them together.

You can't give away my dad's clothes, Mallie said.

I was cutting the peonies. The sensuous splay of their blooms made me angry. My hand on the knife almost sliced through my own skin.

What do you think he'd say if he saw you getting rid of him like that? she said.

We'll never know, will we, I thought.

Look at these beautiful flowers, I said to my daughter, my knife crunching and cracking, ripping through the stems.

In my made-up family there was my mother, Olivia, my father, John, my sister, Laura, and my dog that would be a Labrador with a red collar, named Spike. Quiet days spent in our quiet dark apartment, I played with paper dolls that I cut out of old magazines, whispering their names.

John, you need to pick up the baby, I made Olivia say. She needs to be rocked.

Laura, go play with your little sister, I made John say. Take the dog outside for a walk now, the two of you.

My grandmother knitted, her endless scarves of red and green, building up her supply for the Christmas hospital auxiliary. She always gave the most.

You could knit me a sweater, I said to her one year.

Too many scarves to knit.

Please?

You heard what I said, she said.

I remember a shower Starr and I took together. I was eight months pregnant with Mal, my belly swollen and hard, my breasts large. I remembered his hands holding the bar of soap, running it up and down my back, over my breasts. His hands circling my belly.

This baby can have a dog, don't you think? I said to him.

He started laughing.

What the hell are you talking about? he asked.

The baby might want a dog, I said.

I turned around so my hard belly pushed into his flat one. I started to laugh too. Steam rose around us and swirled out the door.

If the baby wants a dog the baby can have a dog, he said.

Mallie plays with paper dolls. I buy her stiff-paged books of them, with perforated lines around smiling paper people: mothers, fathers, girls, and boys. Some of the pages even have pets. But she prefers to cut them out herself, from old magazines. She makes clothes for them herself, out of scraps of the bright construction paper that Tim brings her from his school art room. Sometimes I watch her playing with Charlie in the next room. She plays only if she thinks I'm not there.

Let's go, she says, one hand on the paper man and the other on the paper girl. Starr, don't forget to stop at the diner. Mallie's waiting for you there. Charlie, don't talk to any strangers today.

OK, says Charlie, one hand each on the paper woman and the paper boy.

What's for dinner tonight? the paper man says to the paper woman.

Anchovies, Charlie says, and laughs.

That's on the Starr dislike list, says Mallie.

Mayonnaise, says Charlie, laughing.

So's that, and you know it.

Tomatoes!

Mallie ignores him and floats the paper man through the air, talking for him out of the corner of her mouth.

We'll have hamburgers at Crystal's Diner, she intones. Mallie and I will have hamburgers, and your mother and you can have anchovies and mayonnaise.

Don't step in the road, says Charlie, shaking the paper boy in the paper man's face. Always look both ways.

Bye, Lucia, Mallie makes the father doll say.

The paper Starr kisses the paper Lucia, unaware of so many things: how she struggles with dreams he can't help her with any-more, how she can't bear the smell of coffee because he used to make it for her, how her marriage quilt, with its intertwining fragile rings, lies folded in a neat pile on the top shelf of a closet that never sees light.

Mallie swoops the paper girl onto the paper man.

I almost forgot, says the paper girl. Don't forget to kiss your dad.

I watch from my silent doorway. Paper people embrace, their bodies thin as the air that is all around us.

TIM WILLIAMS

There was never a moment when I didn't love Georgia. From that first day in painting class on, all my life I loved my wife. But still it happened, what they call an affair. It happened.

When Starr met Lucia he said, Dad, I feel like I know her. Like I've known her for a long time.

I saw why when she came out to the house that first day, in her white T-shirt and her pink skirt. Before Starr introduced us I knew who Lucia was, her face that mirrored Livvy's, her way of moving that's like Livvy's, only not as light.

You do know her, I could've said then. You played with this girl when you were babies. You knew Lucia when you were two, and three.

But I didn't say anything. There was Georgia to protect, and Starr. Lucia was three when her parents died; how much could she remember of that time? That very first day she told us she remembered nothing of them. That was enough I thought, enough to keep the secret safe. I would never have hurt my wife. I'd kept my secret for fifteen years when Livvy, in the form of her daughter Lucia, walked back into my life. Why hurt anyone needlessly? I thought.

How naive I was.

It happened when Georgia worked at the brewery, those couple of years we were trying to make the down payment. I would get home from school and we would all three drive to Utica together, Starr and I waiting while she drove the trolley for the Utica Club Brewery tour. Afterward we met her, Starr and I, in the saloon that they decorated to look like an 1890s saloon, with its player piano and dark shiny-wooded bar. The root beer foam gave Starr a mustache every time, and every time he laughed.

Did his China loving start then? Who knows? He was a baby sitting in his jump seat on my table at The Great Wall while we waited for Georgia to be done. His blue eyes stared up at the mural circling the wall of the room while I ate. They say they don't focus until later, but I don't believe that. His eyes stared into mine on the day he was born. Georgia sleeping the sleep of the dead, and me beside her staring into the face of new life.

The end flowed into the beginning. The mural floated high, a crumbling brick-and-stone painting fading into the wall above the noise and clatter, the sizzling platters and clicking chopsticks. Someone had stood on a ladder and painted it before the restaurant ever opened, the Great Wall of China, twisting around the room like the ribbons Starr used to braid into Mallie's hair, retreating and reappearing in the distance through painted-on green mountains that looked nothing like the Adirondacks.

I have not been back in all these years, not once, even though it is only blocks from the Foothills Home where my daughter-in-law, Lucia, works. She sometimes brings home bags of doughnuts from Hemstrought's Bakery, and I know that that means she was there, just steps away from where her mother spent her days.

Mallie, we need to fatten you up a little bit, I said. I'm taking you and Charlie out to dinner.

Can I pick where?

Sure.

The Great Wall, she said. So I can practice my Chinese.

Oh, no. Anyplace but there. How about McDonald's instead?

McDonald's, McDonald's, Charlie chanted, bouncing between us like a ball.

You said I could pick and that's what I pick. The Great Wall.

Mallie would not be denied. When I got out of the car in Utica I kept my eyes on Hemstrought's Bakery next door. Still the same two huge windows, the slanted tin rows displaying doughnuts, muffins, giant cookies. Wedding cakes, which I knew were not cakes at all but frosted Styrofoam rounds, so disappointing to Starr when he was a child.

Well, there it is, I said to Mallie.

Pagoda arches framed the doorway which was still the same bleached white I remembered. Inside, the floor was the same red linoleum. Posters of China hung on walls that were pink now. The tables were small and square, covered with red oilcloth and set round with the black-legged chairs that every Chinese restaurant must order from the same Chinese restaurant catalog.

The mural was gone.

But I could still match every corner and angle with the room I carried in my mind. I looked to the back, imagining Livvy leaning against the faded stones of the lost mural. Mallie was already inside, standing on tiptoe by the kitchen serving counter.

For a woman so small, Livvy's hands were long, the fineness of all her bones concentrated in her fingers. To me, the purest part of the body is the hands. When I was younger and still painting I used to paint them. Even try to sculpt them, sometimes. Now I watch hands all day long, the hands of my students as they handle the paper and glue and scissors. I watch Johnny Zielinski's hands, the one twisted and clenched, the other grasping his shinies with a stillness that is surprising.

The first time I met her I watched Livvy's hands as they moved in back of her waist and tied the white cotton tie into a bow. Starr was two, standing by the window counting the cars going by. I watched her hands as she held the pen in her left hand.

I see you're a lefty, was the first thing I said to her.

She looked at her hand as if she hadn't realized that she was left-handed.

I am too, I said. That's why I noticed. It's a hard world for us lefties.

She laughed.

That's a weird way to put it, she said. But I guess it is.

I mean it's hard with scissors, I said. Can openers, things like that.

Stuck lids, she said, putting down the pad. I watched her fingers working the air, trying to open the lid of a nonexistent jar.

Table settings, I said, still watching. One finger was circled with a thin gold band.

You're married.

So are you, she said.

Her finger reached out and brushed my own ring. I shivered.

Ni hao, said Mal, straining to see over the ledge, her small feet tiptoed. Charlie ran up behind her.

Ni hao, I heard her say again.

Mallie is a determined girl. Charlie flashed around her thin legs, circling his sister as if they were playing ring around the rosy. *Hey diddle diddle, the cat and the fiddle*, he sang. I watched her calf muscles clench. I remembered how her face looks when she jumps up into the window of my classroom door.

Three murmuring faces appeared.

Ni hao, ni hao, said one while the others watched. Hello.

Wo ai pijiu, Charlie yelled from behind Mallie, clutching the belt loops of her jeans with both hands.

They were surprised. They turned to each other and started to laugh.

He does, said Mallie. He's my little brother, and he does love beer.

Chinese words spilled over each other. If I still painted I would paint the way that language sounds, syllables with sharp edges and angles, bumping into each other in a stormy sea. In the middle of the unfamiliar sounds a name fell like rain: *Starr Williams.* I watched the older man reach his hand over the counter ledge, stretching for Mallie's hand. She reached up and he grasped her fingers.

And again: *Starr. Starr shibushi ni baba?*

Yes he is, she said. Starr's my dad.

She pointed at the man. *Yi,* she said, then she pointed at the other men. *Er, san.* One, two, three. Three men.

Hao, said the man. Your daddy teach you?

He taught me, said Mallie.

From the door I watched her, my bony granddaughter who's getting thinner each week, speaking to the men in Chinese.

Starr, they said again.

Mallie came to the table where I sat frozen, listening.

Dad was here, she said. Dad used to come here. He came here to practice his Chinese, the guy said.

She sat down then and called to Charlie to come sit down too.

Mallie doesn't know that Starr was here long before that. I brought him in first just to get out of the rain while we waited for Georgia to finish driving the tours over at the brewery. I took Starr on the tour once but he hated it. He hated the smell, of hops and malt and ferment.

It stinks! I remember him saying. Get me out of here!

Mallie and Charlie and I sat at a table in the back, underneath a poster of a Chinese toddler climbing the Wall, his little padded jacket a swirl of color next to the crumbling stone. The food came.

My dark-eyed daughter-in-law was at work three blocks away. Like Mallie, her softness was fading away. In Lucia it could be expected; at thirty women seemed to pare down or fill out, as if expanding or contracting to fit the predestined lines of their bodies. But in a little girl, no.

You need to eat, Mal, I said.

I can't eat without chopsticks.

Chopsticks? Since when?

I've been practicing. Me and Charlie are practicing, like Dad used to do. We're mastering the art, aren't we Charlie?

Yuck, said Charlie. What is this?

That's dried crispy and juicy string beans, said Mal.

Starr's favorite, said the waiter. And the bean curd here, Spicy Grandma's Bean Curd. Also his favorite.

We need some chopsticks, said Mallie. Please. *Qing*. Is that how to say it?

Yes, said the waiter. Very good.

Mallie let Charlie break the sticks apart. Mallie read the words on the red paper packaging: Please to try nice Chopsticks. The beautiful and glorious of Chinese Tradition.

I watched as they struggled to pick up a bean each, lifting it off the plate to watch it fall back.

You're not going to gain any weight that way.

It's the only way to learn, said Mallie.

Charlie gave up and started picking the beans up with his fingers. Yum.

Use your chopsticks, Charlie.

No.

Charlie, you're a man of few words, I said, watching the soft curve of his cheek, thinking that Starr at three looked just like him.

Starr zai nar? asked the one who had reached his hand down to Mallie as she strained to see over the counter.

Where is Starr? Somewhere in China, said Mallie. Maybe walking the Great Wall right this minute.

Mallie, I said.

Baby Grandma is in China too, said Charlie. And the cat too, our cat, Road.

Charlie lifted single beans delicately to his mouth, their slim deep-fried lengths bending from the weight of the oil and sauce. Mallie struggled with her chopsticks.

The waiter balanced one stick in the soft flesh between thumb and index finger, supporting it on his middle and ring fingers. The other he held poised above the first.

Here, he said. Like this.

I tipped my head back and searched the pale pink walls. Toward the ceiling the painter had gotten lazy and splotched the paint on carelessly.

Look at that, I said to Mal.

She followed my pointing finger up toward the ceiling.

It's the Great Wall. Can you see it?

She squinted. Pale fragments, ghosts of the mural that had been there, snaked around the rim of the room.

Kind of.

Well I'll tell you a secret, I said. Your dad was here when he was younger than you. These walls used to be white, with that Great Wall circling around up there, above us all. He was here before he even learned to crawl.

Babies crawl, said Charlie. But not me.

Who brought him? asked Mal.

Me. He used to play with a little girl, the daughter of one of the waitresses. First they were babies together, then they learned to walk. We came here while your grandmother Georgia was working at the brewery. The waiters sang them Chinese lullabies when they got cranky.

I don't get cranky, said Charlie.

These same waiters? asked Mallie.

No, I said. Different ones. It was twenty-seven years ago, remember.

Charlie picked up his chopsticks and tried and failed to pick up a peanut. They lay fatly in the little bowl, disappearing one by one as Mallie labored them through the air and into her mouth.

Hen hao, said the waiter. Very good.

Me too, said Charlie.

The waiter watched Charlie try to stab a nut with his stick. With his own longer sticks he plucked one up and popped it into Charlie's mouth.

Wo ai pijiu, sang Charlie. Beer, beer, I love beer.

In winter Livvy used to wear sweaters under her apron, soft thick handknit sweaters of pale blue, cream, pink. They softened the lines of her body, the severity of the black waitress skirt she wore. I asked her about them once.

My mother, she said. She's the one who likes these sweaters. Pastels are what she likes. But not me.

Why do you wear them then?

I've pretended for too long now. She'd be hurt.

What colors would you choose if you could? I asked.

Turquoise, she said. Magenta. The stranger the name, the better the color; that's my opinion.

The waiter brought over an orange cut in half, its flesh separated from the rind. Quartered and nested, so that each bite could be speared with a toothpick.

This is how your father likes to eat oranges, said the waiter to Charlie. I'll bring more.

Starr Williams, said Charlie. Not three. *Thirty*. Hair, purple.

Be quiet Charlie, said Mal.

Starr Williams, said Charlie. Loves oranges. Hates anchovies.

Shut up, said Mal.

Starr Williams is dead, said Charlie. Starr Williams is dead.

I looked around the room, trying to find where the mural began and ended. But I couldn't, it all flowed together. My son's daughter stared at my son's son with burning eyes. The waiter brought over another plate of oranges.

How did you know who we were? I asked him.

He slid a piece of orange into Charlie's open mouth.

Them, he said, nodding at my grandchildren.

I looked at them. Mallie's smoky eyes fixed on her brother. Charlie's soft mouth set in a familiar way that reminded me of Starr at three, climbing Bald Mountain, chanting his nursery rhymes that even then he loved. *I had two pigeons bright and gay, They flew from me the other day.*

What was the reason they did go? I cannot tell for I do not know.

You're right, I said, my heart pierced. They look just like him, don't they?

LUCIA WILLIAMS

She never said a word, Crystal didn't. She melted away like ice cream into the autumn woods of North Sterns, and five months later, in the spring, she came out again, holding a baby in her arms.

My sister Angela is having a hard time, she told people. I'm going to help her out a while with the baby.

I watched Starr when he heard that; I saw the look in his eyes. As if he were thinking: I never knew her. I never knew her at all.

But no one cared about what Crystal said anyway. The way things are out in North Sterns, babies are born and then they grow up. People think, so what?

Years later I knew how wrong I was. I saw the way Mallie and Charlie turned to the door at the sound of Starr's truck on the gravel. I watched the way Mallie stretched in the white tub as a baby while his washclothed hand soaped her back up and down, while his fingers rubbed yellow baby shampoo into her long dark hair. I saw her eyes close from the tenderness in his fingers, saw her thin little girl's body begin to relax and slide into sleep as Starr rocked her and brushed her hair and sang to her and read to her.

At his wake Mallie stood, dark head bent over Johnny Zielinski's pale blond one. In a week her body had molded itself into lines of grief, grief too old for her.

Starr. Look what's happened to your baby girl.

I remember how cold it was standing outside the Utica Public Library, the stolen microfiche card burning in the back pocket of my jeans. I was only sixteen.

My grandparents and I had been living in Albany for years. I took the car one day and drove to Utica, to the cemetery where my parents' headstones stood, weathered from thirteen years of upstate New York winters. I wrote down the date of their death and then I went to the Utica Public Library. They had just put in new microfiche machines.

Can I help you? asked the reference clerk. I could tell she was dying to show me how to use the microfiche machines.

I think I'll just browse for a while, I said.

Disappointed that I already knew how, she left. I flipped through cards until I found the day of their deaths. I had not told my grandparents what I was doing. I was looking for something to touch, a piece of paper even.

There was nothing under the obituaries. I went back a day.

But their deaths weren't in the obits at all. They were on the front page.

My parents' names leaped at me as if their lifeblood was held and contained in the musty library file. Waiting for me, their daughter, to find them.

How weird that they both had heart attacks together, I said to my grandfather one morning early, when he had just opened the newspaper. Trying to catch him off guard.

You know, my parents?

Heart attacks? Who said anything about heart attacks?

You did. When I was little.

No. You must have dreamed that one up. They died in a car crash, he said, a solid, practiced sound to his voice.

Grandma, I said, sneaking up on her in the kitchen. Who was driving? Where did it happen? Was I in the car?

This time she was ready for me.

91

Your father was behind the wheel, she said. A truck came out of nowhere, it was in February on an icy hill in North Sterns, and crashed head-on into them.

Was I in the car?

No.

How old was I?

You were three.

On my wedding day Starr and I came out of the church and there it was, perched like a white bird in the field across the road. He smiled, waiting to help me into the glider. In the long white dress I had borrowed from his mother I stood there, silk-bound pink roses and baby's breath in my hand. I looked at him, this boy I had met not even a year before, his teeth white against his tan, standing in a black tuxedo.

Back in the crowd, Crystal hovered. She wore a dark dress to the wedding, standing on the groom's side to the far back. We were all three of us nineteen years old.

Terrified, I got in. There was another plane in front, to tow us up in the air and then let us go.

No engine! Starr shouted.

Too scared to cry I sat, my long white dress draping like a shroud in the tiny plane. Ahead of us sat the smiling pilot, a white carnation stuck behind his ear in honor of the occasion. I closed my eyes and felt doom around me, a fellow passenger. I opened my eyes. Starr to the left of me took my hand, the crowd waved. A sea of color they were, dressed in their finery. Chanting, *Throw the flowers, throw the flowers.*

No one had ever heard of us, living in Albany. My grandparents were old, too old to look like parents, and tired. They did not come to school conferences nor did they come watch me run track. After I found out how my parents died, I used to sneak in a question every now and then.

Was there a place called Star Hill in Sterns? I asked.

Her knitting sat quietly on my grandmother's lap.

What are you talking about? she said.

I seem to remember something about a place called Star Hill, I said.

I think there may be a place like that near Sterns, she said to the book on her lap.

Something about a ghost there, said my grandfather from the television. Kids liked to go there, isn't that right Teresa?

Maybe, she said.

By that time I knew all about Star Hill. I had topographical maps that I stole out of the library; I had the history of the Adirondacks. Old copies of the *Utica Daily* had an "Adirondacks Notes" page. Every so often it mentioned Sterns, or North Sterns, or the Baron von Steuben's Memorial. I knew Sterns the way you know a place you've been to only in your dreams.

Late that night I heard them whispering in their room that was next to my room in our two-bedroom apartment in Albany. In all our years there they had made no friends, and they had not taught me the language of friend-making. I walked to school by myself. I walked home by myself. Emptied and cleaned my lunch box and did my homework and got up the next day to do it again.

Murder-Suicide on Star Hill. John DeMaria and estranged wife, Olivia Wilder.

After I found it, I slept each night with the microfiche silent and burning under my pillow. I saw the way my grandparents moved, an old defeated way. I saw that there were no pictures of my parents in the apartment, just a few of me from childhood up on the walls. I watched my grandmother with her needles, head bent, lips moving as she counted stitches, the stitches that kept her moving through the days.

Does anybody know where there's a ghost around here? I said to Starr's back in the diner, his lean back in an old blue work shirt.

My grandparents died within three months of each other, shortly after I told them about Starr, and Sterns. I never mentioned the microfiche I still carried, that went with me wherever I went, even though the print was worn down fine from the handling. The furniture I sold at a garage sale in Albany. I put up flyers around the neighborhood. People I did not know came to look, to stare, to paw. After a few hours I owned nothing but my clothes and three crates of soft wool sweaters, folded so long that the creases were permanent.

The first time Tim Williams saw me he stared at me and went pale.

He can tell that this is for real, I thought. He knows I'm not a Crystal Zielinski.

The night Starr died I dreamed a dream I'd dreamed all my life: black legs standing tall around me, and a hand holding my own. The sweetness of a cake that hurt my stomach. Later, at her father's wake, I saw despair in my daughter's eyes. I saw my son sitting motionless under a lace-covered table, black clothes moving all around, and then I knew where my dream must have come from. I had been three years old at my own parents' wake.

Throw the bouquet, they shouted at our wedding. Throw it, throw it.

My fingers clutched the flowers as if for life.

Throw it, said Starr.

The plane ahead of us started its engine.

I couldn't move my fingers.

We started to move, down the field, plowing along a tractor path through the corn just beginning to poke its green heads above the brown. I could smell the earth and the young scent of new corn.

We're going up, said Starr. This is it.

He squeezed my hand.

Up, up, and away, he whispered in my ear. Someday we'll fly to China.

Throw it, the crowd yelled.

The Sterns valley lay spread out below us, a mosaic of green and blue and gold. I leaned forward and held the flowers out the window. The crowd was a blur. Up in the sky we went, my eyes straining toward the earth. A slender girl in a dark dress to the side of the crowd was the only clear picture in my vision. She held a baby in her arms, straining under his weight, and lifted him up to the sky. Even then Johnny Zielinski tilted his head to catch the light. I imagined how we looked from the ground, the boy in black and the girl in her long white dress, gliding into the clouds in a gossamer craft that rested on air.

When we circled round I stretched my arm through the open window and let the pink and white flowers drop. They tumbled through the air, weightless, end over end, pulled by gravity to the longing fingers below.

Crystal held her boy up, lifting him to the sky. I thought of the words she might be whispering in his baby ear: Look. There goes your daddy. Wave bye-bye.

CRYSTAL ZIELINSKI

It might have meant something, said Mallie, that yell when he pushed Johnny out of the way. My dad might have been calling something out. A message maybe.

Maybe, I said.

She sat there with her notebook, the pages that are gradually getting filled up with her penciled lists and codes and words. She thinks she's bad. She's adding herself to her list of World's Worst People, which is something I can understand the motivation for.

Miss, do you know what we mean by cerebral palsy? they asked me when Johnny was just a few weeks old.

That's why I brought him in, I said.

Cerebral palsy is a disability resulting from damage to the brain before or during birth, said the doctor. It is outwardly manifested by muscular uncoordination and speech disturbances. Occasionally it is accompanied by mental retardation, depending on the severity of the birth injury.

My baby boy jerked and shivered.

Miss? Did you hear what I just said?

I watched my baby lying in the bassinet. The lights above him were like floodlights, spotlights. His eyes squinched shut.

Often CP is caused by a lack of oxygen at birth, he said.

I knew what they thought they saw: a girl from North Sterns with a North Sterns baby, something she hadn't thought about.

Didn't want. Didn't care enough to think about, to plan to get to a hospital in time.

A lack of oxygen at birth, he repeated.

I heard you the first time, I said.

I watched my hand go out to baby Johnny, three weeks old, his muscles seizing under hot lights. I watched my fingers cover his eyes, hovering just above his papery skin, so that the brightness wouldn't scare him.

Mallie was quizzing Johnny over in his booth and I listened. She had her notebook out.

What did Dad say?

He smiled at her.

What did Starr say? she asked. The day the rain came down on you. What did he yell?

He started to rock in his seat.

Starr, he said in his way that, now that Starr's gone, only Mallie and I can understand.

Starr? That's what he said? Are you sure?

Johnny moaned and covered his eyes like he did when the sunshower started. Mallie opened her notebook and wrote something down.

Sometimes I look at Johnny and imagine the life he would have lived. Sitting in the booth he sits in now, slurping milkshakes the way the other kids do. Washing his own face. Projects brought home from school, the glue lines straight and the scissor cuts clean. He would know his own birthday. He would have friends on the school bus, or enemies. He would take a shower and let the water run hot and then hotter, loving its wetness and warmth.

The doctor couldn't help himself.

Miss Zielinski, I must ask, he said. Why didn't you call for an ambulance?

I thought of that night, the burning and ripping in the trailer's dark living room. The unpaid phone that they disconnected four months before. I thought of the drive to Utica, down and out of the snowy foothills, Johnny in a cardboard box lined with the red afghan I pulled off the couch. Driving one-handed so I could keep my other hand on his chest, making sure it was going up and down.

If what you're trying to tell me is that it's my fault, I said to the doctor, I can do that well enough myself.

After their wedding Johnny and I watched Starr and Lucia sail away. Up they went, towed behind a noisy two-seater. And then they were set adrift, swooping and gliding with no noise, just air. All around me they were yelling: Throw the flowers. Something creepy about it, like a mob at a kill.

Finally they came, dropped from the end of her white arm. Straight toward me they came. I was hypnotized by them, the pink and white petals drifting down.

Crystal, somebody yelled. They're yours.

But my hands were full. My arms were heavy with the weight of my baby boy. I moved away from the flowers that I couldn't catch. Dena Schumacher darted left and right, her hands straining to the sky. She mowed down all who were in her path, so they moved aside, quieting. It was her they watched instead of the flowers, respectful of someone with so much wanting on her face. She caught them. Six months later Mark Jacobs finally married her, father now of six little Jacobs girls. Eternally hoping for his boy though, which is why Dena's pregnant again.

I remember that day.

Years ago Lucia watched Johnny when she didn't think I was looking, her eyes following the slowness of his arms and legs. She listened to his garbled sounds, his few words that no one but me could understand, until Mallie and Starr learned how. Mallie wasn't born yet when Lucia started school, her stomach swelling tight under the sweatshirts she borrowed from Starr. Johnny was three.

She's going to be an occupational therapist, Starr told me as I pressed the spatula down on his hamburger at the grill. Handicapped kids, retarded. Like Johnny.

She doesn't have to do that, I said.

She doesn't *have* to? he said. What do you mean? She wants to.

But I knew better. Guilt was no stranger to me either, back then. In dreams and waking he came to me, images of my son as he might have been.

A month after Starr died Johnny slept his soundless sleep and I lay in my bed in the room next to him, arms crossed behind my head. Around midnight the coyotes started up. In the dark I went out to the living room and opened up the cupboards where I put Johnny's old little-kid toys, the ones he never used. In the darkness you couldn't see the bright plastic colors. The box of postcards from my father was there, saved from when I was a kid and he worked for Utica Trucking.

Dear Crystal, this is where I am, said all of them, in the same sprawling script.

Landscapes. In each of them something in the distance beckoned, like the oil rigs in Oklahoma that he told me reminded him of giant praying mantises, dipping their heads up and down into flat, baked ground. A water tower in Minnesota shaped like a teakettle. The Rocky Mountains. Look closely and you can see it: far in the distance and outlined against one peak, there it was, a cross made out of snow.

Crystal, there are options you need to consider.

The doctor sat next to us in the office, the fluorescent lights shining down. Johnny was on my lap. At three he was only twenty-one pounds.

You're taking good care of Johnny at home now, he said. But in the future, things may change.

Things like what? I said.

Johnny's needs. Your own. You don't know.

There were brochures on his desk that he handed to me. Johnny reached for one.

No, I said, and pulled it out of his reach.

I think you should consider some alternatives, he said.

Still Johnny reached, and I saw that he wanted the doctor's stethoscope. Round and shiny, it hung from the black cord around the doctor's neck.

Different places offer varying levels of care, he said.

Johnny started to cry, his good hand still stretched toward the shiny disk. Above our heads the fluorescence hummed. I bent my mouth to Johnny's neck, whispering into his ear, trying to calm him.

We're not interested, I said to the doctor. Thanks.

Johnny opened his mouth the way he cries, his shoulders jerking up and down.

Sshhh, baby, I said.

The doctor looked at Johnny shivering in my arms, his twenty-one-pound body bird-boned and huddled. He stood up to leave.

Well, he said.

On his way out the door the stethoscope glittered under the humming lights, Johnny still reaching.

Nights since Starr died I lie awake, drenched in sweat. Johnny comes to me on angel wings, flying at me in dreams.

Here I am, Ma. Look at me.

I look at him, his body thin and muscled, his hair straight and fine and his eyes the same grey as mine.

Look at me. This is who I was supposed to be.

He shows me everything, everything that he might have been. He's playing baseball and running hurdles. He's working math problems on the purple dittoed paper that I remember from elementary school, with the ink that was like sniffing a drug. He's plunging, leaping from the high cliff like the other boys, into the quarry's shocking water. He's reading the comics that come wrapped around thick pink squares of bubble gum, and he's laughing out loud. In dreams his fine hair falls across bitter grey eyes. It stretches before me, his life, filled with these and other things, things that won't ever be.

Johnny called to me from his booth today.

What's the matter, J?

He turned toward the sound of my voice, his head moving back and forth. I went over to the table. He swept his fingers over his shinies, disturbing their neat rows. He never did that before.

What's wrong, baby? Let's pick up your shinies.

But he shook his head. I looked at them, his toys. The dancer earring. An old ball of tinfoil strung round with a thin gold chain. The aluminum swan Mallie had made for him a couple months ago.

I know, I said. You're bored, that's it. You're bored with all these toys.

No Starr to bring him new ones, nor Mallie either. Too busy with her codes, her notebook full of lists and words written in red pen and circled in black.

Nobody's brought you shinies in a while, have they, baby.

I went back to the grill and got the whisk out of the scrambled egg bowl. I rinsed it in hot water and shook the drops off.

Here you go.

But he didn't touch it. He used to love to twirl the whisk next to the window, its curved wires sparkling with sun. It used to be a treat.

How about a Popsicle? I asked.

That was another treat, but not mine. Popsicles were Starr's specialty, cherry ones he pulled out of the freezer case at Jewell's. Johnny was only three when they started that ritual.

How's that sound, baby? A red Popsicle?

He closed his eyes and shook his head. His hand came out and swept over the shinies, the wire whisk, scattering them onto the red vinyl seat and the floor. He started to cry.

Starr, he said, in his voice that only Mallie and I can understand. Starr.

Across the street the screen door of Jewell's opened and closed. People disappeared into the shadowed interior and then emerged, holding sodas and ice cream cones. Johnny shook and cried. I remembered him, three weeks old, lying on the doctor's table, quivering with the seizures that shivered through his seven-pound body. I bent over him in the booth and put my arms around him.

I know, baby, I said. I know.

Another one, the first one in fifteen years, came in the mail a few weeks before Starr died. I keep it in the diner, stuck on one of the order prongs that lined up above the grill. A giant ceramic rodent leers over buildings that look shrunken. *World's Largest Gopher*, South Dakota, it says on the other side.

Dear Crystal, it reads. *I guess this about describes the kind of dad I've been, ha ha. It's been a long time. This is where I am. Dad. PS. Badlands Trucking is the name of the company.*

Jewell's has a rack of postcards. The brewery in Utica, with its red velvet-lined trolley that ferries tourists from the tour to the fake 1890s saloon. Mt. Marcy, highest peak in the Adirondacks, which Starr climbed once. There's a card of the Twin Churches in Sterns, and the village green they front. There's a picture of the diner even, with a little girl disappearing through the door. $.25 each, 5/$1.00, the sign says. They're old cards, curling at the edges. The colors are either faded or too bright, either way looking unreal.

Where Lucia works is one of the places Johnny's doctors have brochures about—Foothills Home for Children. Every year I get another batch. The doctor's office in Utica sends them out. Mr. and Mrs. Dale Zielinski, the fake names I gave them when he was born, is what the address label that hasn't changed in twelve years says.

Lucia is in the latest brochure. She's sitting with a girl who's bent in her wheelchair, her long dark hair falling over her face so you can't see it. Lucia's head is the one you can see, even though it's tilted so her profile is all that shows. She's wearing one of the sweaters she always wears, the pink or blue or ivory ones. She's holding a brush. She's brushing the wheelchair girl's hair.

Mallie's hair is getting worse.

Want me to take a whack at that snarl? I asked when she came in the diner, which she does almost every day now.

I watched her hand freeze on the giant many-inked pen she writes in her notebook with. She traced around the heading of one her lists. She didn't say anything. I watched her hand on the pencil. Around and around she traced.

Whoa, I said, I'm getting a message. I'm getting a clear message even without the Ouija board. Crystal Zielinski, MYOB. That's my message. Doesn't need any deciphering even.

The brochure that Lucia's in, it shows the ways the kids can play there. There's a big vat of colored balls that they lower them into, for stimulation. A music room. A room with different things in it, things they can exercise on or stretch on. Lucia is in a lot of the photos, her head always a little bent, a little hidden.

Mallie saw them in my pile of mail that I pick up at the post office and then stack on a corner of the counter. I was washing out the milkshake can.

What're these?

Brochures.

She looked over at Johnny, eating his cheeseburger in his booth.

You're taking him away?

The water was warm on my hands that were cold from the ice cream freezer. I let it run and run, getting hotter until it was almost too hot for me.

They keep saying it might be better for him, I said.

That was the first time I heard myself say something like that.

You're sending him away?

Look at that one brochure, I said. That's your mom's place.

I know that. I've been there.

Look at that big container of balls, I said. Johnny would like that, don't you think?

She went over to Johnny in his booth and climbed in next to him. Johnny opened his mouth with his special Mallie smile, ketchup reddening his cheeks.

After Starr died I sent my father a postcard, one of the unnatural Sterns Village Green ones from Jewell's. I sent it to Theodore Zielinski, % Badlands Trucking, Badlands, South Dakota.

Dear Dad, I am working at the diner. It's called Crystal's Diner now. Starr Williams and I had a baby. We named him after you; we call him Teddy. Love, Crystal.

Here's the day I try to remember about my father: I am small and he is big. I am sitting on the counter in the trailer while he shows me how to make scrambled eggs.

When you get good, you can crack it with one hand like me, he says.

He cracks and empties and throws the shell away in one smooth swoop.

Now you, he says. Both hands now.

But no, I try to do it like him. Tiny pieces of broken shell gather in the bowl, oozing through the broken spreading yolk and white. But he doesn't yell. He picks out every tiny shard and lets me try again.

That's what I try to remember, that one patient day.

Don't take Johnny away, Mallie said.

She had her head buried in Johnny's shoulder, crying. He still had his cheeseburger, holding it in the air away from Mallie's bent head.

Mallie, he said in his way.

Don't take him away, she said. See, he heard me. He said my name. He doesn't want to go.

Nobody else can understand him, I said. You and me are the only ones. Nobody else would even know he was saying Mallie.

Dad would know.

Mallie. There are things I can't do for him.

I can do them, she said.

My son, Johnny, stepped off the curb; the Popsicle crushed beneath his foot. He lifted his head to the heavens and wept.

You can't watch him all the time, I said. You can't keep him safe.

Yes I can. You don't know all the things I do, to keep him safe and Charlie safe and everybody.

Who's keeping Mal safe? I said. Who's watching over Mallie Williams while you're watching over everybody else?

Don't send him away.

I know you're trying, I said. I know you're on the lookout.

She put her arms around him and rocked. He patted her face with his good hand. I watched the two of them. I remembered the ambulance siren, wailing soft and then louder. Mallie tries but she can't keep him from his fears. She can't give him a bath. She can't save him from the rain that's going to fall on him, that for the rest of his life is going to be falling.

MALLIE WILLIAMS

The waiter asked where Starr was and I told him. Grandpa gave me a look. Charlie knew what I was talking about because we practice. He's digging holes to China now, in the back lawn.

First there's the dirt, he says. Then there's the rock. Then there's the burning lava. Then there's China with Dad and the baby Grandma cat.

He's digging them all over the lawn.

My God, my mother said when she was hanging out the wash. What is that, gophers? Moles?

We didn't tell her it was Charlie digging to China. It's too hot for him to dig for too long. He's only three. When he takes breaks he sings Dad songs, like *Rock-a-bye baby in the tree top when the wind blows*, which is one of his favorites.

Mallie can you help me? he asks.

Just keep digging. You dig far enough, you'll end up in China.

Then I'll see my dad, Charlie says.

It's hard to explain to Charlie that Dad is a baby now. But I try. I tell him, Charlie, Dad's a baby again, smaller than you now.

I want to see my dad, is what he says. Not a baby.

Just keep digging and sooner or later there you'll be.

I sleep now in my closet with the door shut. It's warm in there with the pool and my notebook and the other things. Now I am writing down the opposite of everything the ball and the Ouija board tell me. If the ball says Yes, I write down No. If the Ouija says A, I write down Z.

But still it doesn't make any sense.

Violators Will Be Prosecuted. I spy on the violators. I lay a blue thread on the doorsill before I close the closet door every morning. I got the thread from my dad's blue suit that was hanging in the window of my mom's car, before she drove it away and his clothes disappeared. I pulled it out of the inner pocket, a short blue thread that is only long enough to stretch over the doorsill.

Every day I check to make sure the thread is undisturbed. If it is disturbed that means a violator was there, opening the door and looking in at my closet. All my clothes are still lined up, and the shoes underneath, but move just one or two hangers and a violator would be able to see it all: the pool and the Chinese letters. The Dixie cup of ashes, way in back.

There was nobody I showed it to except Charlie. I only showed it to him once, when he was tired out from digging. He came to me with a baby tomato plant he chopped through by accident.

Look, he said.

He was tired. He's only three.

You want to go in the sprinkler? I said.

I want my swimming pool, he said.

That was the first time he said that. I thought he had forgotten all about the pool.

I want my swimming pool that my dad gave me, he said.

Come here, I said.

I took him up to my room.

You got to promise not to say anything about this to anyone, I said. You promise?

Yeah.

I showed him the pool.

The pool's in a special place now, I said. The pool's filled with dad's air. We have to keep it just like it is.

I know he didn't understand. He will when he gets older, though. I'm saving it for him and for me, so we'll have our dad's air forever.

There's my pool, he said.

He started trying to pull it out of the closet.

No, I said. That's what we can't do. You got to stay away from this closet now, Charlie. The pool is not to swim in anymore. It's got to stay just the way it is.

They turned him into dust. They put him in the coffin and the fire burned him up. The place is in Utica. We drove by it. There's a chimney on the side of the building.

Look, I said to Grandpa.

I pointed at the chimney. He pretended not to see.

At the restaurant they asked me how my dad, Starr, was and I said fine. Fine. He's in China right now, could be climbing the Great Wall.

That was what he wanted to see, said the waiter. That and the soldiers.

The terra cotta warriors, my grandfather said.

After the waiter was gone Grandpa said to me, That plane ticket was nonrefundable, Mallie.

I know, I said.

It has to be used up in the next year. When I was younger I wanted to travel. Did you know that?

Where did you want to go? I asked.

Anywhere.

The big can of ashes is in her closet. She put it on the shelf that holds all her sweaters, the old ones that we're not supposed to touch because they're wool and it's hard to clean wool. He brought it out in his car, the guy from the place where they burn you up. He had a mole with a hair growing out of it.

I wanted to bring it out to you in person, he said. Some of them mail it out, but I think that's tacky.

My mother said thank you.

The jar was in a cardboard box that had tape crisscrossed all over it. After I went to bed I heard the rip of the tape so I watched over the stair railing. The ashes would be in an old gold jar, something special, is what I thought. But they weren't.

You're too thin, my grandpa Tim says.

My clothes are getting looser but still, I am growing. I don't eat much and at night I squeeze myself up, but nothing can stop it, it seems. I saw my grandfather watching me at the restaurant.

There's still some of those good beans left, he said. Mal, why don't you finish them off?

He gave me the extra fortune cookie too. *You will travel far and marry well*, it said.

I wonder if I'll be around when you get married? he said.

The list of my most loved people that could die is still under my pillow. I sleep with it. When I change the sheets I save it and I put it back under the new pillowcase, for luck. When my grandfather said that, I quickly said my new chant.

Youwillliveforever, foreverlivewillyou, youwillliveforever.

He heard me.

Not forever I won't, Mal.

Now Charlie's started digging in the garden. Without enough rain this spring the lawn is hard and the grass is turning yellow-green and sharp like small sticks. So Charlie took the trowel and started digging in the garden, around the little plants. They're wilting too, under the hot sun. Every few days we take the sprinkler and set it in the garden and turn it on. But it's not a very good sprinkler. It doesn't throw the water far enough, so we keep having to move it.

Every day he wears his red boots that are his rain boots, that my dad gave him on his second birthday.

Those are for rain, I say. Put on your shoes that Mom bought you. Boots.

But those boots don't fit you anymore.

Boots, he says. Boots.

He's digging in the dirt between the rows.

Careful, I say to him. You don't want to dig up any of the plants.

Charlie tries. But sometimes he slips. Baby carrots he's brought me, so thin they're see-through, and baby squash from the hills of dirt that we mounded up around the seeds, the green leaves already drooping from the uprooting.

I'm digging to China to see my dad, he says.

In the house is our dad's body, burned into ashes in a can. She hasn't opened them up. I know that because I snooped when she was out in the backyard looking at the holes that she thought were mole holes. The lid was on tight. It was sealed up good, the way I left it after I filled the Dixie cup.

What are you going to do with the ashes? I asked my mother.

Oh, she said.

She knelt down where I was sitting on the grass. Charlie was running through the sprinkler.

I don't know where that pool got off to, she said. But he seems happy enough with the sprinkler, doesn't he?

Have you decided? I said.

Well I thought we might sprinkle them. That's often what people do, is sprinkle them places where the person liked to go.

Like where?

That's the problem, she said. There're a lot of places. There're a lot of places that your dad liked to go. I was thinking Star Hill, maybe.

With that ghost?

It's a beautiful spot, Star Hill. But maybe we should also put up a headstone. In the old cemetery up in North Sterns. What do you think, Mal? Would that be something you would like?

Me?

Something that you could go to, something that you could touch. I thought you might like that.

She reached her hand out to my head, to touch my hair. But I twisted away. She might feel the snarl, bigger than ever.

Crystal, she's thinking of sending Johnny away.

You can't keep him safe, she says.

I can. I can keep him safe and everyone else. Every day I practice Emergency with Charlie, so that he knows his name and his phone number and where he lives. Every day before school let out, I ducked for the tree and in front of Jewell's. Now Grandpa who's taking care of us in the summer takes me to the diner and I take care of Johnny.

Careful with the knife, Johnny, I say to him, loud so Crystal can hear me.

I help him across the street if he wants to go to Jewell's. Sometimes I even help him in the bathroom. I will prove it to Crystal, that I can take care of Johnny Zielinski.

I'm quizzing him, for the notebook.

What did he say? I asked him. Dad, I mean, when the rain started coming down on you.

Johnny says, Starr. Every time I ask him he just says, Starr. So I put that in the notebook. Me, I wonder what he said. Crystal heard it, so did Grandpa and Johnny. Crystal says it was a yell. Johnny says Starr.

I didn't ask Grandpa.

You're too thin, Grandpa says to me. Crystal, fatten this girl up.

I'm trying, she says.

She is. She gives me ice cream and chocolate milkshakes whenever I go to the diner. Johnny and me, we sit in his booth and we eat them. He makes a mess and Crystal comes over with her warm washcloth and wipes his mouth off. Charlie runs around the tables and between the chairs, singing and chanting.

The swimming pool is in a special place, Charlie said to Crystal.

Is it? she said.

I gave him a look but he wouldn't look at me.

And you can never never touch it, he said.

I mess up my bed in the morning so my mother doesn't know that I didn't sleep in it. At night I lie there until it's late, when she comes upstairs and sits on the edge. She puts her hand on my face, itching, but I don't move a muscle. I lie on my back so she can't touch the snarl.

I'm sleeping now in my closet, with the swimming pool wrapped around me and the yellow stickums on the wall, and my dad's ashes, which I took some from.

The can wasn't sealed. I pried up the top with the screwdriver from the toolbox. I put my finger in, to feel. The ashes were soft, like the baby powder we used to put on Charlie. But no smell. I dipped my hand in and put some in a Dixie cup. Then I took the cup back to my closet and set it in the far corner, next to the pool.

Excuse me, where is a restaurant? says the man on the tape.

Excuse me, where is a restaurant? I repeat.

I'm past my dad now. He never got beyond numbers and greetings. I'm up to Popular Tourist Destinations now.

Excuse me, I need to use the WC.

I repeat after the man, but I don't know what the WC is.

He could be walking the Great Wall right now, I said to the waiter at The Great Wall. Or maybe he's at the WC.

I thought, maybe he would give me a hint what the WC is.

It's a popular tourist destination, I said.

Yes, he said. He laughed. WCs in China are different from the WCs in America, you know.

Oh, I know, I said.

But I didn't; I still didn't know what WC was.

She's so pretty, it won't be too long. Don't you think?

That's what I heard Kathy the cash register lady at Jewell's saying. I heard her say it when Johnny and I were at the back of Jewell's looking at the treats in the freezer case. She was talking to Dena Jacobs, who was buying formula for her new baby.

Lucia Williams? said Dena. Give her a little time for God's sake Kathy. It's only been three months.

You watch, said Kathy. Mark my words. I give it another year at most.

She brought home some doughnuts, Mom did. The ones she always used to bring home on Fridays for me and Charlie and our dad, the glazed ones from Hemstrought's. I looked at her when she opened up the bag. Mom is pretty. Even with the dark circles under her eyes. Her clothes are getting looser too, like mine. She pushed her hair back behind her ear.

I brought us a treat, she said.

Doughnuts, said Charlie.

Don't grab, Charlie, she said.

She put one on the apple plate, that's the special plate, and gave it to me.

Here you go, sweetheart.

She's who Dena Jacobs and Kathy were talking about. My mother, Lucia Williams. Her getting married again, to a man who would not be my dad.

I don't want it, I said.

She looked at the plate, the apple plate that she got out of the corner cabinet. She reached out with her finger and pushed the doughnut so that it was exactly in the middle of the plate.

You know what they're saying about you, I said.

She pressed her fingers into her eyes that were getting red.

You didn't love him enough, that's what they're saying, I said. That you're just forgetting all about him, even though it's only been three months.

She took the apple plate with the doughnut on it, and she went into the kitchen and ran the water.

We're digging a hole to China, Charlie said to Crystal. First there's the dirt, then there's the rock, then there's the burning hot lava. Then there's China.

And what are you going to do in China? asked Crystal.

See the baby Grandma and Starr Williams.

Next to me Johnny shivered.

Starr, he said in his way.

Crystal heard him too.

You need a face wash, she said to him. Don't you, baby?

She wrung out his washcloth and brought it over. Johnny, he won't take a bath. He never has, not once. He's deathly afraid of it. Crystal washes him with a washcloth, every night, she told me. He likes it warm but not hot. Never cold.

I have not been bringing him shinies. He's tired of his old ones, I can tell. Grandpa gives him one sometimes, like the tube of glitter that he took from his room at school. He brings things like that home from school for the summer, Grandpa does, for us to make things with when he's taking care of us.

Here, Johnny Z, he said, and he gave him the tube.

Johnny tried to get the red cap off, but he couldn't. I watched him. I was going to help him but Crystal stopped me.

Let him try, she said.

So he tried. He kept trying with his good hand, propping the tube against his bad one, but it was a tiny tube and the cap was stuck in hard. When Crystal went back to the grill I helped him.

There you go, Johnny, I said.

Mal, said Crystal. Mallie.

She had a tone in her voice.

I was helping him, I said. It was too hard for him.

How do you know if you won't let him try?

I couldn't stand it, I said, watching Johnny trying to get the cap off. It was too hard for him; he kept knocking it over.

I've been talking to the doctor, said Crystal. Some things that I do for Johnny, that you do too, he can maybe do for himself. That's what the doctor says.

I looked over at the corner of the grill. The pile of brochures was still there. The tube fell out of his fingers onto the table. All the glitter poured out on Johnny's bowl that had his leftover melted ice cream in it. It was multicolor glitter, like my multicolor pen that my dad gave me for my ninth birthday, sparkles of red and gold and green sinking into the white puddle.

Pretty, he said.

A new word, I said to Crystal. Did you hear that?

He's been working on it, she said. He's been working a long time on that word.

I came into my room and my mother was standing there, her back to me, her arms pressed around her like she was hugging someone. I could hear Charlie's voice.

No, he said. No. You're not supposed to touch it.

It's OK, Charlie, she said.

There was a slow noise that I knew. I knew the noise.

Never, never, said Charlie. It's in a special place.

I knew the noise that I was hearing. My closet door was open. She turned around. She was a violator. She was hugging it. It was flat and shrunken. She was squeezing it out, the last of it, my dad's air.

TIM WILLIAMS

They change everything, the babies do. They come into this world with nothing but their need. What you don't know is how much you need them in return. Livvy wouldn't have left her little girl for anything, nor I my little boy. I wish I could have let Lucia know that years ago. That's one thing I could have given to her. But time goes by and you think it's too late.

The last time I saw Livvy was nearly thirty years ago, the afternoon of the day she died. How can it be thirty years?

Listen, she said. He found your name in my address book.

She was scared.

I told him you were my eye doctor, she said.

Eye doctor?

It was all I could think of, said Livvy. I came into the bedroom and there he was, flipping through my address book. Who's this? he asked. Who's this Tim from Sterns? I said, My eye doctor. How come there's no Dr. in front of his name? How come there's no last name? How come he's in here as just Tim?

He's so weird these days he scares me, she said.

That night sirens and police cars went screaming by in the night. I got up. It was three or four in the morning. Georgia came to the window with me. The ambulance from Utica went by a little later. We stood at the window, watching the red lights fading up the hill that leads to Star Hill. Their twirling lights flashed around and around the dark walls of our bedroom. It was cold. Upstate New York is always cold in January. We stood shivering, staring out at the night.

What do you think it could be? Georgia asked. Some of the kids in an accident up on Star Hill?

High school kids were always going up there, late after parties. Drunk.

Maybe, I said.

Next morning it was on the radio, the murder-suicide up in North Sterns on Star Hill. They kept repeating it. Over and over they repeated it. I listened all that morning, until next of kin had been notified. Until finally they told the names.

Your mother wouldn't have left you for anything, I have wanted for years to tell Lucia, to stop that look in her eyes. Not for me or anyone else.

There was the obituary in the newspaper, a double one for both Livvy and John. In it they called her Olivia, her proper name, which no one that I knew of ever called her by. There was speculation as to why he drove her up to Star Hill and killed her there.

Sundays ever since have had a strange light to me, no matter whether the sky is clouded or heavy with rain. Sometimes I imagine him hitting her.

Neighbors reported hearing sounds of an argument earlier in the evening. Their toddler daughter was found unharmed, locked in her bedroom in the couple's Utica apartment.

I still dream about it. In my nightmare an airplane hangs in the dark night air and Livvy's trapped, with fire roaring toward her. Now Lucia's the same age as Livvy was when she died. Lucia's getting skinnier. She doesn't walk the way she used to walk anymore, the way she walked when I first met her. She's always holding on to things when she walks now, like a countertop or the back of a chair. Lucia walks like Johnny Z walks, as if she's out of balance.

Lucia still wears Livvy's sweaters. She brought them with her when she came to Sterns, three cardboard boxes filled with her dead mother's sweaters. I know that she lived with her grandparents after Livvy was murdered, that pretty soon afterward they moved to Albany. Lucia hardly ever talks about Albany. When she does it's as though it were a place she never wanted to be, where she was forced to visit for a long time.

Sometimes I watch Lucia through the windows of the place where she works. Livvy used to call her Lucy. It's still spooky to me, after all this time, how much Lucia looks like her mother. There's something in the way she talks, the way her voice rises when she's excited or being stubborn about something. It's Livvy's voice that I'm hearing.

I've watched Lucia sit with the parents who come to visit. She'll hold their hands if they need it. You can tell the ones. Usually they've just brought their child in, the first day. Had them at home all that time, years, and then it's too much. They bring them to the place where Lucia works, those huge rooms. If I still painted I'd paint them in big blocks of white, with splashes of yellow and pink and red and green. Like the bright wall hangings they put up, to try to cover the white walls, I guess.

It's still hard, to see the sadness in Lucia's eyes that's always been there. She moves more heavily than Livvy did. There's a weight on her shoulders that Livvy didn't have. But still, Livvy's lines were passed through the bone.

Lucia doesn't know how good she is at what she does. The kids that she works with reach out to her the same way the special ed kids reach out to me in art class: Mr. Williams, Mr. Williams. I can see it with Lucia too. That one with the long hair, who sits lopsided in her wheelchair. Lucia will brush that girl's hair over and over. I've seen that girl start to rock in her chair because she loves the way Lucia brushes her hair.

There was a red geranium that Starr and Lucia had hanging in the kitchen window above Mallie's head when Mallie was a baby still taking baths in the kitchen sink. She used to reach for it, lying back while they scooped water up in a cup and dribbled it over her belly. Then Lucia started night school and Starr became the bath giver. He sang Lucia's lullaby to baby Madeleine, the same Young Shoe song that I remembered the Chinese waiters singing to him when he was a baby himself. That's what I thought of it as anyway, because the first two words of it sounded like young shoe. Mallie used to splash her fists in the water when he sang it. Starr could always make Mallie laugh, which is something that Lucia has always had trouble doing.

Lucia used to stand in the doorway on nights when she didn't have school, watching them play in the water and sing the bathtub song.

The sadness in Lucia's eyes has always been there. Her father pulled the trigger, but I had a part in it. I used to watch Lucia watch Starr and Mallie during the bath and wonder: what did they tell Lucia the first night after her parents died, when there was no one around who could lead her through the ritual, the parent-child routine of bedtime?

When Starr brought her in the door the first day, I knew. Still I couldn't help myself.

And where are you from, Lucia? I asked.

Albany.

Are your parents from Albany as well?

Actually they grew up in Utica. But they died when I was three.

Lucia's body moved into our kitchen, our home, as if she wanted to own it. Her fingers curled into Starr's as they stood at the door. I saw her long fingers.

Are you left-handed? I asked.

Dad! said Starr. What a weird question.

Yes, said Lucia. I am. How did you know?

Just wondered, I said.

We're waiting till midnight then I'm taking her up to Star Hill, Starr said. She wants to see the ghost.

I went to the window and watched the taillights of Starr's pickup going up the hill, then taking the left turn that leads to the road that goes to Star Hill. It was a familiar sight, a route he had taken many times. It's the same route that leads to the trailer where Crystal Zielinski lived. And still lives.

Babies, you can't imagine how they'll change your life.

We loved Johnny Zielinski right from the start. Crystal brought him to the diner, propped him up on the counter in his blue baby seat strung across with a mobile, little stars and suns that shook when the door opened and shut. That was Johnny's first lullaby, the bell pull on the diner door. It jingled when anyone came in or went out. He slept the way babies sleep, as if they're dead, propped up on the counter while Crystal ran around behind the grill. Later his eyes would open and he'd try to focus on us. Johnny's eyes looked like his aunt's even though his are green and Crystal's are grey.

Tim, why doesn't she put him in one of those places down in Utica I wonder? Georgia said after the first few months, when we had all got used to seeing baby Johnny in the diner. In the corner in his playpen, batting at the mobiles Crystal strung up for him.

Some of those places are nice, you know, she said. Like homes.

But I could see how Aunt Crystal loved that baby, how her eyes were always longing over to where he sat in his seat, or lay in the playpen. She was never away from him. He went where she did.

Crystal's a lonely girl, I said to Georgia. Out there in that trailer alone, the baby's probably a comfort to her.

Parents will do anything to save their children. Children will do anything to save their parents.

I used to wonder what baby Johnny was looking for. I wonder what he sees now, tilting his head to catch the light.

Mallie and Charlie and I went to pick up Lucia from work. Her car was in again, and she wouldn't drive Starr's old blue pickup.

Tim, you know I'm no good at standard, she said.

But she was; she was perfectly good with a stick shift. I remember when Starr taught her.

Look, there's your mother, I said to the kids.

She was sitting in front of the big picture window with the girl in the wheelchair, brushing her hair.

When Mom marries the new guy, can we come live with you? asked Charlie.

Shut up, Charlie, said Mallie.

I hate that guy, Charlie said.

Charlie, what are you talking about? I asked.

The one because she didn't love our dad enough. We want to come live with you when she marries him, said Charlie. That guy who's not Starr Williams.

There's not going to be any need of that, I said.

I looked at Mallie in the backseat, twisting her seat belt around so it cut into her waist. I kept looking at her in the rearview mirror until she looked back at me.

They're saying Mom's going to get married again, she said. In less than a year. She's too pretty, is why. That's what Kathy at Jewell's says.

Yeah, said Charlie.

She didn't love him enough is what I think, said Mal.

I remembered Lucia and Starr in the shower, married less than a year. Georgia was sleeping. The noise of the water running in the downstairs bathroom kept me awake and made me restless. I got up to go outside for a walk. On my way outside I heard them laughing as the water ran. They were showering in the dark. Lucia was eight months pregnant with Mallie and huge. They had candles lit. They talked and rocked and swayed, locked in each other's arms. In my mind I can still see that flickering light, reflecting off the water pearled on the shower door.

I looked at Mallie in the rearview mirror.

She loved him enough, I said.

Mallie watched me. Her eyes were narrow and burning.

Crystal loves Johnny, she said. But she's giving him away anyway.

15

CRYSTAL ZIELINSKI

All his life they've been saying it, that it's maybe not fair to Johnny. That it's selfish to keep him with me. I thought of the new words he's been working on: pretty, sun. He's trying for Charlie now, and Tim too.

That's a good word, Mallie says to him when he tries his new ones. Pretty's a good word, isn't it?

Sun, he says, and points to the window.

That's another good one, Mallie says. You like the sun, don't you, Johnny?

She's gone from asking the Magic 8 Ball about Starr to believing that he's there; he's in China, a baby Starr waiting for his daughter.

You think he'll know you? I asked her.

He'll know me.

But he's a baby, right?

He's with the baby Grandma cat, Charlie said.

Shut up, Charlie, said Mallie.

She's carrying her notebook with her all the time now, ever since Lucia found her secret place. As if her secrets will be safe as long as the notebook never leaves her arms.

How's he going to know you?

He'll know me. I'm still Mallie. I haven't changed.

Yes you have, I thought. Skinny, with purplish stains under her eyes from lack of sleep. And that hair that's a rat's nest. I saw her hand go out and try to smooth it down.

My hair's still long, she said. I'm still wearing the same clothes. He'll know me.

You're getting too skinny, I said. What's your reasoning, that somehow if you don't eat you won't grow? You think you'll stay the same forever?

She got down out of the booth and went over to the counter, came back carrying a ketchup bottle.

Johnny was about out, she said. Here's more for you, Johnny.

Mallie, are you walking funny? I asked.

Her toes pointed in and she was mincing a little, rolling her feet to the outside. She climbed back onto the seat and didn't say anything.

Your shoes hurt you, it looks like.

I picked up her foot that was dangling down from the red vinyl.

No wonder, I said. These sneakers are about two sizes too small for you. Plus there's a hole in the bottom.

These are the sneakers he bought me, she said.

I borrowed her book, the one about reincarnation and the afterlife that she carries around with her, stuck inside her notebook. After closing up I gave it to Johnny to hold after I buckled him into the truck.

That's Mal's book. Be careful with it.

Mallie, he said.

He's getting clearer I think. Tim can understand a couple of the words he says now. The brochure for the Foothills Home where Lucia works disappeared from the end of the counter. It must have been Mal, but I didn't say anything to her; I just called them up and had them send a new one. Up and down the hills on our way home Johnny held Mallie's reincarnation book on his lap, squeezed in both hands.

I don't think it's going to disappear, J. You don't have to strain your muscles like that.

Still he clutched it, his Mallie's book. After I washed him and he was asleep, I turned off all the lights except the one by my bed. It was a soft summer night, the air smelling like pine and damp loamy soil, the coyotes quiet.

Sterns Public Library, said the library card in the back. Way overdue. I looked at the date. Four months ago, stamped the week after Starr died, and signed out to Madeleine Williams.

It was full of case histories: a woman who recited in perfect detail the interior of a house she had never been in before. A man who remembered being kicked to death by a horse in a past life and would not enter a barn in this one. A girl with perfect hearing and no knowledge of sign language who, upon seeing deaf people signing, started signing as well. A man who had a near-death experience and saw his lost daughter on the other side of a bridge of white light, waiting for him with outstretched hands. A baby who bore an uncanny resemblance to her dead grandmother and who, when she could talk, looked her mother in the eye and said, Don't you remember when I was the mother and you were my baby?

After Johnny was asleep the trailer was silent, the only sounds from outside, pine trees creaking, once in a while a coyote far off across the field.

I'm going to China with my grandpa, Mal said.

Are you hoping to find your dad?

Did you read that book? she asked. Those are all true stories, you know. It's a true fact about that baby, born to her own daughter.

I took out some books of my own. I printed my name in the back with the yellow library pencil: Crystal Constance Zielinski. Fifteen years since I took any books out of the Sterns Public Library, but the whispery scratch of pencil lead on card stock brought me back. At night in the trailer I read, the pines whispering above the tin roof and Johnny soundless in his room next to mine.

She's in bad shape, Crystal, Tim had said to me last time he and Mallie were in the diner. Lucia wants to send her to China with me. There's Starr's ticket, that you can't get a refund on.

She thinks she's going to find him there, I said.

Mallie was over in Johnny's booth, her head bent over the notebook, but I could tell she was listening in. I went over to the booth. Johnny had pushed aside his rice pudding and was playing with the multicolor pen, clicking each color down in turn.

I've been doing some research for you, Mal, I said. Anyone in the world you want to find, all it takes is five go-betweens before you find someone who knows that person. Degrees of separation, is the name of the theory.

He's there, she said. I'm going to find him.

But even if you don't, I said. Isn't it comforting to know that someone you know knows someone else who knows someone else who knows someone else who knows someone else who knows someone else, completely unknown to you, who's living and breathing right now in Beijing, China?

The sun glinted off puddles in the parking lot.

Roll down your window, Johnny, I said, which is one of the things I used to do for him, that I'm trying not to do anymore. He did it himself, jerking the handle around.

Good job.

We parked in the usual spot. He made a sound that I recognized, that he's been working on.

I know, I said. I see her too.

Lucia through the window was a shadow moving from room to room. She was there, then she wasn't, then she was there again. We knew by the hair and the bend of her neck and the typical color of the sweater. Tim talked about it once, how Lucia was with these kids. It's her gift, he said, as if everyone has a gift.

Johnny made his new sound again.

Oh, I know what you're saying. Lucia. That's your new word, isn't it?

He made it again.

Not bad, I said. You want to go in and see her?

His good hand played on the rear view mirror that's stuck on the outside of the truck. He pushed it in and out of its casing.

Careful with that, I said.

I went around and opened up his door. He shook his head.

No?

I got back in behind the wheel and started it up.

Maybe another time then, I said.

He kept his hand on the mirror, playing with it, turning it to catch the reflection of the sun as we went back to Sterns. Up and down the hills, the beginning of the Adirondacks, he kept playing with the mirror. He squinted in the glare. I thought of it, what it would be like if Johnny were gone. What I would do with his room. Keep it the same I guess, for the weekend visits.

Some of those kids, they can't even stand, Mallie said next day. They strap them up to these chairs and boards so that their bones stay in the sockets. Otherwise they'd slip out. Because they can't even sit up by themselves.

Mallie, I said.

Most of them wear diapers, you know. They crawl around with them. With loads in them too.

She took out her multicolor pen.

Think that pen's big enough? I said.

I brought her a chocolate milkshake, which she ignored.

It's like a hellhole, she said after a while. That place.

It's not a hellhole. Your mother works there.

The kids that go in there, they don't come out.

I've been there, I said. The kids look as if they're having fun. That big vat of balls. The whirlpool.

Which Johnny would hate, said Mal.

This is what I think about: No Johnny in the other room lying under his red blanket that I got at the thrift shop when he was a baby, that he's worn all the satin corners off of. No triple seat belt rigged up on the passenger side of the truck. No drives in the summer up Route 12 to the Kayuta, where he points and laughs at the suspended neon ice cream cone that the bugs all buzz around. No box of Cheerios on the shelf and no more Popsicle sticks for the Popsicle stick house that we've been working on stick by stick for nine years now.

They forget their parents you know, said Mallie. At first when they get there they cry all the time. They're so sad. But after a while, that's it. Forgotten.

She lined up her notebook exactly on the table's edge.

I'm just telling you, she said. Just so you know that that's the way it is. I can only talk about parents, but I bet it's the same for aunts too.

You want to take a drive with me? I asked. Me and Johnny?

Where to?

We're going to get him some new shoes. He's growing. We could get you some new sneakers at the same time.

I don't need any, she said. But I'll come.

Call your mother first.

I hauled up the old black phone that sits on the shelf under the counter and watched as she dialed. Her voice was muffled, her body strained into the angles she contorts herself into when she's around her mother. She kept nodding her head as if Lucia could see her through the telephone wire.

Your mother's all you've got, Mal, I wanted to say to her; don't give up on her.

But I didn't. It's been a few months, but I haven't heard from my father. I won't ever, if he's the same as always. Why I sent it I don't even know. I keep remembering him like he was that one day of my childhood, with the scrambled eggs.

You stir them up good and you put the flame on low, my father said. And you wait until they bubble up. And then you stir them. Slowly and carefully, that's how you stir them. Crystal you're doing a real good job.

Now that Starr's dead it doesn't make any sense to me, a postcard of lies sent to a trucking company in the middle of nowhere. I keep checking the mail though. I can't not, it seems.

Johnny practiced tying his new sneakers that Mallie picked out for him. She brought him two pairs in the store, red and blue.

Of course I knew you'd pick red, she said. I was just testing with the blue ones.

Mallie helped me behind the grill, making orange garnishes. Johnny sat on the step stool chair, bent over his laces.

Thanks, Mal, I said. That's going to help me out with the lunch crowd.

She cut both ends off the orange, then she cut it in half. She slipped the blade around the inside of the skin, then she quartered the orange. She fit the ends back into the rind and placed the quartered pieces onto the rind. She put a toothpick at an angle into one quarter section.

There, she said.

Where'd you learn to do that?

Dad. He learned it at the Chinese restaurant. Chinese people eat oranges because they don't like sweets.

Johnny likes sweets, don't you, Johnny?

I put some vanilla ice cream into a dish and set it on the counter.

Hold tight, I said, and I pushed the step stool chair closer so he could eat. He held the spoon in his good hand and pressed it into the ice cream, not eating. Mallie watched him.

That's the way me and Charlie do it, she said. We smoosh it around so it's all soft before we eat it. Johnny got that from us.

Johnny lifted a spoonful of softened vanilla to his mouth.

Then we lick the bowl after, said Mal. That's what me and my brother do.

No bowl licking around here, I said. Cut me up some more oranges, please and thank you.

I took the hamburger and slapped it into patties, separating each with a piece of wax paper. Mallie worked on the oranges until she had a plateful ready to go. It was quiet before the lunch crowd came in. Across the street people went in and out of Jewell's, where the screen door was propped open.

Johnny slurped.

Look, said Mal. He's slurping, just like Charlie and me.

I turned to see the bowl up at Johnny's mouth, his face buried in it. He set the bowl down on the counter with his good hand and looked up, a vanilla ghost, melted ice cream outlining his eyebrows, his mouth, and the end of his nose. Mallie choked with laughter.

Now there's a sound I haven't heard in a while, I said.

The door jingled.

Mal reached out with the rag to swipe at Johnny's nose. I looked up to see Lucia at the door, watching Mallie laugh. There was a look on her face that I knew. I have felt that hungry look before, on my own face. She walked toward her daughter, arms open to hug.

Mallie? she said, happiness in her voice.

But Mallie was gone, slipped under the grill gate and out the door to Jewell's. I watched her run across the street, away from her mother, her notebook stuffed under her arm. I could still hear her laughter. Lucia's arms came down and hung quiet at her sides. Johnny sat smiling, with ice cream dripping off his nose.

LUCIA WILLIAMS

It's a secret, Charlie said. You can't ever, ever touch it.

I did though. I dragged it out of her closet, her closet that smelled musty and close, like clothes that have lain limp and damp for too long. Like a space that hasn't seen air or sun. Like incense and burnt matches, that faint smell of sulfur.

What are you showing me, Charlie? I asked. Hurry up. I have to get dinner ready.

A secret, he whispered. You have to whisper.

He pointed into the closet. I raked them aside, the clothes, the navy blue dress I got her for Starr's service, the one that she wouldn't wear, still with tissue paper in its sleeves. All hanging so neatly.

What's this doing here? I asked.

There it was, Charlie's swimming pool that disappeared when Starr died, and that I'd forgotten about. And Starr's stickums that used to drive me crazy—fluttering their Chinese words all over the house—were neatly pasted in rows at the back of her closet. A Dixie cup filled with dirt, it looked like, or burnt crumblings from the incense that the kids got at the last state fair and that, from the smell of her closet, Mallie's still burning.

They're born and your life expands, it bulges with their presence for the rest of your days. They change you in every way you can think of, they push mountains up on the horizon and make canyons and valleys in the terrain of your life. But what you don't realize until later, what is unimaginably difficult to see, is that you cannot will your children's fates. I can see it now in Tim's eyes, that awful knowledge.

Maybe that's what Starr knew and what I didn't. I remember being eight months pregnant, leaning into his arms as he soaped my huge taut belly in the shower.

What if the baby's not OK? I said to him. What if it's born deformed, no arms or legs, no feet or hands?

What if, what if, what if, he said. That's not the way to live a life.

But really, I said. What do we do if he's born with something missing, something not there that should be there?

That was when I was still thinking of Johnny Zielinski, when the guilt was still new and immense inside my heart.

Who's not? he said. There's always something missing, isn't there?

But we'll love him anyway, right? I said.

Of course, said Starr. Look at Johnny.

Back then I thought it would be enough, that love would be enough.

Mallie stood there in her room, the ribs heaving in and out on her scrawny chest. Like a baby bird who couldn't breathe, she stood frozen and staring.

Mallie, I said. Honey, what is it?

I squeezed the rest of the air out of the plastic pool and tossed it in the corner.

Mallie, darling girl, tell me.

I knelt by her and put my arms around her heaving rib cage.

What is it, baby?

I tried to rock her back and forth, the same way I had tried to rock her as a baby. But it was the same now as then, she wouldn't let me. It was only Starr who could comfort her. Charlie stood off to the side starring at Mallie, a look in his eyes and his thumb in his mouth like he hadn't done since he was a year old.

You can't never, ever touch it, he said. It's in a special place and it's a secret.

Not now, Charlie, I said. Mallie's upset and we have to help her. Then I stroked her hair, that hair that hangs down her back.

Jesus God, Mal, I said. What have you done to yourself?

Thick as rope and as hopelessly entwined, it hung on her back like an anchor. Still she stood, unable to breathe or speak.

We're going to have to cut that off, I said. We're going to have to cut all your hair right off your head.

She spun away into the corner, crouching beside the emptied vinyl pool, pulling it over herself. Charlie ran. I stood there for a minute more, then I followed him down the stairs and outside.

You try to give them the things you miss, the things you were missing all the time when you were a child. Me, it was parents, a mother and a father, a home where I could walk in the door after school and call Mom and Dad. That's what I wanted for my children. That's what I thought I had found when I walked in that diner and saw that boy standing there, when I saw his mother and his father, their pretty frame house out in the country, with a garden and trees and a road that stretched into the mountains, the Adirondack mountains whose secrets Starr knew.

How about if I take Mallie and we go, just the two of us? Tim asked.

Go where?

China.

We were in the diner on a Saturday morning, Tim and I sitting at counter stools. Treating the kids to pancakes and eggs. Mallie was in the back booth with Johnny. He was eating baked beans with a spoon, and she was working in her notebook, her secret notebook.

Don't cry, Tim said.

The tears kept coming, leaking down my cheeks and turning the napkins I pulled out of the dispenser into sodden balls.

Jesus, I said. We're falling apart.

I looked over at her, sitting in the window with Johnny. She bent forward, her pen over the open notebook, asking Johnny something. He turned from her, shaking his head. I couldn't hear what she was saying.

Look at that hair, I said. Look at how skinny she is.

Silent Crystal stood behind the counter, her back turned to us, stirring eggs and milk together with a wire whisk. I looked at my father-in-law.

You've never really liked me, I said. Is it because I took your boy away? Because I took him away from you and Georgia?

The tears kept sliding out of my eyes. I watched the back of Mallie's hair, moving all in one piece, the snarl she can't hide anymore twitching like a snake.

There was a pile of balled-up napkins on the counter in front of me. Crystal's hand swept them away, and she set a plate of blueberry pancakes and scrambled eggs down in their place.

Here, she said.

She put something into my hand. A warm washcloth, a faint scent of soap and heat rising from it. I laid the cloth across my eyes.

It's not that I didn't like you, Lucia, said Tim.

Too late now, I said. They're both gone, Georgia and now Starr. You're stuck with me.

He sat, drawing his fork through puddled syrup, making little patterns. He looks older all the time, as if his sixty years are making their presence known all at once: his grey hair, the lines of his cheeks, the way the lumber jacket he's had since I first knew him hangs forward over his shoulders that have started to curve.

You don't know, I said. You don't know how simple it was, what I wanted. A family, parents.

You think that's simple? he said. Lucia, you have no idea.

Finished? asked Crystal.

My plate was still full, the eggs floating at the edges of the syrup I poured on the cakes. They were brown and soggy with it, the syrup, the blueberries clumped together in the centers and oozing dark juice.

Because I can leave it there if you're not, she said.

She handed me something from the end of the counter. The new brochure from the home. Grace on the front cover, with me brushing her hair.

I'm thinking of sending him there, she said.

I watched my daughter with Johnny in the corner booth. I imagined him at the home, stepping into the vat filled with colored balls. Watching James Howard hitting the orange button so he could hear his music. Sitting in the whirlpool, which there was a picture of in the brochure.

Why? I asked.

Because. There's things he can't do, that I can't do for him either.

She pointed to the whirlpool.

Like water, she said. Which he hates.

Mallie turned her head and saw us staring at them, her and Johnny. Still as prey she sat, her eyes on the brochure that lay open between us. Johnny sat, his head tilted, staring out of the window. I remembered flying in the glider, no sound but the rush of air around us while down in the crowd Crystal reached her baby boy up to the sun. I remembered walking into the diner, seeing Starr's hand on her bare arm. In his red booth Johnny rocked and stared, something about the curve of his child's cheek reminding me of someone I loved.

My girl is disappearing, I said to Crystal. She's going someplace where I can't.

The parents come to visit their children, they sit beside them in the orange vinyl armchairs that are scattered through the rooms.

The children who know their parents are happy to see them. Grace leans forward in her wheelchair, smiling and reaching, her head bending down even as she strains to lift it up. Days when her mother can't come I do it for her, put her hand in mine, brush her long dark hair.

There are lives you were going to live but you didn't. Unlived, they take shelter in your soul. They feed off the hungers you don't talk about, like the starving cats that used to moan outside our Albany apartment windows. Nothing turns out how you think it will; you make your plans but the world makes others.

My husband's nonsense rhymes echo in Charlie's voice. They float in through open windows, high and faint. *Bye baby bunting. Daddy's gone a-hunting. Gone to get a rabbit skin, to wrap the baby bunting in*. Mallie hides in her closet and won't let me in. I see the life's she's living, and I know that my child's fate is her own. She has her own code to follow, her own footprints to leave, in places I never imagined, places I will not know.

MALLIE WILLIAMS

He'll know me. The eyes are the windows to the soul. It might happen at any time. I might be walking on the Great Wall. I might be eating in a restaurant. I might be seeing the clay warriors when it happens. If he's a Chinese baby I'll speak to him in Chinese. He'll know me by the way I say my numbers and greetings.

Ni hao, I'll say to him. *Wo shi Mallie.*

That way he'll understand the Chinese because he's a Chinese baby, and he'll also hear my name in English, and he'll remember. There's a baby in the reincarnation book whose mother used to be her daughter. That baby remembered. She looked her mother in the eye and said, Do you remember when I was the mother and you were the baby?

That might happen to me. He might say, Do you remember when I was the father and you were my baby?

And I'll say, *Shide*, which means "That is so," which is the closest thing I can come to saying yes in Chinese. They don't have words for yes and no in Chinese.

My grandpa saw me. I tried to be inconspicuous but he noticed anyway.

What's the matter? he said. Your seat belt too tight?

I was scrunched down below the dashboard with my eyes closed.

Hey. Mallie. You OK?

His voice kept coming into my head so that I couldn't concentrate. I kept losing count. One, two, three, I kept having to start over. The rule is that you have to keep counting straight, with no interruptions, until you get up to eighteen. Then you can stop and sit up again. But he kept saying Hey! Mallie!

The car pulled over to the side of the road. I was only on eleven. He reached over and kept shaking me. I stayed scrunched and tried to keep on going.

But I couldn't.

Mallie, Mallie. It kept coming into my head and messing me up.

He pulled me up so my head was up above the dashboard. I opened my eyes.

I'm trying to concentrate! I started to say.

Then I saw where he stopped. Right by the tree. Right on the side of the road where her car went off, and I was only on eleven.

It disperses, that's what Crystal says. It's never lost. The air molecules of everyone's breath who ever once lived are still around us; they're still being breathed in and out of our lungs. She doesn't understand it either, but it's a scientific fact.

It's true, she said. Julius Caesar, for example. A few molecules from his last gasp are in every breath we take. That's the example they used in the book.

Smile, the passport man said.

But I forgot. There was the flash and the click.

Well that's going to be a beauty of a passport picture, the man said. You're going to look like a skinned rat in that picture.

It came in the mail and I got it before Lucia saw it. If that picture's what I look like now maybe he won't know me. I was wearing my blue shirt and the four-leaf clover earrings that he gave me on my ninth birthday, but still. I had on my same sneakers that he gave me, but in a passport picture your feet don't show.

In my duffel I have the tapes and the stickums. Extra batteries for the tape player. I took a little bag from the bag box in the kitchen and I dumped the Dixie cup into it. I closed it up with a twist tie. The customs people, they'll never know what it is.

I'm going to China, Charlie, I said.

Me too. I'm digging a tunnel.

He doesn't understand. He's only three.

I'm going in an airplane, I said.

I'm going through the ground, he said.

Lucia, she's started filling in the holes.

It's like a John Wayne movie around here, she said. I expect a horse to fall into one of these prairie dog holes and break its leg.

She's filling them in when she finds them. Charlie's putting them in weird places now. He stops digging when it gets hard, like when he hits tree roots or rocks.

Keep digging, Charlie, I tell him. You got to keep on digging. You're not going to find a hole that's easy start to finish.

Johnny can say my mother's name now. That means he can say everyone in my family's name: me, Charlie, my dad, Tim, Lucia.

He's getting good, I said to Crystal. See, he doesn't have to go anywhere.

She didn't say anything. I stole the new Foothills Home brochure from the pile of mail on the counter when she was cutting up tomatoes.

Crystal brought a milkshake over to the booth.

It's for all of you to share, she said.

She gave us each a glass, real for me and plastic cartoon ones for Charlie and Johnny.

It's green, I said.

It's a special shake. Mint chocolate chip.

Me and Charlie can't eat mint.

You can't?

She kept pouring the shake anyway. She made sure the three glasses were exactly even. Johnny took the long spoon and dipped it in. Charlie picked his up like he was about to drink.

Put that down, I said. We can't eat mint and you know that.

I want it, Charlie said.

It's on the list. We can't eat anything that's on the list. Anchovies. Mayonnaise. Tomatoes on anything except in spaghetti sauce. Mint.

What list is that? Crystal asked. Because if I'm not mistaken you just ate a tuna sandwich that had plenty of mayonnaise in it.

She was right. Me and Charlie and Johnny all ate a tuna sub cut up into quarters. Crystal mixed up a batch that morning, in the big bowl, with spoonfuls of mayonnaise dumped in. I tried to think then, how many times had I eaten tuna fish since my dad died?

Is this related to one of your secret notebook lists? asked Crystal.

Foods Starr Williams doesn't like, Charlie said. Anchovies. Mayonnaise. Mint.

Shut up, Charlie, I said.

I'm covering it up with a baseball cap. I took my dad's from the top drawer where Lucia put it, that has the twined NY on it. It's the kind with an adjustable band so first I memorized the hole that my dad had it on, so I will always know his head size. I marked it with my multicolor pen, then I adjusted the cap for me.

Why do you call me Lucia now? she asked.

Why do you call me Mallie?

Because it's your name.

Well there you go, I said.

Charlie started calling her Lucia too.

More milk please, Lucia, he said at supper.

None of that, Charles. My name is Mom to you. And that's final.

But she doesn't say that to me. I still call her Lucia and she doesn't say, Don't be smart, the way she would have before. She and Crystal were talking at the diner. Words came floating in the air over to where me and Johnny were in the booth making pictures with my multicolor pen that my dad gave me. I heard the words: Johnny, Mallie, Johnny, Mallie.

They're talking about us, I said to Johnny. That's you and me they're talking about.

We're going to Jewell's, I said to him.

Then I yelled it over to where they were huddled together.

Me and Johnny're going to Jewell's!

Be careful, Crystal said.

Crystal thinks I don't know how she watches us when I take Johnny to Jewell's. But I do, I do know how she watches. She wants to say, Be careful crossing the street, but she holds it back. We went into Jewell's.

You want a Popsicle? I asked.

He shook his head.

You sure? Not even a red one?

No, he said.

Good. That no was a really clear no. Help me pick out a notebook, OK?

We went to the bin of notebooks. They were getting ready for school even though there's another month. Back to School Special, Notebooks 2/$1.00. They had them stacked up. Packs of pens and pencils next to them. Snoopy erasers.

Which color do you think, Johnny?

Of course he picked red.

Surprise, surprise, I said.

So how's your mother doing? Kathy asked when we went up to the register. She had a tone in her voice.

Lucia's fine.

Lucia? she said. You call your mother Lucia?

That's her name isn't it? I said.

She had a look on her face.

She's looking thin these days, your mom is, isn't she? I mean Lucia; Lucia's looking thin these days. But so are you too. I guess that's natural. After what happened. Of course she's still pretty.

My birthday is the week after Labor Day. Not a good one. It's too early in the year for the teachers to notice. They don't like you to bring in cookies for the class that early in the year. But better than a summer one, which is what Serena who used to be my friend has. I will be ten on my birthday. There's no way to stop it from coming.

The passports came in the mail.

This is an old man's photo, my grandfather said. You look at it, Mal. Does this photo look like me?

Yeah, I said. It looks like how you look now.

He reached out to pull my hair. I didn't twist away in time.

What's this? he asked. He had his hands on it, the big rope of snarl.

Madeleine Williams, how long has this been here?

Crystal looked over from behind the grill.

Leave it alone, I said. It just needs a brushing is all.

I think it needs more than that, said my grandfather.

He reached out again to try to take the baseball cap off. I ducked and he missed. Johnny thought it was a game and he reached out with his good hand.

No, Johnny, I said.

Crystal was watching from behind the grill. Johnny reached out again and swiped at my cap.

Cut it out, I said. That's my dad's cap.

Johnny reached again. He started to laugh the way he does, shaking and moaning.

Shut up! I said. Shut up!

Crystal was there behind me. She put her hands on my shoulders and pressed.

Don't you ever talk that way again, she said.

Her voice was so quiet I could hardly hear her. Johnny shook his head and cried the way he does, that's so close to the way he laughs you can barely tell the difference.

What happened in the car the other day? my grandfather asked me when we went to get the shot for China. It was a big needle that they give you in your bottom. The shot streams through your butt and down your thigh. I could feel it.

When you were crouched down below the dashboard and you wouldn't look up at me, he said.

I was playing with my multicolor pen. I started drawing the Chinese characters for the numbers, one through thirty, which is how old my dad was when he died. Every number I made a different color by pushing down on another color in my multicolor pen. Mr. Roy. G. Biv is the order I put it in.

You were doing some kind of chant or something, weren't you?

I concentrated on making the characters for the numbers as perfect as I could. I can count all the way to one thousand in Chinese, which is more than my dad got to. He didn't know that it's easy, that once you get to ten that's all the numbers and all the sounds you need to count forever.

Look, I said. These are the numbers from one to thirty, written in the order that the rainbow goes in.

There was a rainbow in the sky the day that my dad died. I saw it on the school bus. Me and my dad, we made up other codes for the Roy G. Biv color order. Rude Old Yak Gives Birth In Vehicle, was one. Rhyming On Your Green Back In Vain. Roses On Your Grave Back In Vermont.

I'm trying to talk to you, Mallie.

You didn't even notice where you stopped the car, did you? I said to him.

He took the multicolor pen out of my fingers.

I noticed, he said.

I put them in a resealable bag. I zipped it up and I shook it to make sure that none would fall out. Then I put that bag in another one and zipped that one too. Then I put the double bag into a pair of socks that were balled up, ones that I might wear in China, and I put the socks at the bottom of the duffel. That way if the customs people bring out a drug-sniffing dog it won't be able to smell them. Dogs can't smell through two resealable bags. Anyway I don't think people ashes even have a smell.

A few days before we left I held out the multicolor pen to Johnny. Which color?

Red. I opened up the new notebook to the first page. *Johnny Zielinski*, I wrote in big letters. I made them swirly.

What do you think? I asked him. But he didn't say anything. He was dipping french fries in his ketchup and dragging them around the plate.

This is going to be your notebook, I said. The book of Johnny Zielinski that you picked out yourself. We'll start with your favorites.

Favorite Color: red.

That was an easy one.

Favorite Food.

This might be a little harder, I said. You tell me, Johnny. What's your favorite food of all?

The french fry he was dipping got soggy. He got another one from the pile and started dragging it through the ketchup.

What are you doing? asked Crystal.

I didn't hear her come up behind me. I closed the notebook.

Johnny Zielinski? she said. You've got a notebook going for him now?

I put it underneath the other notebook.

Favorite foods? Favorite color? Favorite toys?

She reached for the notebook. I put my hands on top so she couldn't get to it.

You don't have to start making lists about him too. Johnny's not dead.

If you send him away he might as well be, I said. I need to have something to remember him by, if you send him away.

LUCIA WILLIAMS

It happens in a second. On a summer day I open the freezer door. Icy air plumes out at me and there I am, walking into a diner in a pink cotton skirt. I can feel the cold mist from the ice cream freezer. I can see Crystal's hand frozen on the scoop, her arm that's reaching toward Starr already beginning to fade away. Knowing that I have the power in my hands, in my voice, in the way I'm holding my head, to make my life change. To put myself on a different path. The girl that I was is still walking the beach, but Lucia, she set down roots right then, into the creaky wooden floor of an old diner in an old upstate New York town.

Still I search, still I keep my eyes open for signs of my mother, Olivia. When Mallie was born I looked at her, into her eyes that were depthless blue until at six months they changed to brown.

Were my mother's eyes like that?

When she did something I didn't recognize from me or from Starr, when she tilted her head in a certain way, when she loved apricots, when she spit out blueberries, I wondered: Was my mother like that?

Starr Williams, says Mallie, and I can hear it, how she longs for him. Every day she quizzes Charlie.

Starr Williams's favorite color?

Blue.

Favorite food?

Oranges, quartered.

She's got him well trained, Mallie does. I listen to them some-times when they're eating the breakfast that Mallie gets for them both. She asked for frozen waffles, so I put a box in the freezer. They're almost gone now. Two by two, she puts them in the toaster and then draws two knives across them to cut them into pieces for Charlie. I can smell the waffles from upstairs, that hot lazy smell of butter and syrup.

Other favorites?

Waffles. Like these.

Charlie knows. He's got them down, Starr's favorites and Starr's unfavorites. Mallie's worried that he won't remember his dad, that already he's fading. She doesn't see what I do. She doesn't know that Charlie's got his own rituals, his own routines. He holds the railing like Starr told him always to do when he goes downstairs. He won't ever not hold that railing. Rain or shine he wears his red rain boots that were Starr's gift to him on his second birthday. He's saying Starr's rhymes and singing Starr's songs, but he won't let anyone else. He whispers them to himself. *Once I saw a little bird come hop, hop, hop, So I cried Little bird, Will you stop, stop, stop? And was going to the window to say, How do you do? But he shook his little tail, and far away he flew.*

Silently they sit in their sealed can, above the hanging blouses and below our double-wedding ring quilt. The man brought them out one afternoon when I was waiting for the school bus, waiting to see Mallie's dark head in her seat five rows behind the bus driver they call Tiny even though he's huge. I wasn't expecting that, that they would just arrive one day, be hoisted out of a beat-up green station wagon, the kind you see up in North Sterns.

I try to always deliver them in person, he said. I think it's cheap to make you come pick them up. Or send it through the mail, God forbid.

Thank you.

He stood there.

So, how are you? he said. How's it going?

I saw how he looked at me, the way men have been looking at me. I can tell they want to sleep with me, they want to touch a woman whose defenses are gone, who can't hide from them.

I'm fine, I said.

Disappointed, he got in his car and drove off, up the hill that leads to North Sterns, disappearing up the road the way Starr's truck used to disappear.

I sit in the dark on the porch that grows cool on these August nights. Nearly five months since he died and the ax still sits where he left it, embedded in the chunk of wood he used for propping smaller chunks. For splitting.

At night, hanging up my clothes, I touch his sealed ashes in apology.

Gradually he is disappearing. Except for the labeled can, the house is losing signs of Starr. His suits that I took to the thrift shop, his good shoes that I gave to Dena Jacobs's husband who wears his exact size, his fingerprints that I never saw but that were everywhere. His mail that is slowing to a trickle.

Congratulations Starr Williams, you may already be a winner.

I found a box under the bed that I put up in the attic, a cardboard shoe box that Mallie's first shoes we bought her came in. Filled with cards Mallie made him, and one from Charlie, his first. Mallie must have helped him make it, a squiggle of black and green, labeled *Dear Dad, This is a crocodile.*

I used to sit by Mallie's crib when she slept, thinking of the things that she'd know about me. Things even I didn't know about myself, like the way I smelled, the way my hands felt around her when I picked her up, the way my voice sounded when I whispered or yelled or sang to her. Everything my baby would know about me that I don't know about my mother.

I try to trace things back to my mother. Her low gravelly voice that haunts me, the wool sweaters in the soft colors that I know she loved. My secret is that I don't even like them, these dull pastels. The colors I like are big and bright. They shout instead of whisper; they have complicated and beautiful names like *turquoise* and *cerulean* and *magenta*.

But still I wear these sweaters, for the same reason I took piano lessons when Mallie was a baby. There was a picture in my mother's yearbook of her playing the piano, alone on the stage. I willed my fingers to behave on the keys, to translate the printed black circles and flags into music. I remember the whispery sound of Mrs. Delany's pencil as she wrote instructions across the pages of *Beginner Tunes*.

Imagine that your hands are cupping a baseball, she said. Imagine there's a string pulling the top of your head up to heaven.

I was terrible though. My fingers don't carry the same talent my mother's did. After six months Mrs. Delany made me quit.

Babies have no defenses.

Babies. You can drive yourself crazy thinking about it. I see that sometimes, with the new parents. I see it in the way they sit straight and tight in the armchairs next to my desk. I hear the tension in their voices when I ask the questions for the initial forms.

The six-month ultrasound showed something maybe was wrong, but it was too late to do anything by then, a mother will say.

There was nothing we could do by then, the father adds.

I see their defensiveness, how they yearn to tell me the reasons why they cannot care for their child at home. They were long pregnancies for these parents, who gazed early on at the mysterious flickering dots of black and white on the sonogram screen and heard those words, *Something is wrong*. Their baby in its muted water world, tumbling and floating, something already fixed in place, changing the course of its life.

Then there are the birth traumas.

Everything was fine until the birth, begins the mother.

I keep my eyes on the form.

But something happened, the father says. He got stuck and they couldn't get him out fast enough.

She didn't breathe on her own, and they couldn't get her breathing fast enough, another will say.

I listen to them, the parents who force out every word and the ones who can't stop the words from coming. They're young, most of them, some of their babies only a few months old, but already these parents look old. The weight of guilt and love hangs heavy on their shoulders.

The cord was wrapped around her neck, said one mother who came in alone. It was wrapped right around and she couldn't breathe.

She rocked her baby as she talked. I could tell she'd been rocking that baby ever since it was born.

It was like you read about, she said. Like an old wives' tale, like something you always hear about but you disregard. A ghost story, you think. But then it happens.

Back and forth she swayed, rocking.

There must have been something I did that was wrong, she said. Every day I'm thinking, what was it? What was it that I did?

I saw Crystal and Johnny. They didn't come in but I saw the pickup, Crystal's same truck that she's had since Johnny was born. That she painted herself, roaring red, when it became clear that that was Johnny's favorite color.

I wonder about it, what it was like for Crystal.

It happened when he was born, she said. He came too quick, there was no one to help. My sister said there was a lack of oxygen at birth and that's what caused it, the CP and the slowness.

That was about all Crystal ever said. But me, behind my desk that puts space between my womb and theirs, I wonder. Because I knew there was no sister, there never was an Angie in Albany. I don't know where Crystal spent that summer or how it was for her when Johnny came into this world.

Grace, she's missing part of a chromosome.

James Howard, he's hydrocephalic.

That was before the sonogram things, James Howard's mother says when she comes visiting. It's just as well. I don't know what we would have done if we'd been able to see it, that big old head growing inside there.

She laughs. She hands me a jelly doughnut from her white waxed bag. Powered sugar floats onto the paperwork on my desk.

Give me some music honey, she says to her boy.

He hits his orange button and smiles.

I mean, what would I have done? she says. He's my boy.

Out in the parking lot Crystal sat with one arm over the wheel. Johnny leaned forward against the spiderweb of belts that years ago she rigged for him. I put the brush down that I was using on Gracie's hair and went back to my desk as if I hadn't seen it, the splash of red outside the big picture window.

Mallie says I didn't love Starr enough. That people are talking about me. She won't name names, she just says people.

She believes them too; I can see it in her eyes. Mallie turns to Crystal, not me. She tells Charlie secrets and she says not to tell me, not to say a word to me. She won't call me Mom anymore. Lucia, she calls me. I've heard her with other people: Lucia this, Lucia that.

The day after I saw Crystal spying on me from the parking lot I drove up to her trailer. There's not too many houses that far up in North Sterns. Crystal and Johnny were sitting outside on the grass in the last slanting rays of the sun. Smoke from the barbecue grill spiraled up into the pine trees that leaned over the rusting tin roof of the trailer. I killed the engine and the only sound was the wind in the pines. Charlie jumped down.

Hi, Johnny, he said.

Mallie, said Johnny.

Mallie's with her grandpa right now, Johnny, I said. They're getting traveler's checks for their trip to China.

Crystal's washcloth fit over her hand like a mitten. She dipped it in a basin of soapy water and ran it over Johnny's face and neck.

I see you've got your red boots on, Charlie, she said.

Is that your bath, Johnny? asked Charlie. You need to sing the bathtub song if that's your bath.

Johnny smiled. The washcloth wound its way behind his ears and passed over his hair. Charlie started singing in his tuneless three-year-old way: *young shoe yeah fa la la la*.

That's what we sing at our house when we wash, he said. That's the young shoe bathtub song.

La la la, repeated Johnny.

Not bad, J, said Crystal.

She dipped the rag into water again and eased Johnny's T-shirt over his head. His scrawny chest slumped in from fragile shoulders. She traced the outline of each curved rib and one by one ran the washcloth down each finger. Charlie leaned against the picnic table and sang the bathtub song, repeating its one verse over and over. Johnny smiled and hummed. Above the pine trees pinpricks of light came sparkling into the sky.

It's getting dark, said Crystal. The stars are coming out.

We've got to be going, I said, without having said why we came.

Charlie got in the car. I slid behind the wheel. Charlie leaned out the open window, his small body jackknifed at the waist, waving.

Bye, Johnny, he chanted. Bye, bye, bye.

I backed out, tires grinding on the stones, and headed back to Sterns. Behind me on the cool grass Crystal dipped and wrung and washed, her grey eyes as calm at our departure as they had been at our arrival.

Did she have her baby by herself? Was she alone when he came? Would he have been whole and perfect if someone had been there to help?

Johnny, Crystal, Starr, Mallie and all her secrets. The can of ashes sits, silent presence, on my closet shelf. Charlie sang himself to sleep with the bathtub song while I drove. White lines on the dark road flashed underneath the truck and spun away into the darkness.

At the airport we stood by the big window, watching little shadowed heads bob along the row of plane windows.

Is that my Mallie? asked Charlie. Where's my Mallie?

It's too hard to tell, I said.

But which one? Which one is her?

I pointed.

That one, I said. That's Mal. See her, walking along there with Grandpa behind her?

She's keeping track, Mallie is. She's writing it all down. She's listening and she's planning and she's longing: to keep her father alive, to keep him safe and strong in her heart and her brother's. I can't argue with her, because I know she's right. It ends in a second, I'm thinking, and she knows it.

It was a lie; I couldn't tell one head from another. But it made Charlie happy. He waved and waved, until the plane lumbered around in a graceless circle, then started down the runway, gathered speed, lifted its heavy nose in the air, and flew.

TIM WILLIAMS

The state doesn't pay too much attention to a place like North Sterns, up in the Adirondacks where hardly any people live anyway. Over the years there's the occasional car and truck that keeps coming, swooping around the bends and curves, not noticing that it can't stop until it's too late. Even that yellow-and-black sign with its picture of the tilted truck on the steep incline has been hit so that its stake is bent and rusty. Like the houses and trailers that people live in up there.

Every time I pass skid marks on the pavement I remember seeing her car, crushed up. The windshield caved in. When I stopped the truck and got out, there was the silence. I went over to where Georgia was leaning in the seat. I reached in the side window that was also broken and touched her hair and her shoulder that was bent like shoulders shouldn't be.

I drove to the pay phone outside Jewell's and called the Utica police. Then I went back and sat beside her car until they came.

I thought: I should have been with her.

I knew about her tiredness, her night blindness, the way she wouldn't wear a seat belt unless I made her. The sun started coming up over the valley. Then the twirling light of the police car came up behind me.

For weeks I couldn't stand to drive by the place. There was a curve of burnt rubber on the pavement. A section of barbed wire fence was knocked askew so that the wire hung down. The Welsh fitted-stone wall was undone, the long flat rocks flung in the ditch. And the old tree that she'd hit, its ripped trunk started turning grey.

Lucia and I sat in the backyard watching Mallie write in her notebook and Charlie dig holes to China. Whenever he found a worm he tossed his toy shovel to the side.

Worm! he yelled.

He'd dangle it between his thumb and finger and stroke it, singing, *Tickly, tickly on your knee, If you laugh you don't love me*. He brought the worm over to Lucia and me, still chanting.

Tickly, tickly on your knee, he said. That's a Dad song.

Put that poor thing back in the ground, said Lucia.

He ran back and picked up the shovel again.

My mother had a funny voice, said Lucia out of the blue. It's one of the very few things I can remember about her. Low and growly. Husky I guess is the word. She used to sing to me all the time. The only one I remember of her songs is the bathtub song.

The Young Shoe song, I said.

Young shoe fa la la la la. I wish I could sing like her. She had a beautiful singing voice. Low. I can't remember the words to that song. But I remember the feel of water, and the smell of soap always brings it back to me, so I know it must have been in the bath that she sang it to me.

Charlie kicked off his red rubber boots. They must be hot but still, he wears them every day.

It was the first time since I knew her that Lucia'd talked about her mother.

There's a forest of dark legs, said Lucia, that smells like mothballs. There's a plate with a big piece of something on it that hurts my throat, like a cake that's too sweet. And there's a bath, my mother giving me a bath and drying me off, singing the bathtub song to me.

And that's it, she said after a while. That's all I remember about her.

Look at those petunias, I said.

I know. They're a mess. That was Starr's department, the flower beds.

I started deadheading the flowers and tossing the withered ones at Charlie. He didn't notice though. Too intent on another hole.

Look at them, said Lucia. My babies. There's nothing I wouldn't do for them, to keep them safe, to keep them happy. That's what makes me think that the ghost of Star Hill is actually my mother's spirit, up there searching for peace.

Crystal has old postcards clipped up like breakfast orders to the rim of the vent. Some I recognize, like the Jolly Green Giant statue that I know is in Minnesota somewhere, and the Corn Palace that I know is somewhere out there too.

The World's Largest Rodent?

That's in South Dakota, said Crystal. The Badlands is the name of the place where it's at. These are from my dad. That world's largest rodent card is from out there where he's working now. Badlands Trucking.

He know about Johnny?

If he got the card I sent him he does.

Johnny came swinging across the diner from his booth, his plastic cartoon glass in his good hand. He had a milk mustache.

Finished that whole glass already? said Crystal.

He smiled and held it out. She took out the gallon jug and filled it halfway with more.

Drink it here at the counter, J. So there's no spill.

I unclipped the rodent postcard from its clothespin: *Dear Crystal, I guess this about describes the kind of dad I've been, ha ha*. Crystal took the card out of my hand and turned it over, studying it. The rodent's mouth was open. It had big teeth.

I sent him one of the Sterns Village Green, she said. From that rack at Jewell's. I haven't heard back, but still, I'm hoping.

The day before Mallie and I left for China, Lucia sat in her kitchen with her hands around a mug of coffee. I picked up the carton of cream and poured some into my own cup. It sank and then reappeared, tiny spots of white dotting the surface of the coffee and turning it ivory.

It's funny, the things you remember, said Lucia. The things that stick out in your mind. Remember that glider Starr and I went up in when we got married? I've been thinking about that a lot these days.

Why? I asked.

I remember looking down, seeing everybody waving and yelling. You and Georgia way off to the side looking up. Crystal with Johnny.

She sipped at her coffee.

I remember looking down from that glider. Seeing Crystal with Johnny. Already you could tell something was wrong with him.

She got up and took the mugs over to the coffeepot on the counter. Through the kitchen window I watched Mallie and Charlie outside. Charlie leaped into the air, grabbing for the lowest branch of the weeping willow and swinging, while Mallie worked in her notebook.

There's a couple more things I remember about my mother, said Lucia. Hands under me and the sun shining down above, hurting my eyes. Her same low voice, telling me to kick.

Swimming lessons probably, I said.

And I remember her holding my hands, both of them, and swinging me through the air. One, two, three, swing. One, two, three, swing.

Look at Mallie, said Lucia. She's writing all her memories down. She's got enough for a hundred of those notebooks. A forest of black legs is all I have. And a funny low voice singing me a song that I can't even remember the words to.

Once in our seats I tried to look through the window and spot Lucia and Charlie, to wave. But we were on the wrong side of the plane. There was nothing to see except a long line of suitcases, jostling up a black conveyor belt into the belly of the plane.

Don't snoop, said Mallie.

I quit trying to read over her shoulder.

She worked on her notebook until she fell asleep. Every new entry she chose a different color of ink from her multicolor pen.

What exactly are you putting in there?

Things.

It was hours into the first leg of the trip, the flight to Tokyo, when she finally fell asleep. Then I slid the notebook from under her pillow and opened it up. The pages with their different inks looked like a coloring book.

Likes was at the top of one page, with a list of foods I recognized from Starr's earliest days. Oranges, fig bars that he called icky cookies because of the filling but wolfed anyway, chocolate ice cream, New England clam chowder.

Dislikes—mint ice cream, anchovies, Manhattan clam chowder. There were pages of scribbles, letters and numbers printed out in Mallie's neat block letters, none of which made any sense.

Dad came home and said, Where's my girl? We went into the cornfield. Charlie cut his finger on a blade of corn leaf.

Reply hazy, try again

y 8 4 n g g g i 4 3 r t 9

I closed the notebook and slid it back under Mal's sleeping arm. I eased past her to the empty window seat and pushed up the armrests on our three-seat row. Then I stretched her out so that she would have more room. Mallie slept on. The flight attendant came by with a tray of soda and peanuts. I shook my head and she glided past. Then she came back with a dark blue blanket for Mallie and tucked it in around her shoulders. She pointed to the baseball cap digging into Mal's forehead and smiled at me.

Kids, she said.

The plane was quiet and dark except for a few beams of light over seats here and there. Way high up the night sky is darker and deeper than it appears on earth. Stars everywhere. I pulled the blanket tight over Mallie and looked out at them. Most of them are already dead and gone, with only their light left to survive.

Mallie woke and pulled at her cap, adjusting it over the thick nest of hair. She leaned over my lap to peer out.

Why are they so bright? she asked.

We're that much closer to them, I said.

She hunched into the dark blue airplane blanket and pulled out her red notebook. Halfway to Tokyo the sun came bursting up over the horizon.

Johnny would love that, said Mal.

Later she asked me about Starr's last word. I was reading the in-flight magazine, the section on gourmet vacations. She turned her multicolor pen around in her hand and pushed down the magenta ink plunger, holding it ready over her notebook.

What did he say?

Who?

Him. His last word, that Crystal says was nothing and that Johnny says was star.

A smiling Balinese maiden stared up at me from the page. In my mind my son, Starr, flung himself again out the door of Jewell's, his white shirt like the flash from a Fourth of July sparkler. Johnny moaned and wept, his twisted foot touching down on a fallen red Popsicle and jerking back up. Inside the diner my breath stopped.

Well? What did he say? Mallie repeated.

Sun, I said. He said, Sun! Then he was gone.

She wrote it down in magenta ink.

Because he knew how much Johnny hated the rain, she said. That must be it, he was trying to get him to ignore the rain and look at the sun instead.

I tried to peek over her shoulder but she slapped the notebook closed.

Everybody thinks he says something different, she said. There's not one that says the same thing.

Mallie got nervous at customs. She stood hugging her duffel as if it were her only friend.

Do you see any drug-sniffing dogs? she whispered when I put my arm around her.

Why? You brought some drugs you didn't tell me about?

The line inched forward. All around us people sat and stood by their luggage, holding their passports.

Look, said Mal. They got that guy.

Three officials went through an Asian man's mountain of luggage. He stood staring straight ahead as they riffled through his passport. Then they unzipped each bag and went through every shirt, every pair of pants, every compartment and pocket.

You worried about something, Mallie?

No.

She walked up to the counter when the man barked, Next, and stood quietly while he flipped through her brand-new passport.

My thought is that it's her, said Lucia on the lawn the day before we left. That the ghost of Star Hill is the spirit of my mother, restless and searching. Laugh if you want.

I'm not laughing.

I used to read books, she said. The supernatural, the otherworld, like that. There're many cultures that believe a spirit can't be at rest until it reaches atonement.

Atonement for what? I asked.

For the way she died, Lucia said. That's what I think. For the way my father killed her, took her life away from her. Murdered her.

That was something she'd never talked about before.

They were that murder-suicide up on Star Hill, she said, dead-heading the zinnias. The one that people talk about every now and then.

You're snapping off new ones, I said.

She was. Flicking away bright blooms and buds along with the dead ones. She made a face and sat back on her heels. She looked me in the eye.

Tell me something, said Lucia. Did you know?

We sat in the Tokyo airport for two hours, waiting for the connection to Beijing. Mallie was hungry. I got her a big bowl of the noodles that the Asian passengers were eating. She watched to see how they were eating, then copied them exactly, twirling the noodles around the chopsticks, raising the bowl to her lips to slurp the broth. Loosen up, Mallie, honey, I thought. The world's not going to fall apart if you don't eat your noodles exactly the right way.

They have some fish- and seaweed-flavored crackers to go with that if you want, I said.

She smiled.

Yum, she said.

The rim of the white bowl hid her face so that only her dark eyes and the circles under them showed. Steam rose in wispy spirals and curled around the brim of her baseball cap.

I hadn't told Lucia that some people in Sterns who still remembered the murder believed it too, that the ghost is her mother Livvy's unquiet spirit, searching for her baby daughter. Parents, there isn't anything they won't do. Beyond the grave even, some people think.

Mallie finished her noodles and started to sing.

There was an old woman tossed up in a basket,
Seventeen times as high as the moon;
Where she was going I couldn't but ask it,
For in her hand she carried a broom.
Old woman, old woman, old woman, quoth I,
Where are you going to, up so high?
To brush the cobwebs off the sky!
May I go with you? Aye, by-and-by.

I can only sing it when Charlie's not around, she said. That's one of Dad's songs.

I know, I said. I taught it to him.

20

CRYSTAL ZIELINSKI

I could see it in Lucia's eyes when she pulled into the driveway. She's pulling herself out of herself, Lucia is, searching for who she is. Turning her skin inside out. There's much she wants to say. She looked at Johnny full-on instead of sideways for the first time ever, and spoke directly to him.

Mal's with her grandpa, Johnny, she said.

The pines scraped on the roof of the trailer, scratching the way they do when there's even a slight breeze.

The boughs are too long, I said. I've got to prune them. Climb up on the trailer some night when Johnny's asleep and cut them down a bit. It's too scary for him if I do it in the day. He sees me climb up on the roof and he starts to cry. Mowing the lawn, that does it too. I do it with that old rotary mower so he doesn't wake up.

You mow the grass at night too?

Mmhm.

I rubbed soap into the basin with my hands, making the warm water slippery. On soft summer nights we wash outside, Johnny sitting on the grass like he loves to do. He sits between my legs, leaning into my arms until it's time to wash his back.

It's the blades, I guess, I said. Scares him. Turning and turning and shaving off the grass that he likes better the longer it gets.

I took Johnny back to the Foothills Home the day before Tim

and Mallie left for China. All the way down to Utica I sang to the radio, loud. Johnny opened his window the way he likes to do on the way down Star Hill, to let the wind that's always cold under the old pines blow his hair back and his eyes shut. He kept sticking his head out the window like a dog, trying to eat the air. He pulled it in when the wind got to be too much, his hair blown back. A big grin.

You got your seat belts on, Johnny Z?

He did. He always does. His head was out the window, his good foot tapping on the floor, his hair blowing.

He looked like the boy in my dream, the one that stands in front of me with accusing eyes.

You like that air I guess. Don't you?

He stuck his head out the window again. We headed down the big slope that opens out onto the flood plain outside of Utica. Pines on either side of the road, blocking out the sun and chilling the air. He pulled his head in again. We came onto the flat, and the marshes swept away on either side of the truck, water glinting blue among the cattails and long waving march grass.

They were going to cover this all up, I said. Pave it over.

But they didn't; the marsh people wouldn't let them. Lucia's building is in the middle of Utica, past the brewery where Starr and I went for a tour once. We were eighteen, it was just at the end of high school. I remember that day, holding his hand and losing the tour on purpose in the brewing room. Huge white vats filled with fermenting beer.

This is where my mother used to work, he said, when I was a baby. Running the trolley. My dad used to drive her down and wait with me in a restaurant until she finished her shift.

Stinks in here, I said.

He pinned me in front of one of the vats. Behind me I could feel the cold painted steel. He put his eyes close to mine. Two eyes blurred into one the closer he got. The eye was huge, one huge brown Starr eye with a fathomless black center.

We were at the Foothills Home. I pulled into the same space we were in before.

Baby, your hair's a mess.

I put out my hand to pat it down but the wind had done its job. Filled it with its own wildness and made it stiff and unsmoothable.

Better watch it or you'll end up like Mallie. With a snarl that's never going to come out.

Mallie.

I know you miss her, but she'll be back. She'll be back.

Lucia passed in front of the picture window, her hair tied in back of her neck. She had a red bow like the kind that come stuck on top of birthday presents on the top of her head. She was carrying something in front of her with both arms. A little head jumped up and down beside her.

Come on, J. We're going in.

Charlie was the bobbing head beside her. She was lighting candles on a cake. It was still sitting in its white bakery box, Hemstrought's Bakery stenciled on the side. Kids were grouped around an oversize white crib with steel bars painted white, some in wheelchairs, some sitting on the carpet. Johnny and I stood by the door.

Happy Birthday, James Howard, Happy Birthday to you, sang Charlie.

The girl with the long brown hair reached her arm out to Lucia.

In a minute, Grace, said Lucia. We've got to blow out the candles first. Who's going to help me?

Me, said Charlie.

A woman sat by the crib. She had on white waitress shoes like the kind I used to have to wear at the diner.

Make a wish, son, she said to the boy lying in the huge crib.

He smiled and raised his hand to hit an oversize orange button. Music, a guitar and a flute, started playing from a tape recorder propped underneath the crib.

Look at all the candles, I said to Johnny, but he didn't hear me. His eyes were turned up to the ceiling, fixed on it as if a string were pulling him up to heaven. I turned my head up too. Sparkles of gold covered the ceiling, sprinkled in with the white paint it looked like. In the sun that poured through the domed skylight they glittered.

Like stars they are, aren't they?

Starr, he moaned.

Johnny kept his head tilted back, turned away from the party for the boy with the big head who lay on his back in the crib. Johnny kept his eyes turned to the painted-on glitter stars.

Lucia looked up from where she sat with the white box in her lap, cutting small square pieces of birthday cake. It was chocolate with fluffy white bakery frosting, the kind they make with shortening and sugar. Johnny was still staring at the ceiling, leaning against me for balance.

Johnny? said Lucia.

He looked down from the stars when he heard her voice.

Johnny, you want some cake?

The boy in the crib hit the button again and the music under the crib switched on. The cake was scattered with musical notes made out of brown frosting squeezed out of a tube.

You like chocolate, J, I said. Go get a piece if you want.

He limped over to Lucia and took the piece she gave him on a white napkin.

I found the box the next day, out at the end of the driveway. It was too big to fit in the mailbox, even with the dent in one side. Crystal Zielinski, the address label said. He had tried to wrap it. It was covered with a brown grocery bag that he taped all over, but with narrow Scotch tape so it was all coming undone.

Well what do you think, Johnny, I said. Looks to be a box from your Grandpa Zielinski. No stamps though. How do you suppose it got through the U.S. mail with no stamps?

I started pulling off the tape and brown paper and opened it up.

The stamps fell off probably, I said. Not a very professional wrapping job after all. A liquor store box even. Surprise, surprise. But what have we here?

A red bow, crushed from its journey and stuck to the top of the box. Immediately his hand was reaching.

Your favorite color.

He plucked at it and I pulled it off and stuck it to his nose.

Just like Rudolph, I said.

He batted at it, laughing the way he does.

Don't even try, my boy, I said. Get that thing away from my nose.

Crumpled newspaper lined the box, surrounding a brown stuffed bear. The *Winner Gazette*, from Winner, South Dakota.

Look, J, I said. This bear's got a red bow too. A red ribbon around its neck.

He went to sleep that night curled around it. I sat up going through Johnny's old toys that he never used anyway, all the ones from when he was a baby straight on through. They were mostly up in the cupboard over the kitchen. There was the walker I got him too, when he hadn't even barely learned to crawl. Because if he was going to have as much trouble learning to walk as he did learning to crawl, I thought why shouldn't he have something that he could stand up in.

So you can feel like a big kid, I had said to him, all those years ago.

I remember he was inching around on the floor, finning around and wiggling his way over to me wherever I would go. Brushing my teeth, I'd feel a pat on the foot. There he'd be. Washing dishes at the kitchen sink, staring out at the woods and the field, there he'd be. Sitting at the table paying the electric bill or the taxes, there he'd be.

Me and you, boy, we're a team.

That's what I used to say to him.

There was the tricycle that I bought him when he turned four, that I saved my tips for two months to buy. He never rode it. His bad foot didn't hit the pedal right. It still had its tassels hanging from the handlebars. There was the stacking toy still in the box that said on the outside for ages six to nine months, that he could never do. I remember him reaching out to the little orange circle and trying to fit it over the pole.

The big one first, I said. The big one goes on first and then all the others stack up on top of it.

He tried to maneuver the little one over the top of the pole, but he couldn't do it. He kept swinging his good hand over, leaning on the other one so that he was propped up on the carpet in the trailer living room. Still I can see him, his bad hand crumpled up on the floor, swinging the little orange ring over to fit it on the pole. There was an old burn from one of my father's cigars next to him, on the carpet next to his stomach that was hanging over his diaper. Johnny was a baby. I loved him.

Lucia sat at her desk, surrounded by toys and piles of papers. She was almost hidden behind them. A boy crawled up to her and lay his head on her knee.

Whew, she said. I think we need a diaper change.

I looked at the boy. He was about Johnny's age. He crawled with his butt up high in the air like a monkey. A woman in a blue coat came and led him away to be changed. The girl with the long hair came wheeling up to Lucia, a pink plastic hairbrush in her lap. Johnny reached out to touch Lucia's sweater while she was brushing the girl's hair.

You like that? asked Lucia.

He patted her shoulder through the blue wool.

I don't think I've ever seen you when you weren't wearing one of those sweaters, I said.

They were my mother's, she said.

Johnny stroked the wool. Lucia leaned forward and pulled the girl's hair over her shoulders.

Let's braid all this hair up. See how that looks, what do you say, Gracie?

Her hands started moving, dividing the dark hair into three strands. Johnny watched, hypnotized like me. Grace's eyes closed with pleasure and she leaned against the back strap of her wheelchair.

Over and under, said Lucia. The strand on top becomes the strand on the bottom. That's how braiding is done.

Mallie, said Johnny.

I don't think so, J, I said. Mallie's not one for braids.

Not with the hair she's got these days anyway, said Lucia.

Mallie. Mallie.

Look, Johnny, Lucia said.

Across the room a woman dipped a big plastic circle into a dish of bubble mix and waved it. Huge lopsided bubbles bounced lazily into the air. Johnny bent his head, squinting to see the bubbles bouncing, falling, disappearing.

I never thought of that, I said. Of course he'd love bubbles.

They all do, said Lucia.

The morning after I went through Johnny's toys I brought a photo to the diner and clothespinned it up with the postcards on the grill vent. It had come with the teddy bear in the package for Johnny, fell out of the empty box when I was collapsing it to be burned. Charlie caught sight of it up on the vent when Lucia brought him in for a shake. He laughed.

Kids don't smoke cigars, he said.

Let me see that, said Lucia.

My father's plaid shirt was unbuttoned over his belly that was big even when I was a baby. I sat on top of it. His feet stuck out over the end of the couch that was dull green then.

That's our same couch, I said. I recovered it in red for Johnny though, once I found out how much he loves red.

Is this your father?

The one and only.

I was three that day, but I remember it. He had a cigar stuck in his mouth, and he stuck one in mine too.

That's my family portrait, I said.

Is he playing the bouncing game with you? asked Charlie.

Yeah.

Where's your mom? asked Charlie.

Her you can't see, I said. She's the one taking the picture.

Charlie and Johnny played in a big vinyl swimming pool filled not with water but with colored balls. Charlie kept diving under and yelling, Help, help, I'm a shark!

I think your son's got his signals crossed, I said to Lucia. The shark's not the one who calls help, help.

Charlie dove under again and put his fingers together like a fin, pushing his hand above the surface of the balls. I watched as he wove his way around the pool, his position betrayed by undulations of the colored balls. Johnny sat straight against one curved side of the pool. Balls pushed and bobbled against his blue shirt.

Dive with me, said Charlie. Dive with me; I'm a shark.

He dove again and the fin came up, heading for Johnny.

I'm a hungry shark, said Charlie. I'm going to get me some lunch.

The fin poked Johnny in the stomach. Johnny laughed in his way, the colored balls shaking and wobbling against him. Charlie started to sing *Rub-a-dub-dub, three men in a tub*. Then he stopped. No, two! he said, holding up two fingers. Two men in a tub!

Johnny'll never be able to do that, I said. Figure out how to say two with his fingers.

That's right, said Lucia. He won't.

You were three too, weren't you? When your mother and father died, I said. Do you remember anything about them?

Not much. You?

My mother? Nothing.

A lie. What I didn't tell her was that it's true, it was my mother who took the photo that I call my family portrait. I remember that day perfectly. She stood by the kitchen table, holding the camera in front of her eye.

Cheese, she said. Limburger cheese!

She had on a black-and-white checked shirt and white shorts. Her hair was brown and curly.

Wait, said my father, and he stuck a cigar still wrapped in cellophane in my mouth.

She laughed. He laughed too. She waved at me and squinted some more. I sat perfectly still on the big stomach that my father played the bouncing game with me on. My mother took the picture.

Pretty baby, she said. My pretty baby, Crystal.

21

MALLIE WILLIAMS

Babies, they're everywhere. Strapped to backs. Lying in carriages made of the Chinese wood that the tourist book says is bamboo. Sitting on laps.

You can see why the one-child policy, my grandfather said. My God.

Look, I said. See those pants; they're split in the back. That's the Chinese version of diapers.

I could use something like that at this point, he said.

That's because of the Montezuma's revenge, which we both got after three days, me and Grandpa. He was the first. It happened at breakfast.

Toast? the guy asked.

He had a little metal cart with squares of bun on it, two squares each he put on our plates. Then he went on to the other tables.

Doesn't look like toast to me, my grandfather said.

It's Chinese toast I guess.

He took one bite, then he started looking around.

Mal, what's the symbol for bathroom? he asked.

I don't know, I said, then it got me too. We both ran for it. We couldn't eat anything it seemed.

Mallie, Grandpa said, you're wasting away.

I am. Thinner than before even. But still I keep growing, growing out of the body that my dad knows. My right sneaker gave out on the Great Wall. The top came undone from the bottom, and it flopped with every step. I started limping to make the flop less noticeable.

What are you trying to do, walk like Johnny Zielinski? my grandfather said.

Then he saw the sneaker, flopping.

Whoa, Nellie. What's happened there?

We're stopping right here at this shop, he said. We're buying you some of these Chinese sandals to wear.

They were pretty, dark blue with sparkles sewn on in the shape of the bird they call a phoenix.

Now you'll look like a Chinese princess, he said.

They don't have princesses in China, I told him. Empresses, but no princesses.

I tried but I couldn't fasten the seat belt. At home I never would have ridden in a car like that cab. The rules at home are: fasten the seat belt, make sure the door is locked, duck your head by the tree where Grandma died. The cab driver climbed in through the window because his door didn't open at all. My grandfather shook his head.

Got a meter here? he asked the cab driver.

The cab driver spread his hands and talked fast in Chinese. I heard a number that I knew was three hundred.

One hundred, *yibai*, I said in Chinese because the book said bargain, bargain hard. The cab driver looked back at me.

Very good Chinese!

One hundred, I said.

Two!

I wanted to say one-fifty but I forgot how to say fifty. He kept saying two! and I kept saying one. Finally he shrugged his shoulders.

One, he said.

One hundred is what it's going to cost, I said to my grandpa.

Good job, he said.

The cab driver knew about us. About our digestive condition, which is what my grandfather Tim started calling the Montezuma's. That's how I learned what WC was.

WC? the cab driver said every once in a while. Then he laughed.

Every time my grandfather had to go I went too, just to be sure. Old ladies sit outside the trenches selling toilet paper, *wukuai* for two little squares. Me and Grandpa, we bought our own roll that we kept inside the cab. It was green, which is a weird color for toilet paper.

WC? said the cab driver.

Xiexie, said my grandfather, which is the only thing he knows how to say in Chinese. Thank you, except he says it wrong so he sounds like a foreigner. Me, I listened to the tapes, so I know how to say it right.

The cab driver sticks his head out the window that won't roll up so he can yell at the Chinese people in the road. There aren't any traffic lights here in China. There aren't any road signs like stop or yield. Bikes and cars and buses and people-pedaled carts all twist into one big stream, like a braid.

I bought a Chinese army hat with a red star on it at one of the little stores without a door. It's green, like the toilet paper only darker. It keeps the snarl hid. I roll it up like a snake and then I cram the hat on over. It pushes out in a lump in back, but still, nobody can tell.

So you're a disciple of Mao now? my grandfather asked.

It's green, I said. Matches the toilet paper.

The phone rang when I was watching Chinese television and Grandpa was drinking Chinese beer even though he says it worsens the revenge. All the actors on Chinese television wear more makeup than Kathy who's behind the register at Jewell's wears. My mother, Lucia, wears it sometimes, concealer that goes under your eyes. Look at these bags, she says. Sometimes she wears lipstick too. Wildberry or Ginger Creme, which are both shades of red.

Hello? my grandfather said.

You're supposed to say *Wei*, which means hello on the telephone. When in China, do as the Chinese do, is what the tour book says.

Hello? he said.

Let me talk, I said.

Wei? Ni hao, I said. *Wo shi Madeleine Williams.*

There was a long pause with clicks in it.

I know you're Madeleine Williams, the voice said. I'm the one who named you Madeleine Williams.

Oh, I said. Hi, Lucia.

There's a cable that carries voices across the ocean, is what my dad told me when I asked him about it a long time ago. It lies like a big snake on the bottom of the ocean floor, filled with thousands of voices at the same time, all of them trying to get to the person they're missing. Her voice kept getting lost on its way to me, because of the long distance.

Here's Grandpa, I said.

She was still talking.

Do you miss me, Mal?

That's what I heard coming out of the tiny holes in the big black receiver when I handed it over to my grandfather.

The cab driver took us to a dumpling restaurant.

Very famous, he said.

All they served was dumplings. First they brought out a bowl of steaming water. Grandpa tried to dip his fingers in it, but it wasn't finger bowl water for washing. It was dumpling water. Everybody at the table stared at him.

Oops, he said. Sorry.

An old lady bowed her head to my grandpa. Welcome, she said. Her English was good. The dumplings came in big bowls. The Chinese people snatched them out with their chopsticks. I tried to grab one, but my chopsticks slipped. Grandpa picked his up with his fingers. There was a Chinese family at the table with a little baby. I tried to figure out how old the baby was, but I'm not good with baby ages. I tried to ask its mother.

How much? I asked, pointing at the baby.

That was the closest I could come to how old.

She stared at me.

How much?

She picked up the baby and put it on her lap. It opened its eyes and looked at me. She said something in Chinese. The cab driver started to laugh.

Baby not for sale, he said to me.

No I mean how *old*.

Five months.

I looked at the baby. It looked back at me.

Ke ai, I said, which means cute. It was; the baby was cute.

All the Chinese people laughed and clapped.

You speak Chinese very well, said the cab driver.

Thank you, I said.

I went back to eating dumplings. After a while the mother put the baby back on the seat next to me like I hoped she would do. She started to relax when she thought I wasn't going to try to buy her baby.

Five months could be a possible right age. The book didn't say how long it takes for a soul that's just died to get put into a new baby. If it happened right when the baby was born this baby could be a potential reincarnated Dad. But if it happened when the baby was still inside the mother then it wouldn't be a potential.

Dad? I said when everyone else was talking.

Dad? I whispered. *Baba?*

Grandpa was still picking up dumplings and eating them with his fingers. Then he got the Montezuma's revenge look on his face and zipped out of the room. The baby on the seat opened its eyes. I pretended that I dropped a chopstick so I could bend down and stare into the windows to its soul.

Dad? *Ni hao.* Give me a sign; it's me, Mallie.

The mother saw me whispering to the baby and she quick picked it up again.

I didn't take the little plastic bag out until the day the cab driver took us to see the warriors. I put it in my shorts pocket and buttoned the button.

It rose out of the ground on the way to the warriors. A big pyramid of grass with no trees.

Look at that hill, I said. It's a triangular hill.

The cab driver saw where I was pointing.

Qinshihuangdi, he said.

That was a word I knew. I looked it up especially when I was making my list.

That's him, I said to my grandfather Tim. That's where they've got the Yellow Emperor buried.

The hill was a tomb. Underneath the green grass was a vault with gold and silver and jade and the bones of thousands of dead men and their emperor, the Yellow Emperor. They haven't uncovered it yet. All around Xian, the City of Western Peace, treasures and the bones of men are buried. Under roads and fields and houses lie the bones of the dead.

It's true, what Crystal said. I looked it up in a book, that every breath of air you breathe contains some of the air from Julius Caesar's last breath. Meaning that some of Hitler's last gasp must be in my lungs right now too. The Yellow Emperor, Genghis Khan, all the world's worst. Just a few molecules I think. But still.

I wrote down the explanation in my notebook, but I still don't understand how it is that the evil air molecules get from one side of the earth to the other.

They buried them alive, is what the warrior pamphlet said. Of course the Yellow Emperor was dead already when they buried him. But all the others were alive. The cab driver had a tooth with gold on it. In the sun it glinted, like the metal on my grandma's car that crashed.

Johnny would like that tooth, I said.

WC? said the cab driver. He pointed to the outdoor toilet across the way from the big white building where the terra cotta warriors were. Signs stood along the line to the tomb. *Not photographing. Not spitting. Not touching the terra cottas.*

There were a couple of babies strapped to backs in line. I walked up close behind them and stared into their eyes, the windows to their souls.

Ni hao, I said. *Shi wo, Mallie.*

Then I said it in English, in case my dad's soul still remembered its original language. Hi. It's me, Mallie. They stared right back at me with their slanting brown eyes. I know that I'll know. When the time comes I'll know. For as long as it takes, I'll be waiting.

The cab driver reached his hand out beyond the rope and scraped at one of the soldiers, one that had a mean look on its face.

Not touching, can't you see the sign? I said to him.

He had his hand cupped together. He took my hand and opened it up.

Dirt, he whispered. Dirt from the Yellow Emperor, ten thousand years old.

There were guards all around. They might have dirt-sniffing dogs, I thought. I put my hand into the front pocket of my shorts and let the sand go. It trickled off my hand into the corners. The cab driver smiled.

If Crystal is right about the degrees of separation then there's only five people between me and my dad. I already know someone who know someone who knows someone who knows my baby father, wherever he is.

Dad was right; every soldier face was different.

None of them have given me a sign. That baby in the dumpling restaurant finally started screaming. His mother rocked it back and forth, but it kept staring at me and screaming. She picked apart a dumpling with her chopsticks and poked a piece into its mouth, but it spit it out and just kept screaming. She pulled up her shirt and tried to nurse it, but it screamed harder. She gave me a dirty look and took it outside.

Yangguizi, is what one of the people sitting at the table said.

That's another word I know from the tape. Foreign devil, which is what the book said we might hear some of in China.

I'm not a scientist, said Crystal when she told me about the air molecule theory. I don't understand it either. But I do know this. If you're breathing in Adolf Hitler's air, you've got to be breathing in Mother Teresa's at the same time. Mahatma Gandhi's. Jesus Christ's even.

Starr, said Johnny.

Him too, said Crystal.

Crystal says it doesn't matter, that the molecules are evenly dispersed around the world. They're so tiny you can't see them even with a microscope. You can't help it, you breathe them in, the bad air with the good. It's all mixed in together, she says.

No more shinies? she asked before we went to China.

I was working in the notebook, Johnny's red one.

I keep forgetting, I told her. It's a lie though. I haven't brought him any because of my secret, the one that I can't tell anyone. He looks at me when I come in.

Mallie, he says.

Hi, Johnny.

He reaches out his hand to me. That's the way we always used to do it. He stretched out his hand and I brought out both my fists, closed up.

Which one? I used to say.

He'd smile. He'd start to laugh.

Come on, which one?

He'd stretch out his good hand and lay it on one of my fists.

Nope. Choose again.

He'd be laughing by then, the way he laughs. He'd take his hand and lay it down over my other fist.

Good job. Here you go.

I would open my fist and he would pick it up with his thumb and pointer, the shiny. A piece of tinfoil that I made into an animal the way my dad showed me. A silver earring that my mother Lucia'd lost the other one to, or a paper clip bent into a curvy fishhook. He would hold it up in the window. Dangle it so the sun could flash off it.

That was what Johnny and me did every time I came into the diner. But I don't do it anymore. It's in the notebook, why I don't. I put it in tiny printing on the back of the last page. *You killed my dad*, is what I wrote down. Upside down in code, backward and tiny, so that nobody will ever see it and know that Mallie Williams is not as nice to Johnny Zielinski as they think. That she's changed from who she used to be.

There're some times when I go into the diner and he holds out his hand to me with his fingers stretched out. I stop myself from making the fists. I can feel how his hand would feel on top of mine. The way he lays his fingers down spread out. Slow. Like a skin whisper, is how Johnny touches.

I looked around. They didn't have any ashes-sniffing dogs that I could tell. He was up at the rim of the pit, my grandpa Tim, staring down at all the dead soldiers in their rows. On the other side of the world my brother Charlie is digging his way through earth and rock and fire to get to where I am. On the phone Mom put him on and he sang to me. *Little Tee-wee, he went to sea, in an open boat. And when it was afloat, the little boat bended. My story's ended.*

That's a Dad song, he said.

The ashes were warm in my hand. I went up to where my grandfather leaned against the railing and reached out my hand like I was waving to the warriors. The army hat pressed down on my snarl that was curled up tight against the back of my head. Chinese voices made sounds like running water all around me, and I stretched my fingers out like Johnny does when he's reaching for a shiny in the sun. They drifted down into the pit, the ashes that were my dad, little flakes scattering on the heads of the blind mud soldiers, falling like smoke, like tiny grey flowers, slower than the tears that were dropping out of my grandpa Tim's eyes.

Finally I started singing to that baby in the dumpling restaurant to make it stop crying. The only thing I could think to sing was the bathtub song. My grandpa was still gone with the Montezuma's. The baby did not blink the whole time I was singing. I whisper-sang the bathtub song, but when I finished the whole table was looking at me.

Hen hao, said the old lady who knew English. Very good.

She started singing too. The rest of the table joined in. They knew the song, the bathtub song that my dad taught me. It didn't sound the same as when he sang it. The cab driver smiled and sang too.

Yangshu ye hua la la
Xiaohai shuijiao zhao ta ma
Guaiguai baobei ni shui ba
Mahuzi laile wo da ta

What are you doing? I said. That's the bathtub song. How can you know that song?

It is a Chinese song, the old lady said.

It's my dad's song, I said.

The aspen leaves murmur la la la, sang the old lady who knew English. *Sleepy baby wants his ma. Darling baby close your eyes, go to bed. Any ghost that comes, I'll knock it on the head.*

Her voice was high and thin. She rocked as she sang. The people at the table smiled and nodded.

An old Chinese song, said the cab driver. A what do you call it, lullaby for Chinese babies.

That's my dad's song who's dead, I said to the old lady. I'm looking for him here, for the reincarnation.

Baba si'le, the old lady said. She said something to the other Chinese people, and they all bowed their heads. I saw Grandpa coming back from the bathroom.

I've been looking a long time, I said to the lady.

Changnian leiyue, she said. A Chinese proverb. For many years and months on end, you are looking for your baba.

What that old lady said is right. As long as it takes, is as long as I'll be looking.

22

TIM WILLIAMS

China wasn't what I thought it might be. When I was young I imagined it to be like the painted border of The Great Wall restaurant, that ribbon of crumbling stone that stretched along the borders of a country. Silence, the absence of sound and color. But north of Beijing it was a tourist attraction: flags and souvenir T-shirts, bottles of soda and water for sale, tiny plastic replicas. Buses lumbered through the tiny Chinese streets. The whole thing reminded me of the New York State Fair in Syracuse.

Mallie was leaning up on the Wall itself when I backed out of the toilet that was just a hole in the ground. It's hard squatting down over a hole like that when you're sixty years old. Mallie's lips were moving, as if she were singing a song or humming a tune to herself. Her hands were free, dangling at the ends of her arms. As I watched she lifted her face to the sun and closed her eyes.

It's been a long time since she looked that way, like a little girl. I moved behind one of the parapets and watched her. A flood of Chinese people moved around her carrying straw bags, plastic bags, hats. Babies. Mallie stood at the edge of the crowd, her face lifted to the sun.

A baby cried. I watched as Mallie's eyes opened and she leaned forward to stare as it passed by, bound to its mother's back with a long strip of cotton. She leaned into the baby's face, and it stared at her with big dark eyes. Her lips moved. I could read them.

Who are you? she asked the baby. What's your name?

I called Lucia that night from the hotel after Mallie was asleep. I would have done anything to protect my wife, to shield my child from my wrongdoing. But Starr and Georgia are both dead and what's the point anymore? Lucia's alive. Lucia is hurting. The time has come.

You know, Starr and I never went up to Star Hill that first day, said Lucia over the crackling long distance.

I sat on my bed, Mallie asleep on the other one, the black phone cord twisting around my hand.

That first night we met, she said. We never actually made it up to Star Hill.

Starr told us that you left and went up to see the ghost, I said.

He lied, said Lucia. We drove around North Sterns instead, up the hills and down. Then we went down to Utica and ate Chinese food at a little restaurant instead, that one that's right near where I work. He loved Chinese food.

Yes he did.

It was me, said Lucia. I'm the one that chickened out from going up to Star Hill. Because I think it really could be her. The ghost could be my mother.

They say the ghost is hard to see, I said.

So actually I've never been. All this time and I've never been. All I remember is her singing. A bath. Black legs that smelled like mothballs and a sweet taste that burns.

There's more, I said.

Of course there's more. But that's all that I have. I don't even know how she smelled, or what she liked to eat, or if she had a sense of humor.

She did.

What do you mean, she did? How would you know?

You asked me if I knew. If I knew that they were the murder-suicide. I did know, Lucia. That and lots more.

What do you mean? she asked again.

I knew your mother, I said.

Silence.

Right away I could feel it through the distance, greater than her confusion, her anger that would soon begin to bloom. But greater than that was her longing.

Is that why you looked that way when you met me? she asked. Like you'd just seen a ghost?

You look just like her, I said.

I listened to the hum. I ground my cheek into the Chinese telephone, with the Chinese characters on it that I didn't understand. I thought of all the knowledge we carry within us in this world, and how that knowledge dies with us, is turned into ash and smoke and returned to the air that we all breathe.

How? she asked. Where?

She was a waitress at that Chinese restaurant. I used to take Starr there.

Starr?

You knew him long ago, I said. You played together when you were babies.

Lucia didn't say anything. Then she hung up. I listened to the buzz for a while; then I lay the phone back in its cradle.

Mallie slept on her narrow Chinese bed. She was still in her clothes. One of her embroidered slippers had fallen off her foot and lay half-covered with the rough white Chinese sheet. I opened the notebook that lay under her sleeping arm.

Starr Williams's Last Word Possibilities
Johnny: star
Crystal: nothing
Grandpa Tim: sun
Ouija:8gh33efl
Magic 8 Ball: signs point to yes

Mallie had tried to turn the Ouija board message into something that made sense, attaching letter meanings to numbers and vice versa, turning it backward so that it read *lfe33hg8*. I closed the notebook and tried to ease the army cap off her head. But even in her sleep her arm came up and batted my hand away. She seems to think that no one's going to notice if she just keeps it on all the time. It's a Mao cap. It's even got the red star.

Did he kill her because of you? asked Lucia the next night. I have to know.

I don't know. I don't know what happened that night. All I know is that your father drove her up to Sterns, which is where I lived, and killed her and himself on Star Hill. The rest is a mystery.

The long distance hummed and clicked.

Do I look like her?

You look exactly like her, I said.

But she doesn't, not really. There's a weight that Lucia carries that Livvy didn't. They started with the same kind of sculpting, the same bones and blood and skin, but the world has marked Lucia in ways that her mother didn't live long enough to know.

She was young, I said. She was only thirty when she died.

There's Charlie now, she said. Out on the lawn digging another of those holes that goes nowhere. Poking away with that plastic shovel Starr gave him. He's the same age I was when my father murdered my mother.

I looked at Mallie, asleep on the bed, her eyes hidden under the brim of her Chinese army cap.

You were three years old, I said. You were a little girl wearing a navy blue dress.

The long distance hummed.

It had white on it, what do you call that stuff. Fringe?

Rickrack.

Three-year-old Lucia had stood between her grandparents, those two people grown suddenly old. The line filed past them, snaked around the pews and past the coffin draped with flowers. Where his was, I don't know. They had only hers, their only child's, with a closed lid and lilies strewn on top.

You were quiet and still, I said.

The line shuffled forward; the church filled with the murmurs of those ahead of me, grasping the hands of the man and woman grown old. Some bent down to the little girl standing between them. I heard the words *Lucia, Lucy.* I stood behind a couple dressed in black, ahead of an old man who told everyone who would listen that he was Livvy's uncle.

I'm her uncle, he said. I'm Olivia's uncle. I can remember when she was born. Such a head of hair on her, just like little Lucy here.

It was my turn and I went on past. I shook their hands, this mother and father. I put my hand on the head of the little girl in the navy dress with white rickrack.

I have new shoes, she said. Size five.

You had new shoes, I said to my daughter-in-law. Black patent leathers, size five.

I don't remember, Tim, said Lucia. You don't know how I hate that I can't remember.

You can't tell Mallie anything, so I don't try. But at night when she can't stay awake any longer even though she wants to, it comes curling out like a hibernating snake. My granddaughter tries to keep everything under wraps, but her hair betrays her.

It's out of control, I said to her. There could be things crawling around in there.

Every couple of years at school we have a lice epidemic. The parents come in looking embarrassed and haul their infested kids away. They're back in a couple of days, hair smelling of the harsh shampoo that washes out the tiny bugs, the nits that are almost invisible to the naked eye.

WC? says the cab driver. Every few minutes there he is, peering into the rearview mirror that has the big crack running through it, back at Mallie, his darling. She has him charmed with her numbers and greetings, her phrases that she's got down perfectly: *wo ai pijiu, changjiang shangyou hen feiwo.*

What does that one mean? I asked the first time I heard it come rolling out of her mouth.

Changjiang shangyou hen feiwo, she said. The upper reaches of the Yangtze River valley are very rich and fertile.

Oh, of course, I said. How could I not have known.

I like the way it sounds, she said. They said it on the tape and it sounds like hills to me. Rolling up and down, like the hills at home.

Charlie still digging? I asked Lucia next night over the phone.

He's given it up. He told me he was too scared of what he'd find once he'd gotten through the bedrock and into the hot lava. Didn't want to burn himself.

Mallie's got the cab driver charmed, I said. He's impressed with her command of Chinese.

Like father, like daughter, said Lucia.

Her sneakers finally gave up the ghost, I said. Even she had to admit it. We bought her some new Chinese slippers. They have gold sparkles on them in the shape of a phoenix.

I can't remember a goddamned thing about my mother, Tim, said Lucia. Nothing except a song, a bath, a bunch of black legs. Now I look at Charlie and I think, is that what it's going to be like for him?

Not if Mallie can help it, I said. She's determined.

Did you love my mother? said Lucia.

I loved her.

But not enough. Not enough to keep her safe.

You can't keep the people you love safe, I said. That's the dirtiest secret in this world.

I read over Mallie's shoulder in the cab.

Possible Dad Sightings:

1. Jacobs #6?

2. baby at dumpling restaurant?

3. baby in bamboo carriage next to pig in cage?

Don't snoop, she said.

I'm your grandfather, I said. Grandfathers can snoop every now and then.

She took something out of her pocket and let it fall from her hand over the railing when she thought I wasn't looking. Probably the dust, I thought, that the cab driver scraped off the face of one of the soldiers.

You can't do that, I told him. I pointed at the signs.

He pretended not to understand. He spit out a stream of Chinese that Mallie understood. Or seemed to. He slipped the dust into the pocket of her shorts.

The Yellow Emperor, she said. Now I'm contaminated.

Her mess of hair bulged the dull green cap out in back like a nest of snakes. She leaned over so that the tips of her new Chinese slipper sandals dug into the dust of the walkway. I watched her hand slip around back and unbutton the closed flap of her back pocket. She brought out a pinch of dust and opened her fingers over the pit.

I saw her watch it flutter down and I knew; it was not dust, but ashes. She doesn't know how closely I keep track of her, how much I know of who she is. How familiar her desire is to me, to make him live again. And failing that, to keep him in this world, whatever it takes.

MALLIE WILLIAMS

The sea urchin was like a rubber cement ball, the kind you roll around in your hand until the cement starts to dry and balls up in your palm. That's what it looked like, anyway.

Also called sea slug, is what the waiter said.

My grandfather Tim ate a piece with his chopsticks.

Not bad, he said.

I couldn't. I covered up my pieces of slug with white rice. I hid it at the bottom of the bowl and fluffed the rice up with my chopsticks. Around us other people were holding their bowls up to their mouths and shoveling in the slug and rice with their chopsticks. Like dump trucks. The waiter came back and looked at my bowl that looked like just a bowl of plain rice.

Very good! he said.

He plopped another scoop of sea slug into my bowl. My grandfather Tim laughed.

That's what you get for trying to be polite, Mallie.

It was right after I sprinkled the ashes on the soldiers that Grandpa put his hand on my cap. I stood still and didn't move my head, so he wouldn't feel how hard the lump was. But he knew, he knew already.

Should we do something about this? he asked.

About what?

But he knew I was pretending.

It's time, don't you think? he said.

The haircut shops are all over China, on the back streets that are called alleys. Sterns doesn't have any alleys, but that is the name for these tiny twisting streets that the doorways open onto. There aren't any sidewalks. Sterns has sidewalks on the main street, the one that Jewell's and the diner is on, and on the two cross side streets. And around the village green in front of the twin churches. That's it.

But China, China is different. People squat in the doorways that don't even have doors, some of them. Everyone in China squats. They squat to drink tea out of little glasses. They squat to stir bowls of noodles with their chopsticks. They squat to talk to each other. The babies squat to do their business, so that the slits up the back of their pants open.

I have started to squat too, on my walks in the afternoon when my grandfather Tim is sleeping.

It's time for my siesta, he says. Now what would you call that in Chinese, I wonder? A Chinese siesta.

Xiuxi, I said, which is the word for rest that I learned from the tape.

That's thank you, isn't it?

No, that's *xiexie*. This is *xiuxi*.

He made his face that he makes, that means, What's the difference? then he lay down on the Chinese bed that his feet dangle off of.

I'm going to the restaurant, I said.

But I didn't. I walked past the restaurant that's actually just one little room where at breakfast they wheel in the tin cart with stuff that they say is toast but that isn't toast.

Zaijian, I said at the front desk, which means good-bye.

They all waved, the three Chinese men that work behind the

189

counter. They look the same, the Chinese men. They are the same height that's a lot shorter than my dad. They all wear black glasses and red vests that belong to the hotel.

Meiguo xiaojie, zaijian. Good-bye American miss.

The hotel has a door. You step out of it into the alley, which is hot and sticky. Smoke plumes out of the little firepots that people squat around, cooking. Babies sit propped up in laps and bamboo carriages. Or strapped to backs, they stare around. They stare at me, the *yangguizi* foreign devil. Some of them scream when they see me.

I pulled my Mao cap down low to hide my eyes that are not Chinese eyes. It is 2 a.m. on the other side of the world where my brother, Charlie, lies asleep. If I concentrate I can send him vibrations from this side of the world.

It is hot here, Charlie. The cabdriver contaminated me with dust from the evil emperor. I am carrying it in my pocket. I'm looking for Dad. I'm looking everywhere.

The Chinese people stare at me when I walk by. My Chinese slippers are size 32, which is a size we don't have in America. Lots of the Chinese men's slippers are not as big as mine, because my feet keep growing and growing.

Some of the doorways are people's houses and some are shops. Some of the shops have wooden cases outside with things for sale on them, dried-up things that look like wood but are actually Chinese medicine. Some smell bad. Some have no smell.

On my walks I only look at the babies that are tiny, that look as if they were born less than six months ago. Sometimes their mothers are nursing them so it's hard to see their eyes.

The eyes are the windows to the soul. That's what you have to stare into, in order to recognize the person.

On Star Hill where the high schoolers go there's a ghost. It only comes out at night. You can only see it when you don't look at it. When you let your eyes slide away, then you can see it out of the corner of your eye, is what they say.

Have you seen the ghost, Dad? I asked my dad when he was alive.

I've tried.

But did you?

Not yet, he said. But I'm on the lookout.

I'm trying to look like a Chinese girl. Then maybe the babies won't scream at me. They'll let me look at them. This would be the place that my dad would come back to life, I think, here where he wanted to be so bad. That's my prediction. That's why I sprinkled the ashes on the soldiers, so that he'd be here in the City of Western Peace.

Some of the alleys are food alleys, with stalls that sell green vegetables, big watermelons, oranges. Bunches of things that look like huge brown grapes but are not, that are fruits that you pop out of the brown skins and into your mouth, round white fruit with a big seed in the middle. They taste like the word *supple*, which I learned from the dictionary.

Dad would love these, I said when I tried one. I said it in English and all the Chinese people who were selling them, the fruits, laughed and nodded their heads.

Can you understand what I'm saying?

They laughed and nodded their heads again. But I don't think they did really. Some of the alleys are crammed with little stalls that sell deep-fried dough twists. A boy stands with the dough and tosses it into the air, twirling it around and around and looping it in on itself. Then he dips it in the boiling oil, and it comes out brown and fried.

Like a Chinese Hemstrought's, I said when I saw that. Sort of.

Friday afternoons my mom brings home a bag of doughnuts from Hemstrought's, the glazed kind that's everybody's favorites. Except me; I don't eat them anymore since my dad died. They were his favorite, that's why. That's why I gave them up.

Other stalls, they sell fish. Fish that's still alive, swimming around in buckets. You pick the fish you want and they kill it right there, with a mallet. There's a lot of blood.

Others, they sell orange fruit speared on big toothpicks. Fruit-on-a-stick, like at the Boonville County Fair that we're missing because we're in China. Every year my dad used to throw dimes on the plates to win more china for my mother. She hated it though. She says it's cheap crap, the china. To tease her, is why he does it.

Did it.

Mom brings home only three doughnuts now. One for her, one for Charlie, one for my grandfather Tim if he comes by. If he doesn't, she gives it to the squirrels. Squirrels will eat anything, even glazed doughnuts with cinnamon on top.

The man selling Chinese pancakes gave me one. He put it in a piece of wax paper and handed it over.

Meiguo xiaojie, lai, lai, he said. Come here American miss.

Xiexie, I said.

It was hot and it didn't taste like the kind of pancake we have at home. There were bits of green and white scallion in it and egg fried onto it. It was salty.

Hen hao, I said.

It was true. It was the best thing I'd tasted since I came to China, much better than the sea slug and the chicken soup that had the whole head of the chicken in it including the eyes and tongue.

Mallie, I don't think I knew chickens had tongues, my grandfather said. And I'm not sure it's something I really needed to know, if you want the truth.

He turned the chicken head over on his spoon and looked at the eyes and the beak and the tongue that stuck out. Then the Montezuma's got us both and we had to run for the trench.

There were a couple of chairs in the shop, with big Chinese sinks behind them and running water.

Lai'a, lai'a, is what the ladies said.

That was not a word I knew from the book, but you could tell what they meant by the way they waved their hands in circles, with their fingers twirling toward themselves.

I went in.

Meiguo xiaojie, they said. They always know, they always know you're from America. There was an old Chinese lady in the other chair, leaning back so her black hair swam in the running water. A lady with a blue smock rubbed her fingers in the old lady's hair, back and forth, scrubbing over her scalp. The old lady opened her eyes to stare at me. Then she closed them again.

There were no babies there.

The lady in the blue smock took my Mao cap off.

Mao Zhuxi, she said, which I knew meant Chairman Mao. My hair didn't fall down my back like normal hair. It stayed twisted up next to my neck. Hot and sweaty. Through the door of the shop I stared at the alley, at the life going by: babies on backs, little kids playing with balls, old ladies shuffling on tiny feet that I knew were bound feet.

Aiya, said the lady to the other lady. I felt her fingers on my hair that wasn't moving, even when she pulled at it. *Aiya*, said the other lady. Together they pulled.

Ouch.

Ouch, they repeated. *Ouch, ouch.*

The old lady pulled her head up from the water and wrapped a towel around it. She hobbled over to where the ladies had pushed me into the other chair. She bent and smoothed her hand over my hair.

Hao kelian, she said. *Kelian de haizi*. Words I didn't know, but still, I knew what she meant. She meant what everyone wearing black at my dad's memorial service meant when they walked by me in the buffet line, talking in that same tone of voice, putting their hands on my hair. My hair that wasn't tangled yet, back then.

The blue-smock lady held the scissors up in front of my nose. Big black scissors that looked a hundred years old. The light from the open doorway poured in and made a space of sun around the chair I was sitting in. She snipped the scissors open and shut in front of my eyes and spoke Chinese words that I didn't understand. The sun sparkled off the broad sharp blades.

Johnny Zielinski would love that, I said out loud in English.

She nodded and smiled, then frowned and snipped them open and shut again. She held up a hank of her hair and pretended to cut it. Then she raised her eyebrows and looked at me.

Go ahead, I said.

They looked at each other, all three of them. The old lady with the towel around her head took it off and started combing her hair with a black comb. They talked in Chinese, fast words with no breaks in between.

It's OK. Go ahead.

She bent forward and rubbed her hand on my head, the old lady with the comb. She whispered into my ear. I could tell it was a question.

Go ahead, I said. There's nothing I can do. No matter what I do it's going to keep on growing.

Charlie, I am getting my hair cut. I am wearing Chinese slippers. I am eating Chinese food. I don't know if I still look like Mallie; you might not know me when I get back.

The sun poured in around the chair, and little kids came in from the alley. They crowded around the chair while she tipped my head back and ran the warm water on it. She held the big knot of hair in her hand and soaked it. It was heavy. It pulled my scalp and hung heavy off my head.

Ouch, I said, but not out loud.

The little kids pressed in around the chair, touching my bare arms with their fingers. They talked to themselves in Chinese that

I couldn't understand. That's how Johnny talks, so only a few can understand him. You have to practice, to be able to hear what he means to say. I started to sing a dad song. *Ladybird, ladybird, fly away home. Your house is on fire and your children burn.*

If Charlie heard me he'd scream. But Charlie is on the other side of the world.

I closed my eyes, but still the sun was too bright. I felt the scissors behind me. They cut through my heavy hurting hair. I opened my eyes and looked down at my Chinese slippers, shining in the sunlight. Sequins and glitter on the phoenix bird.

Charlie, here I am on the other side of the world. Grandpa is taking a Chinese siesta. I had to eat sea slug. It's 7 a.m. where you are. I'm looking at the babies, but I can't tell which one is Dad. Keep practicing because I will quiz you when I get back. Remember everything.

Charlie, they're cutting my hair off.

Meiguo xiaojie haoma? said the lady who was cutting. How are you doing American miss?

Hao, I said.

But it was a lie. The sneakers that were my dad's present to me my grandfather Tim already threw out. My bones, they hurt all the time, and my hair keeps on growing, growing. There is nothing I can do to stop it, to stop me from going on and living in this world where he isn't anymore.

CRYSTAL ZIELINSKI

Johnny was three when Mallie was born, just starting to walk in his crablike way. They brought Mallie into the diner, still strapped into her car seat, screaming her newborn's scream, and put her up on the booth table. Johnny limped over to where she was and crawled up onto the seat next to Starr.

Hi, Johnny Z, said Starr.

Lucia hovered over Mallie, hushing and murmuring. Still, baby Mallie screamed, angry at having been brought into this, the world. Three-year-old Johnny plucked at the blanket covering her.

This is Madeleine, said Starr, which is what they were still calling her back then. Loud, so Johnny could hear her name over the crying. Lucia bent down, trying to comfort the baby.

Mal, said Johnny. He was the first one to shorten her name, to call her Mallie. A nickname giver, Johnny was.

I was behind the counter, whisking eggs and milk, pouring pancakes into rounds on the grill. Three years since the day that Lucia walked into the diner, wearing her pink skirt and her white cotton T-shirt, three and a half years since Johnny came sliding out, his life almost ended before it began. I took the spatula and made perfect rounds with the pancake batter. I ladled a spoonful of blueberries onto the exact center of each. The crying stopped.

She likes you, said Starr to Johnny.

Over at the table Johnny was stroking baby Mallie's face. My head bent over the bowl of eggs and milk and I looked up from under my hair so no one could see me, just my eyes, watching the booth where the three of them huddled over the baby.

Baby Mal opened her eyes and looked up at Johnny, whose finger reached out to trace the faint curve of her shadowy eyebrow.

Johnny Z, you've got a friend, said Starr.

Johnny smiled. Starr gave him a kiss. Lucia watched them, the brother tracing the lines of his sister's baby face, no expression at all in her dark eyes that flared up at me and then as quickly, away.

Look, there's a Chinese girl, said Kathy from Jewell's who was eating her lunch, tuna melt as always. We got some Chinese people moving into Sterns?

She's pretty, said Dena Jacobs who was sitting on the stool next to her, not able to reach the counter because of her growing belly.

I saw the Chinese girl too, getting out of Starr's blue pickup that Tim has started driving again.

Mallie, Johnny said. Before she was even halfway out the door of Jewell's, he was bouncing in his seat.

Mallie, Mallie, he said. Singing it, even.

Mallie? said Dena. That little Chinese girl is Mallie Williams?

Mallie crossed the street and I saw the sparkles on her feet.

Now what do you suppose she's got on those feet of hers? I said.

Johnny saw them too, glinting in the sunlight of a September day. He smiled the way he does. His old shinies were scattered on the table, the ones he doesn't like anymore. Some of them are tarnished, like the silver dancer earring that used to be his favorite. The swan Mallie made him out of tinfoil got crumpled a while ago. You can't even tell what it used to be.

She came in the door, a green Chinese cap pulled over her eyes.

Hello, Miss Mao, I said. Did your eyes start slanting while you were over there?

She tipped up the brim and looked at me straight on.

Guess not.

Malliemallie, sang Johnny, reaching with his good hand.

Johnny, she said.

I saw Tim through the glass front window come out of Jewell's and look around for Mal. Up the street and down. Then he saw her through the window of the diner. He lifted his arm in a wave and I waved back.

Hello, Crystal, he said when he pushed his way in through the screen door. The bell jingled.

Lost some more weight over there I see, I said.

Ten pounds. It got us both, Montezuma's revenge.

We looked at them in Johnny's corner booth. She was bent over the table toward him. He was still bouncing and grinning, humming the way he does sometimes when he's excited. The green army cap covered up all her hair so she looked like a skinned chicken.

What's with the hat? I said to Tim.

Then I saw. She took it off and laid it on the Formica table between her and Johnny. He reached out for the red star on it. A small red thing for Johnny.

Johnny? Mallie said.

Star, he said, reaching for it.

Her hair swung blunt against her jaw, with Chinese bangs marching straight across her forehead. Each hair in line with the next. She looked over at me with a scared look on her face, as if she were afraid to show me that she'd cut her hair.

It's beautiful, I said. You're beautiful.

Johnny? she said. Johnny? Do you still know who I am?

She wanted his reaction; she was afraid he'd be scared. Or worse, that he wouldn't recognize her at all. But he never even looked, he was focused on the red plastic star on her Mao cap.

Don't even think about it, I said to Mal. He had you pegged before you were out the door of Jewell's.

You want a shake? I asked Tim. A burger?

Whatever you've got I'll take, he said. Mallie'll have some sea slug if you've got it.

Johnny got out of the booth and limped over to the grill.

What are you looking for, Johnny Z?

He made his sound, his new one.

Oh, your new teddy? You want to show it to Mallie I bet.

He took it in his arms and made his way back, holding onto the backs of the chairs for support. His good hand held the bear out to her.

What a nice teddy. Did Crystal give it to you?

It's from his grandfather, I said.

I didn't know he had a grandfather, she said.

Everyone's got one, I said. It's a law of nature.

Johnny smiled the way he does and reached the bear to Mallie so she could touch.

He can't be separated from that thing, I said. He sleeps with it. He sits it on his lap and puts his seat belts over it when we drive.

Bear, he said.

When we got home he held it while I soaped the washcloth.

We've got to do hair tonight, baby, I said. It's been more than a week.

Johnny hates shampoos. The only way he lets me do it is to dip the rag into the basin and drape it over his head, over and over until his hair is soaked enough to take the shampoo.

Bear, he said.

You can hold it. That's fine. Now dip your head back.

He squinched his eyes.

I know. God forbid you should ever get any water in your eyes.

The bear sat on his chest, clutched in his good hand, while I dipped the rag in the water and set it on his head, water dripping back into the basin. I draped a towel around him to keep him warm in the late summer night air.

It's your stars-and-sun towel, J. If you opened your eyes you could see it, your favorite towel from Starr.

Starr, he said.

Or star, maybe. Who knows. Baby shampoo oozed into my palm. I spread it into Johnny's fine hair. When he was a baby his hair was so silky and white-blond you could barely see it. I used to wash it with a soapy rag, just run it over his warm head, careful on the soft spot that scared me to touch even though they said the pulsing was normal.

The night he was born I breathed into him. Crazily, thinking, Out with the bad air, in with the good.

You like that bear, don't you?

Bear.

I finished shampooing and rinsed his hair with the rag again, this time holding it under the tap until the water ran clear.

Open your eyes, Johnny; you can see the sparkles in the tap.

But he wouldn't. Still afraid that the shampoo bubbles might hurt his eyes, even though it was only once in his life when he was a baby that it ever happened. It was baby shampoo that's not supposed to hurt if you get it in your eyes, but it still hurt him.

Never going to forgive me for that one time I got them in your eyes, are you, baby?

His clean hair ran smoothly along his scalp, a faint curl in the ends where water dripped off. I pulled the stars-and-sun towel off his chest and rubbed it over his head. He held the bear.

That bear has a name, probably. Let's check on the tag.

Made in China. Teddy. Next to the name on the tag were pen marks, faded from Johnny's bathwater that had dripped on it. I held it up to the light from the trailer window to decipher.

Teddy Zielinski.

Oh.

Oh, said Johnny in imitation. He opened his eyes under the towel that hung over his head like a burnoose and smiled at me.

Your grandfather thought your name was Teddy Zielinski, I said. Because I wrote him that we named you after him.

Teddy, said Johnny. He plucked at the white tag with his good hand and offered up the bear to me. It was a cheap little bear, made in China like other cheap toys. Filled with plastic pellets and bound round the neck with a red ribbon.

A teddy for Teddy, I said. A present from your grandpa.

Johnny was nine when Starr came out one day, a can of spray paint in each hand.

It's time you painted that old tub, don't you think? It's about to rust through.

It was my dad's old white truck, used when he bought it, that he left to me when he took off.

Not true, I said. It's only fifteen. That thing'll outlast us both.

Well then we're in for a short life, said Starr. Come here, Johnny. Take a look at this color, see what you think. I got it specially for you.

Johnny limped over and held on to Starr's pant leg with his good hand. Starr popped off the top of the can and sprayed a stone on the ground.

Jesus, Starr, I said. Trying to blind us?

Bright red, like blood, the color glowed up from the transformed rock. Johnny laughed. The sun shone down on the red paint and made it spark with light.

I knew you'd like that, Johnny Z. You can help me paint it.

You're supposed to get your vehicles painted at special places, I said. Vehicle-painting places. You can't just spray on paint like that.

This old thing? Who cares?

He handed Johnny a can.

Hold it tight now and push the nozzle, he said. This truck is going to be so pretty when we're finished.

I sat and watched them, Starr and Starr's son. Together they covered every inch of rusty white truck with the red paint that gleamed in the sun. Brighter even than the red zinnias nodding against the trailer wall. All afternoon they worked, Starr going over Johnny's drippy lines, wiping excess off the chrome where Johnny faltered. Sometimes he covered Johnny's bad hand with his own, holding him steady so Johnny could reach up high with his can that hissed and dripped with flaming red. Sometimes he leaned over him and whispered into Johnny's ear.

That night when Starr was gone I washed Johnny outside as the sun set on the blood-red truck. Splotches were everywhere, clotting strands of his hair together, between the toes of his arched foot, dripped into his ears even.

That was the one time that Starr came out to the trailer after Lucia took him away from me, the time he turned the truck into a red jewel for Johnny.

Mallie's asked me what Starr's last word was. She's got her list with everyone's answers on it, everyone who might have heard it. Even Kathy from Jewell's with all the makeup. I saw Kathy's answer in there, written down in Mallie's faithful script: *Eeeee.*

They screamed when they saw me, said Mallie. The Chinese babies.

That doesn't surprise me, I said. If what you were doing was trying to pull up their eyelids like you did in the post office with Dena Jacobs's baby number five there.

Number six.

Whatever. Did you?

No, she said, running her hands over her notebook. They screamed because I looked like a foreign devil. That's when I cut my hair. So I'd look like a Chinese girl, and he wouldn't be scared if a Chinese Mallie came up to him. It was a mistake, though. How could he recognize me if I was Chinese?

He'd recognize you, I said. Johnny did.

I put my hand out on her short hair, the blunt swing of it dark and shiny, angling around her jawbone. Bangs hung heavy over her eyes that are dark and deep. Unchildlike.

You forgotten how to sleep? I asked.

Johnny limped over and held onto the back of Mallie's stool for support.

Star, he said.

He held out both fists.

You want me to choose? said Mallie. OK. This one.

His bad hand unfurled, revealing the plastic star centered in his palm. He laid it in her hand and made his way back to the booth. Mallie's slipper lay on the table where she had put it, the sequins shining in the sun. She let the star drop on the counter where it fell, the flat plastic sound of it like a clap.

You want to see something? she said.

She dragged her hand out of her shorts pocket and opened it up to me.

Looks like dirt to me.

From the cab driver. He snuck it into my pocket when I didn't know. Scraped it off the face of one of those soldiers.

The terra cotta warriors?

Yeah. He said, Here's some ten thousand-year-old dirt from the Yellow Emperor.

Oh, the Yellow Emperor, I said. Your old buddy.

Mallie looked down at the dirt in her palm.

I'm contaminated now.

Mallie, said Johnny from his booth.

He had one of her slippers in his hand. He held it up to the window so the sequins glinted in the sun.

There's dirt that's evil on me, said Mallie. Air that's evil in me.

There's nothing you can do to make yourself pure, I said. There's nothing you can do to stop yourself from changing. Look at you; you don't want to but already you're growing.

Johnny slid out of the booth and made his way among the tables to where she leaned against the counter. He reached his good hand out to her new bangs and brushed them off her forehead. With his finger he stroked her cheek, her forehead, the line of her tears.

He wouldn't want you to stop even if you could, Mal.

I'm bad, she said. I'm evil.

You think no one else is? Look at Johnny. He's got his good

hand and his bad hand. Mallie, listen to me. We're born not into this world but out of it, and there's bad and good wherever you turn.

I didn't kiss my dad, she said. I didn't hug him that last day. I'm the reason he died.

Johnny started crying too.

You think somehow you can keep the people you love safe, Mallie?

She didn't answer.

Well, you can't, I said. However much you might want to.

Down on the floor the sparkles on her Chinese slippers glittered in the sun, the bird spreading its wings, trying to lift off her toes. Johnny knelt, crying, and laid his cheek on her feet.

We went back to the Foothills Home next day. It was bright and sunny, white clouds chasing each other across the sky. Johnny unbuckled his belts and leaned against the glowing red of the pickup, holding Teddy Zielinski. Smiling.

Your favorite color on your favorite kind of sun day, I said. Let's go inside and maybe you can blow some bubbles.

The girl came over and took Johnny away, to the place where sun was streaming through the skylight. He loves the bubbles. They're like a gift to Johnny that he expects to see whenever he comes to the place where Lucia works.

Did you recognize Mallie when she got back? asked Lucia.

Sure, I said. She's the same Mal she's always been.

Do you remember when she was born? asked Lucia. And we brought her into the diner, and laid her on the table, and she was crying and crying. And Johnny came over to see her.

I remember, I said.

Maybe she knew, said Lucia, and that was why she stopped crying.

Knew what?

Knew that he was her brother.

Over in the corner the girl blew bubbles for Johnny. He waved his arms, the good one and the bad one, over his head, trying to catch them. Every one he touched popped.

Look at that, I said. You'd think Johnny'd cry, when they disappear like that. But he doesn't; he loves them anyway.

I'm sorry, Crystal, said Lucia. I'm so sorry.

I know you are, I said. And so am I.

JOHNNY ZIELINSKI

remember this sun is what he said
   sun i love you
   there isn't anything i wouldn't do for you sun

LUCIA WILLIAMS

You got some new clothes, Mom?

Charlie and his eagle eyes. Mallie doesn't care; she wears the same things day in and day out. Smells are what she loves. I scoop her clothes up while she's sleeping and put them in the washing machine. But Charlie notices. He comes to me, fingers the newness, rubs his cheek against fabric if it's soft. Velvet he particularly loves and lamb's wool.

Yes I do, Mr. Observant.

I'm not Mr. Observant, he denied automatically, in the way of three-year-olds.

Yes you are.

Am not.

He came up and pressed against my cotton sweater.

What is this color? This is not a Mom color.

This color is turquoise.

Turquoise, he said, pronouncing the word carefully, tasting it.

Turquoise. Like the ocean. Like the deep blue sea.

Sea, sea, like the deep blue sea, he sang in a tuneless tune. The deep, deep blue, blue sea.

Off he spun, twirling his arms as he whirled. He tilted his head back and smiled at the ceiling, then closed his eyes and spun harder.

You're spinning so fast I can hardly see you, I said.

From the depths of the whirling child came his reedy child's voice, overlaid with laughter: *the deep, deep blue, blue sea.*

Out there where no one knows who she is, that girl walks the beach. So long now my thoughts have turned to her that it's habit to think of that other Lucia, the Lucia who might have been, free on the sand while morning fog rises around her and the sun threatens to pierce through. No one knows who she is on that beach, no one knows that her father killed her mother, nor do they know that she has no memories of the woman who gave her birth. They look at her and see a girl in a pink cotton skirt that floats around her ankles. They see the footprints she leaves in the sand, the cartwheels she turns when she thinks no one's there to see.

Charlie, have you seen that little cup full of dirt that was in Mallie's closet? I asked.

He lay on his back in the grass beside one of his holes, his child's rake embedded in the dirt he'd unearthed. Singing *Twinkle, twinkle little star.*

It went to China to see the dead dirt soldiers, he said without opening his eyes.

The stickers still hung on the wall, the incense ring that Starr got her at the state fair with its little cones of blue and green incense in their brass box. But the Dixie cup was gone.

Is that what all that digging's for? I asked Charlie. So you can fill Dixie cups with soil samples and hide them in closets?

I'm digging to China, he said, and went out to start another hole.

Late at night when I couldn't sleep I looked in the closet. Hoping to discover my daughter, the secrets she carries within her, in the totems she set up there. She hid in the closet that whole day, after I dragged the swimming pool out of the closet and deflated it. Charlie stared at me, his eyes shadowed like a three-year-old's shouldn't be, when she ran into the closet and shut the door.

Mallie? Mal? Is it something I did?

Crystal brought Johnny down again. I saw her hovering around the edge of the doorway as I sat with piles of forms at my desk. Johnny was already well into the room, limping along the wall, his good hand out for support.

Lucia, he was saying.

I could understand him, the first time that I could except for when he says Mallie. Mallie was his first word, back when he was three years old. Rita looked up from where she sat on the piano bench. Some of the kids love the music she plays for them, the lullabies that she intersperses with bits of ragtime. They come up to her, tug at her jeans and rock back and forth, the same way James Howard does when the music pours forth from his tape player.

Crystal watched him as he went to Rita and held his hand out to her. His Johnny smile making her smile back.

Well hello, friend, she said. I bet I know what you're here for, don't I?

She went to get the jar of bubble liquid and the big plastic wand, the special one. She poured the liquid into a shallow bowl, a bowl like a dog dish, and dipped the wand into it. Waved it around like a languid tennis racket. Giant lazy bubbles floated free, set spinning amid the dust motes that danced in the light streaming through the skylights. He reached his good hand up for them.

Crystal looked at me with her Crystal eyes that have not changed since the first day I saw her.

Where would he be happier? she asked. Where would be a better place for him, here or Sterns?

Johnny across the room rocked back and forth on his crossed legs, laughing in his silent way as bubbles drifted onto his outstretched fingers, touched his head, and disappeared with a tiny liquid pop. His crooked hand shook as he stretched it up, trying to draw the bubbles toward himself.

Crystal, what happened when he was born? I asked.

She was following him with her eyes, every line of her body leaning toward her boy, longing. A cloud passed over the sun and momentarily obscured the light. Then it was gone and sun poured in again, into this huge room where children lay and sat scattered in its warmth.

It was dark, she said. It was dark, a late winter night. I didn't know it was happening already. I tried to hold it back, but I couldn't. It wasn't the way I'd planned it. I was already registered at the hospital in Utica.

Johnny reached too high for a bubble and fell over, onto his chest. I watched Crystal's hand clench as she stopped herself from jumping up and running to him. He lay on the floor, then heaved himself up, back into his sitting position. Still smiling. Still reaching.

But I couldn't stop it, said Crystal. He came out. I thought I would die.

Rita dipped and spun, gigantic bubbles spiraling in the sun.

It was the cord, said Crystal. Wrapped around his neck, cutting off his air. That's when he got the CP.

She looked at Johnny, sitting next to Rita at the old chipped piano, rocking and clapping his hands together.

See, he can't even clap his hands right, she said. I failed him before he was even into the world.

It wasn't you who failed him, it was me, I said. If I hadn't taken Starr away you wouldn't have been alone.

We're all alone, she said. It's over and done with. And I'd say you've paid your dues.

There was a toy that Johnny and some of the kids were playing with. A round plastic ball with different-shaped holes in it and different shapes to drop in: triangles, circles, squares, and stars. Johnny limped over and leaned against Crystal. He held out his hands, fists clenched, and smiled.

He wants you to choose, said Crystal.

I pointed to the crooked fist. He turned it over and opened it up. A red plastic star. Across the room the other kids were busy, trying to fit circles and squares into the plastic ball.

I recognize that star, I said. It's from Mallie's hat, isn't it?

Mallie, said Johnny.

He put the star into my hand and closed my fingers around it.

Would it be better for him here? asked Crystal.

I've watched you with him all his life, I said. Rocking him, talking to him, washing him with that little washcloth.

That's the only kind of bath he's ever taken, said Crystal. He's filled with fear, he screams and cries. At a distance is the only way he likes water.

Mallie was days old when Starr started bathing her. He filled the tub with warm water and laid her belly to belly, her newborn head lolling on his chest, too heavy for her to move. The bathroom filled with moist warmth from the running of the water that he made sure was not too hot for her. I was afraid to do it myself, but Starr wasn't. Every night he lay in the tub, cradling his baby against his skin that was warmed by the warm water. That was when she was still called Madeleine.

Well let me try, I said.

The whirlpool was a room painted blue and pink and yellow, a pastel sunrise blooming on one of the walls. Starr did it. He walked in one day with three buckets of new paint and sponged it on, soft mottled color on the bare white walls.

Surprise, he said when he was finished.

That's an unusual sunrise, I said.

For you, he said, touching my sweater that like all my sweaters was my mother's. Your favorite colors.

Which they aren't, although it's too late to tell him that now. Johnny held his arms up in the air while Crystal peeled off his T-shirt. He took his pants off himself, leaning on her for support. The steam rose from the whirlpool that's always at the same temperature, not too hot and never cold. Wisps of mist spiraled up and disappeared. Johnny gestured at Starr's sunrise painted on the wall.

I know you like that, said Crystal. It's nice, isn't it?

Sun, said Johnny.

I picked him up, his twelve-year-old body lighter than skinny Mallie's at nine.

We'll leave your undies on, I said. Don't worry.

Submissive, he hung in my arms, his arms and legs drooping down, his head tilted to catch the light streaming in from the skylights.

There's skylights everywhere here, I said. You love that light, don't you?

First one pale foot, then the other, Crystal plucked off his white socks that had bagged around his ankles. I lowered him into the pool until his bottom was sitting on the bench; then I sat on the rim and dangled my bare legs in too.

I don't believe this, said Crystal.

Johnny lay back in the warm water while mist rose around him. His head still tilted to catch the light reflecting and splintering off the surface of the clear water turned blue-green from the painted sides of the tub. He reached his bad hand up to the mist that twined up out of the warmth, twisting his fingers in its vapor.

How long's it been? I asked. Since you tried.

Years.

That might be it, I said. The years go by, and things change. You look at yourself, you look at your child, and he's doing something you thought you'd never live to see.

Johnny said something, his eyes focused on us as we sat talking.

No, your bear can't go in the water with you, Johnny Z, said Crystal. He'd drown.

Johnny said it again, the word, and reached for his stuffed bear that sat on the floor, propped against the wall below the pastel sunrise.

That's a nice bear, I said.

That's the Teddy Zielinski bear, said Crystal. A gift from his grandfather Zielinski.

I dumped in some toys, the ones that the kids who can play by themselves in the whirlpool like to play with. Johnny reached for the rubber shark and piloted it through the bubbles. *Rrrrr*, he groaned, maneuvering the shark through the bubbles, its peeling grey fin barely visible above the manufactured waves.

In sleep the old dream comes back: the faceless man who is my father, driving at night up hills and down, heading into the mountains where he turns the weapon on the woman who is my mother and with the crack of the gun blows her face apart. Somewhere in the dark I follow, running hard but not hard enough. I wake freezing, damp sheets pulled to my chin, and turn to Starr for his warmth. But he isn't there.

In the tub Johnny turned and floated, supporting the lightness of his body with his good hand propped beneath him. Forgotten, the toy shark churned in the bubbling water. Crystal bent forward on the rim and splashed warm bubbling water onto his back.

If my father'd loved me like you love Johnny, my mother would still be here, I said.

How so?

You stay alive, if you love someone like that.

Starr loved his kids like I love Johnny, said Crystal. And he's dead anyway.

Later they drove away, the pickup leaving the parking lot drab and colorless, no unearthly red splotched in the middle like a drop of spilled paint. Johnny strapped into his seat next to Crystal with the complicated web of belts she put together for him years ago. Years ago it was darkest night when she gave birth to him, depthless dark the way it can be in North Sterns when the only light comes from the far-off glitter of the stars.

There was still sweet corn. Mallie took Charlie down the green rows to pick some ears for dinner. Tim helped them shuck it on the porch and I boiled the water. Charlie came in with his mouth dripping sweet juice.

You eating that stuff raw again? I said.

Me and Mal, that's how we eat it, said Charlie. That's the secret way Starr Williams taught us.

Are you ever going to call him Dad again? He was your *dad*, you know.

My dad is a baby in China with dead soldier dirt on him, he said.

Later Mallie soaped him with the blue soap shaped like a dinosaur, running the warm washcloth up and down between his thin shoulder blades. The ends of her blunted brown hair swooped against the line of her jaw.

Did you wear those Chinese slippers down to the cornfield? I asked.

She nodded.

That'll ruin them. The sequins will start to fall off, and they'll turn dusty and fall apart.

Wo ai pijiu, sang Charlie in the tub, pouring water into a bath cup and pretending to swig it. Mallie sat back on her folded legs and wrung the washcloth out.

Hair, she said.

Obediently he bent back, as far as he could without getting his eyes wet. His face with the wet hair streaming underneath his skull looked tiny, smoothed, as it did when he was newborn.

If you'd close your eyes you could get your whole head wet yourself, you know, said Mallie.

Never, never close your eyes, he said.

She swished water up on the part of his head that wasn't submerged, ran her fingers through his hair, and helped him sit up straight. Tim joined me in the doorway, and we watched as she rubbed shampoo onto his sculptured skull and scrubbed her fingers through his hair.

Ow, ow, ow.

She lay him back down again and smoothed his hair in the water, rinsing and rinsing to rid it of bubbles. I watched my daughter's gentle fingers and memory came to me, flooding over my body like warm water, like the sun from behind a cloud, like a gift.

I am three and the water comes up to my armpits. She doesn't like me in water so deep, but he keeps one hand on me. It's our secret. He runs the washcloth over my head and down my shoulders. He plays the washcloth game. He sings me the bathtub song, his voice low and gravelly. He swings me out and wraps me up in a rough white towel that smells like sun.

Something has just come to me, I said to Tim. It wasn't she who sang to me. It was my father. It was my father who was always singing. It's his voice in my head.

Doesn't surprise me, he said. Your mother was tone deaf. She couldn't sing to save her life.

Mallie started to sing, the old bathtub tune that I taught to Starr and he taught to them. But she was putting different words to it. *Yangshu ye hua la la, Xiaohai shuijiao zhao ta ma, Guaiguai baobei ni shui ba, Mahuzi laile wo da ta.*

Her little girl rump in old stained shorts jutted into the air as she bent over the tub, singing softly to her brother.

Is she singing the bathtub song in *Chinese?* I asked.

So did you, said Tim. When you were three. The waiters at the Chinese restaurant used to sing it to you and Starr when you were babies.

Jesus, I said. I was three and so is Charlie. If I remember nothing of that, then how will Charlie remember anything of Starr?

You haven't forgotten. We don't forget anything.

Mallie sang on, her voice high and reedy like a Chinese girl's, her shorts splashed with water and soapsuds.

Aren't those her Chinese shorts? asked Tim. They're all stained.

They were full of dirt, I said. Dirt and some kind of weird Chinese dust, crammed into the pockets. I washed them and they turned into mud shorts, stained forever with Chinese dust.

Mallie lifted Charlie out of the tub and wrapped him up in his Mickey Mouse towel.

Charlie, did you know that they love Mickey in China? she said. *Mi Laoshu*, is what they call him.

We put them in bed, stories and songs for Charlie, nothing for Mallie who says she's too old. Tim and I cleaned up the kitchen and put the corn husks in a paper bag to dry so Mal can show Charlie how to make husk dolls in the fall. I went to her room. She lay in soundless sleep on her narrow child's bed, her face older than nine even in sleep. Her Chinese-cut hair lay arrow-straight on the white pillow, her dusty glitter slippers flung across the room.

All these years and the eighteen-year-old Lucia that I was still walks the sand, unchanged. Her footprints have no beginning and no end.

But me, I have both. My choices have already been made. They gave me Grace's thin hands, reaching for the hairbrush that soothes her fretful nerves; James Howard's music, filling his crib; his tired mother who comes every day on her lunch break. My choices live with me here in this house, in the secrets of my daughter and son, in the bones turned to ash in my bedroom.

I remembered my father bending over the tub, his dark eyes full of reflected light.

Come on baby Lucy, he said. Sing with me, that song you taught me. *Young shoe yeah fa la la*.

His hands rubbed the towel over my body, my three-year-old's legs and arms. *La la fa la la*, he sang on, a meaningless sound replacing the words of a language neither of us could speak.

What are you crying for? asked Mallie in her father's voice, awake, her eyes open and fathomless in the dark.

Nothing, I said. A man I used to know, is all.

MALLIE WILLIAMS

Charlie's stopped now. Lucia didn't know about Charlie's crying, it was our secret. The first night is when he started it. I heard him, but she was still downstairs with the funeral guy.

Hug, he said, which was the routine. Bath, towel, pj's, hug. He could never sleep without it. So I went in.

It's OK, I said.

But he wouldn't stop the crying so I snuck into their room, my mom and dad's. I snuck into my dad's dresser where he kept his T-shirts.

Here's a T-shirt for you, Charlie. Dad left this for you because he knew you wouldn't be able to sleep without him.

He put it on over his head. It looked like a dress on Charlie, a white dress almost because my dad was big and Charlie's only three, I mean four now with his birthday.

Hug.

Every night he said it. Every night I got him the T-shirt. I kept it in my closet for him, for the routine that after my dad died we did every night. But now he doesn't cry anymore. So I folded it up like my grandma Georgia showed me to fold, arms in, sides in, top to bottom, and I put it underneath the red notebook that I'm saving for me and Charlie and Johnny.

Lucia's wearing red. Red and black and bright, bright blue, that she never wore before. She's thinking of cutting her hair, is what I heard her say to Crystal.

Go for it, is what Crystal said.

Crystal took a little bit of the ashes when I showed her where they were. She thought I wasn't looking but I was. The same way I used to look at the babies in China after I got good at it, so they didn't know I was looking. But I was.

He's in there, I said, and I showed her the can.

She was at our house bringing Johnny to the birthday party. Johnny was holding one of Charlie's rubber dolphins, that he'd gotten for his birthday.

Well happy birthday, Charlie, said Crystal when he showed them to her. Thanks for inviting Johnny to your party.

Yeah, said Charlie. But Starr Williams is not here. He's in China.

The party was for Charlie's fourth birthday. My mother had it for him: four friends, one for each year. Pin the Tail on the Donkey. Drop the clothespins in the bottle, which none of them could do unless they stood right over the bottle. But they're only four.

Mallie, will you help me organize this party? my mother asked.

It wasn't my mother's job to organize the birthday parties; it was my dad's. He was the one who bought the streamers and the balloons and did the decorations. He was the one who played games with the kids.

No, I said.

Crystal came and got me and we went to the cemetery. That's the day she stole the ashes, a little handful that I saw her put in her pocket when she thought I wasn't looking but I was. I sat in Johnny's seat.

You don't have to put on all those belts, said Crystal. They're special, for Johnny.

But I did. I put them on anyway, all three of them. Over the stomach and crisscross across my chest.

This is how it feels to be Johnny, I thought. I concentrated on feeling how Johnny feels. It was hard. I couldn't move very well. Up at the cemetery it was bright, with the sun falling on all the old stones. Warm for the end of August. Crystal had her hand in her pocket where my dad's ashes that she stole were. There was an old stone wall running around the cemetery, the kind the old Welsh settlers built. They set them on top of each other, the stones, fit them together, but they didn't use cement or glue. They just fit them together, like puzzle pieces.

Look at them, said Crystal. Young girls and their babies, most of them.

Young men too, I said. Evan Evans, 1866–1896. That's how old my dad was and he wasn't old.

Your dad liked this cemetery, did you know that? He told me he wanted to be buried here.

Her hand went in her pocket where the ashes were. She thought I didn't see but I did. There's not much I don't see. I've got sharp eyes. I'm on the lookout.

I'm going to go look around, I said, so she could be alone with her ashes that she thought were her secret.

I went over by one of the white birch trees and climbed up in it. White birches are easy to climb, with their trunks that start splitting from the ground up. Some of the leaves were starting to fall on the old worn-down stones and the grass and flowers that grow wild because nobody takes care of this cemetery.

She let them go. I watched through the leaves. She sprinkled them around; then she lay down in the grass with her eyes closed and the sun on her face. Across the road the truck gleamed in the sun, its redness so red I couldn't look at it very long. After a while we got back in it and drove around North Sterns.

Didn't want to go to the birthday party? Crystal asked.

No.

Why not?

It's not my mom's job to do the parties, I said to Crystal. It was

219

his. It was only her job to get the cake. From Hemstrought's, a decorated one however you want it, that was her one job.

Crystal nodded.

And a party means that Charlie is another year older, she said. And he's just going to keep getting older. Without his dad around. That's the real kicker for Mallie Williams, isn't it?

You know what they're saying, I said. She didn't love him enough, my mom.

She didn't love your dad enough?

It's true. See the clothes she's wearing now? She didn't wear anything like that when he was alive. She hated colors like that, bright ones. She gave away all his clothes, and she squeezed out his air. And now she's wearing different colors.

Crystal turned the truck up the road that goes to Star Hill and then to our house.

His can of ashes, it gets lighter all the time, I said. And she doesn't even notice that he's disappearing.

Don't be so sure, said Crystal.

Lucia was wearing a red T-shirt and black shorts.

See? I said to Crystal when we drove in. Those are new. She didn't have any clothes like that before.

Nice T-shirt, said Crystal when we got out of the truck.

Thanks, said my mother. Johnny's favorite color.

That it is, Crystal said.

Crystal got the present for Charlie out of the truck. I helped her get it down from the cupboards above the table in her trailer. That was the first time I was ever in Crystal's trailer. It was still in its box, a red tricycle with black pedals. Multicolored tassels like the pen my dad gave me hanging down from the handlebars.

Think Charlie'd like that little bike? asked Crystal.

He's been wanting one, I said.

Well that's good. This'll be from Johnny, his present for Charlie.

Brand-new, it looked like. Never been used, but its box was old and caved in. We loaded it into the truck, in the back, and headed back down to Sterns.

Is he in the cemetery too? I asked Crystal. Your dad, I mean, who gave Johnny the Teddy Zielinski bear?

No. He's somewhere in South Dakota, somewhere out there driving a big old truck.

The sun started to go down over the hills that were the beginning of the Adirondacks. The sun goes down faster in North Sterns than it does in Sterns even though it's just a few miles beyond. The start of the hills, that's why.

It's flat out there, Crystal said. Out in the badlands out there.

We drove past Star Hill.

I'll tell you a secret, I said. I've never seen the ghost.

I don't actually know anyone who has, said Crystal.

It was just Johnny and Charlie when we got back. Sitting in the pool that my mother put new air into, playing shark.

They're not sharks, they're dolphins, I said. Rubber dolphins.

They're sharks, said Charlie.

He aimed his dolphin at Johnny so its fin glided through the water. Johnny laughed the way he does. He was sitting on the side of the pool with his shorts still on, wet, bouncing so that the water spilled out over his legs.

Want a piece? my mother asked.

She had the birthday cake knife out, and the birthday platter. It was a big lemon cake from Hemstrought's, half-eaten.

What kind of a cake is that? asked Crystal. It's so yellow.

A Chinese baby cake, said my mother. It used to look more like one before they ate the head off. I agree though, they made it too yellow. Probably never saw a real Chinese baby before.

Crystal had a look on her face.

I can't help it, said my mother. It's what Charlie wanted. It's his fourth birthday, who am I to stop him?

Charlie and Johnny came up dripping. Johnny held out his fists to Charlie. Charlie patted them.

Pat-a-cake, pat-a-cake, baker's man, sang Charlie. *Bake me a cake as fast as you can. Roll it and prick it and mark it with a C, and put it in the oven for Charlie and me.*

That's a Starr Williams song, he said to Crystal.

Johnny smiled and curled open his closed hands. Nothing at all inside them, just water dripping.

Grandpa Tim went to school and I went with him, to open up his art room before the kids come back. The shades were down and the air smelled tight and hot and closed up, the way my dad never smelled because he was outside all the time.

That's the special end-of-summer smell, Mal, said my grandpa Tim. It's a smell that never changes. It's the before-the-kids smell.

My job was to pull up the shades and open the windows with the long window hook. The janitors were polishing the floors with their big floor polisher. Down the hall they went in slow circles, whirring and humming. Everything in my grandfather's classroom was neat, like it never is when the kids are there. The tubes of glitter and the jars of finger paints were lined up. The easels were stacked in a corner. Johnny's red box with his shinies was inside my grandpa's desk drawer.

The school buses were lined up at the garage, empty and locked. I looked for me and Johnny's, P32. I jumped up, but I couldn't jump high enough to see our seat, fifth on the left behind Tiny. Maybe the shinies are still there. They're hard to get off if you put them on right.

It was also my job to sharpen the pencils, the new yellow ones in the box that they give my grandfather every year. It takes a long time to grind them down to the perfect point, the kind that my grandfather likes. The window in his door was clean and polished. I practiced jumping up and down while he sat at his desk writing in a notebook. His head flashed into the window for a second every time.

Gets easier every year doesn't it, Mal? he said when I came in. Every time I look at you, you're taller.

The tree is greyer and more bent. I know because I forgot to duck down. My grandfather was talking and I was listening. Before I knew it I was staring right at the tree where she died. It was starting to die too, it looked like, too hurt to heal.

And I'm happy to see you're putting some of that weight back on, said my grandfather. Not that you'll ever be anything but skinny, built like your father the way you are.

He's growing up in China. He's a baby still, but soon he'll be walking. Soon he'll be talking. All the stickums are still in my closet, along with the notebook that's filled up now. The notebook is mine and Charlie's. Johnny's too, so that we can remember him forever. The tapes are there too, with his voice on them. I am still practicing, so that when I meet him again he will be able to understand what I'm saying to him. The swimming pool is blown up again, with my mom's air that also has the air of everyone else that ever lived in it. The bad and the good, all mixed up together.

Don't worry, Crystal says. Starr's air is everywhere.

Lucia's hair fell on me the night she sat on my bed and cried. She didn't know I was awake. She was singing the bathtub song in a humming kind of way and crying, my dad's bathtub song that he used to sing to me and to Charlie.

But then I remembered. It wasn't just my dad's. She used to sing it too. They used to sing it together. Better write that down in the notebook, I thought, that it belonged to both of them. You have to be fair. You have to remember everything.

Your mom likes red too, is what Crystal said when we drove in to the birthday party and saw them, Charlie and Johnny playing shark and my mother sitting in the sun. Your mom's allowed to like red too, Miss Mallie.

She does, too. She does like red. The cashier said it wouldn't be too long, but my mother still cries at night when she thinks I'm asleep. She doesn't know I can hear her. She pours warm water over Johnny and he loves it.

My mom and dad used to sing the bathtub song together.

Your mother's doing the best she can, said Crystal when we drove in.

Before he died I used to do the What if there was nothing? routine. That's what you say: *What if there was nothing? What if there was nothing?* You say it over and over. You think about it. What if there was nothing: no house, no sky, no middle of the earth with hot lava and China on the other side, no father, no mother, no Charlie, and no Mallie; no baby Dad growing up somewhere where I don't know him. An inside-out world.

If you think about it long enough all you see is nothing, a whiteness that looks blank but Crystal says is not really. Really what white is is every color of the spectrum put together. Not the absence of color but the overabundance of it, the unimaginably vast spectrum of light, Crystal says. She read that in a book.

I don't do it anymore, because what if there was nothing?

Every night I smell the T-shirt but it's fading. It's faded away and he's gone, my dad. His smell is gone, but I close my eyes and I say remember. *Remember.* And it comes back, what his smell was. Wood and soap and the color green and grass and sweat and sun. It comes back.

28

TIM WILLIAMS

You would've thought that Lucia'd be angry with me for keeping silent so long, but she wasn't; there's too much to learn, she says, too much to remember. Some has started coming back to her, bits here and there about her father as well as Livvy. She can't put him out of her life, much as she wants to.

But he *killed* her, Lucia says. He killed my mother. I don't want to love him.

You can't help it, I say. You can't unremember, once you start.

It's the same as with Mal. Wanting to believe that if she'd just done her routines right he'd still be alive. That somehow she must be evil, to justify the pain. I went through it too, when Georgia died. But there's no one who's all bad or all good.

Up on Star Hill, Lucia held the can of ashes between her hands and rolled it like the special ed kids in art roll lumps of modeling dough between their hands. Worms and snakes are their favorites to make.

I could swear this can seems lighter than it did before, she said. Even though I know no one's touched it.

She handed the can to me and headed back to the truck. The door creaked as she climbed in and then thunked shut with its little scream that I keep meaning to stop with oil but don't. She didn't turn the key that sat in the ignition like it always does. Nothing disturbed the silence. With one hand I reached in my pocket for the Swiss army knife, the other propped the can steady; then I pried the lid up. I sifted a little into my palm and walked down the dirt road to where the hill falls away, down the steep slope where the little pines and white birches are taking root. The kind of breeze that sometimes comes after the sun goes down came up and rustled the leaves. Already they're starting to turn.

I let him go in the breeze. It was too dark; I couldn't see where the ashes went after they left my hand. It was where we made him; only right that some of him should be laid to rest there.

Back in the truck Lucia had rolled down her window and turned the key so the battery fed the radio. A thin twangy wail floated out to me from the dark as I made my way back.

You think my mother's still out there somewhere? she asked.

Could be, I said.

There's another secret that will stay a secret. I will not tell Crystal that I saw her father in Sterns. It's been fifteen years, but still I recognized him. I grew up with him after all, Ted Zielinski from North Sterns. Rode the same school bus even. It was the day before Mallie and I went to China, but I haven't said a word to Crystal.

Ted Zielinski? I said before I thought.

He was just disappearing into Jewell's, the screen door banging onto his shoulder as he quick wheeled around like someone was after him.

Yeah?

Still driving a truck, if that was his parked up along the curb by Jewell's. It was white. It reminded me in a way I hated of the truck that killed my son.

You don't remember me, I said. I'm Tim Williams. You back to see your daughter?

He stared at me from the dark of Jewell's door. It was Monday, Crystal's one day off when the Closed sign stays on the diner all day. She was up in North Sterns no doubt, playing with Johnny.

You see your grandson? I asked.

He got a look on his face.

She wrote me I had a grandson, he said. A baby, she said it was. So I made a detour off my route. I went up there to see, to see my grandson, named after me she said he was.

The comb marks were on his head, pulling his remaining hair across his scalp. Gone grey mostly. Like me.

It was a retard, he said. And not a baby either. He was a kid. A retard kid named after me.

He backed into Jewell's, the door slamming against the flannel shirt he was wearing even in the August heat. His white semi leaned up against the curb, making me think of death.

In the diner Mallie worked on her slippers with Lucia's sewing scissors and a needle and thread. Charlie sat next to Johnny, sharing a plate of french fries they were dipping into a little bowl of ketchup. Thunderclouds growled across the sky.

Those slippers have seen more than their share of life, I said. Tromping around Xian and the Great Wall, down to the cornfield and all around Sterns.

That's why I'm taking them apart, said Mal. They're reincarnating.

Johnny reached for the big-holed needle she was trying to thread with embroidery floss. She jerked it out of the way, but too late. Johnny moaned and held his finger to his heart.

Let me see, said Mal.

A tiny splash of bright red fell on the white T-shirt he was wearing. He held his finger in the air and watched the drops gather slowly and fall to the tabletop.

It's only a little puncture wound, said Mal. Give me your finger.

She dipped her napkin in her glass of ice water and held it to his fingertip for a moment, then let go.

That's what we learned in health, she said. For puncture wounds all you can do is clean the surface and let the blood flow.

She used the wet napkin to swab up the few little drops on the table. Johnny held his finger in the air.

Gone, said Mal. See? Doesn't even hurt anymore I bet.

Crystal watched from behind the counter.

It's his favorite color, she said. He's probably hoping for more.

Look, said Mal.

She held a bracelet up in the air, one she'd just made from her discarded Chinese slippers. All the sequins were strung together on the embroidery floss.

Let's see if it fits, she said to Johnny. Hold out your hand.

He held out his twisted hand, and she eased the bracelet on.

Perfect, she said, tying the ends of the floss in a thick tight knot.

In between the thunderheads the sun flashed and winked on Mallie's sequins.

I followed the code to string them together, said Mal. Roy G. Biv, the rainbow guy. Red, orange, yellow, green, blue, indigo, violet, so that Johnny's got a rainbow bracelet. Better a bracelet than a necklace, because you can't see a necklace and you can always hold your hand up to see a bracelet.

She pantomimed, straining to see an imaginary necklace strung round her own neck. Charlie laughed.

Don't make that funny face, he said.

She mimed again, stretching her mouth into a grimace. Again he laughed.

I remember Starr doing that, I said. He used to stretch his mouth just like that.

It's a special talent, said Mal.

Behind the counter Crystal filled ketchup bottles and smiled.

You want a doughnut? she asked. They're fresh.

She had them arranged on a red plate. Cinnamon and glaze spread out from the center of each.

That's the kind Lucia gets, I said. Hemstrought's.

That's where we got them, said Crystal. Me and Johnny, when we were down there today. Playing in the balls and taking a whirly bath, right, J?

He held up his twisted hand with the bracelet and smiled.

Since when's Johnny taking a bath? I asked.

Since last week when Lucia put him in one. We're going down now and then, Johnny and me, so that he can play with the balls and the bubbles and sit in the whirlpool with Lucia.

Crystal laid the spatula down on the counter and started rinsing a rag in running water. Johnny said something to Mal.

What? she said. I can't understand.

He said it again.

A Popsicle? Come on, I'll get you one.

Me too, said my grandson. Don't forget Charlie.

They left, the three of them, squeezing through the open door. Mallie's voice floated back to where we stood, Crystal and I, at the counter.

Hold hands, she said. Look both ways.

Mallie's bare feet slowed, patient, adjusting her pace to theirs, the four-year-old child and the twelve-year-old boy. They disappeared into the dark door of Jewell's.

That's the first I've heard you do that, said Crystal. Mention Starr's name like that to Mallie, as if nothing had ever happened.

He used to make that exact same face, I said. I didn't even remember it until I saw Mallie doing it.

Crystal squeezed out the rag.

He'll be out of my mind for a minute, I said. And then there he is again, in Mallie's face, in Charlie's eyes. Things you think you've forgotten.

It'll be that way forever, said Crystal.

She still had her dad's old postcards pinned up over the grill as if they were orders to be filled. The world's biggest rodent leered above the vent.

You heard from him? I asked.

Him being my dad? she said. In a way. I told him about Johnny, that he's living with me. That's when he sent Johnny that bear, the one he can't be apart from.

She wiped down the sides of the grill that don't get wiped very often. She knelt down to scrub at the drippings of fat and ketchup that were making streaky lines on the steel.

That's all though, she said after a while. Didn't hear anything else.

I went in after him that day. Into Jewell's where I had only been a couple times since Starr came flinging out that day.

Ted, I said.

He was digging in the cooler for a soda.

Ted.

He wiped the top of the can and popped it open. Root beer, which I remember him always drinking in high school.

I drove up that way, he said. Took a couple days off the route after I made the delivery. It's all the same up there, Star Hill and Carmichael Hill and the rest of it. That old Welsh cemetery.

He tilted his head back and drank deep.

There she was, he said. Crystal. Sitting outside that same old trailer, like nothing's ever changed. There she was, washing the kid's hair. I had a present for him, but I didn't even stop when I saw.

I watched him drink his soda again, half the can in one gulp. Hate came up in me and made my stomach twist, but then I saw he was crying.

I peeked in that diner where she wrote she's working now, he said. She's got those postcards up on the vent. All those old cards I sent her. You seen them?

He finished the soda and started out the door. I watched him go, the screen door slamming behind. Then he was back, a brown paper package in his hand.

Give it to the kid, he said. I'm gone.

I leaned against Mal's stool while Crystal wiped down the counter. She came around front and wiped down each red twirly stool. She got a bottle of window cleaner and sprayed a fan of blue onto the front door window.

I can do that, I said, taking it and the roll of paper towels from her hand. The crumpled paper squeaked on the glass as I rubbed.

Make sure you get all those streaks, said Crystal from behind the counter, where she was scraping down the grill with a tin spatula.

Yes, ma'am.

They emerged from the dark door of Jewell's, Johnny clutching a red Popsicle, Charlie licking a cone. Mallie held a paper soda cup. Then the thunder clapped and it started down, a torrent of rain, and all three turned their heads to the sky. Crystal laid her spatula on the counter and ducked under the latched grill gate. We stood watching while drops of rain hit the window and slid downward like tears.

Charlie danced in the rain, holding his mint ice cream cone above his head like a Statue of Liberty. Mallie lunged for Johnny and dropped her cup. Ice cubes clattered on the sidewalk, and the spilled dark soda speckled Mallie's narrow bare feet. She reached again for Johnny.

Don't worry, Johnny, I heard her say as Charlie whirled near the street. Don't move.

Mal held her hands out, trying to keep them safe. But it was over. Just a storm cloud passing on into the hills where North Sterns begins. The sun came burning and blinding out.

Starr Williams, I heard Charlie chant from the middle of his dancing. Starr, Starr, Williams, Williams.

Red melt from Johnny's Popsicle dribbled down his cheek, and he turned his face up to catch the last drops raining down. I watched his face, the retarded boy not named for his grand-father. I have watched that face for twelve years, seen it define itself by the life lived behind it, like all the faces I love define themselves. The years pile up like leaves on a forest floor. They hold the living, and the dead.

Sun, said Johnny.

His free hand lifted to the sky in imitation of Charlie who twirled and danced in front of him. Mallie's reincarnated phoenix slippers sparkled on his wrist in the sunlight through rain. He stood on the sidewalk smiling, whole foot and twisted one in perfect balance.

Johnny, Johnny, look. There's a rainbow.

Mallie's voice was tight with longing. He turned his eyes to the colored arc, reaching as if to draw it into his body—Johnny Zielinski, who loves shinies.